"Sit." He gestured to the chair in front of him, frowning in his hand.

Sit. One word. Sit. Like I'm a dog, a stray dog, full of fleas, about to be put out of my misery.

"I'd rather stand. I doubt that this will take long."

"It will." He flicked cold brown eyes over her serviceable navy blue suit. It fit her like a glove, the pencil line skirt ending just below the knee. "Sit."

She didn't. Even if she had to stand for hours, she wouldn't sit.

Philippe took out an eight by ten white square, holding it up as if to compare against her face. "I prefer you with your hair down." His lips twisted disapprovingly at the tight chignon she was sporting. He tossed the glossy piece of paper, print side up, across the desk.

Before her brain told her hands to resist, Anne clasped the photo. *Mistake.* That was exactly what he wanted. *Why would he want that? To shock me.* It was a shot of her face, her hair tumbling down all around, the fitted tee shirt, she recognized as the one she wore on Saturday, grocery shopping. *Shock me?* Consider it mission accomplished. Anne sat down with a thump.

"Why do you have a photo of me?" she asked, her voice not betraying any of her wonderment. Later, she would be proud of how calm she sounded.

"Not a photo, photos." Philippe dropped a couple more in front of her. "I like this one." It was of her laughing, out walking her elderly neighbor's energetic Jack Russell terrier, the lease tangled around her legs.

"But this." He tilted the photo up so she couldn't peak. "This one is my favorite." He looked at her, thoroughly entertained, the devil dancing in his eyes.

What They're Saying About Breach Of Trust

Breach of Trust read like a great movie; smooth, very vivid, detailed, and one that you rush to tell your friends about.—*Simply Romance Reviews*

…never a dull moment, and there were lots of twists and turns that keep the reader really enthused. Hot steamy love scenes only compliment this story like whipped cream on apple pie. An exceptional read.—*CoffeeTime Romance*

Champagne Books Presents

Breach Of Trust

By

Kimber Chin

Lorraine,
No Guts,
No Glory!! :)
Happy Reading!
Kimber Chin

Champagne Books
www.champagnebooks.com
Copyright © 2008 by PKCS Incorporated (Written By Kim Chin-Sam)
ISBN 978-1-897445-75-4
May 2008
Cover Art © Trisha FitzGerald
Produced in Canada

Champagne Books
#35069-4604 37 ST SW
Calgary, AB T3E 7C7
Canada

Acknowledgments

I'd like to acknowledge the following sources for their business expertise and research;

Guy Kawasaki (http://www.guykawasaki.com/) is the managing director of Garage Technology Ventures, an early-stage venture capital firm, and the author of my favorite book on start ups, The Art of the Start.

Ladies Who Launch (http://www.LadiesWhoLaunch.com/) is written specifically for female entrepreneurs-to-be. Victoria Colligan, and Beth Schoenfeldt (with Amy Swift) bring their real life experience to both the book and the website.

WomenEntrepreneur.com (http://www.WomenEntrepreneur.com/) is a website affiliated with Entrepreneur Magazine yet dedicated to the female business owner. If information needed is not found within the articles, blogs, and message boards, there is a helpful "Ask Entrepreneur" option where questions can be posted.

Dedication

Thank you to my husband (for proving that true love does exist and can survive a career change), to my best friend Gilly (for patiently playing the business idea of the day game these past two decades), and to my fabulous writing coach Aprille Janes from Creative Light And Power (for pushing me to submit that first writing contest entry)

One

This was the one, and it was about damn time. Venture capitalist Philippe Lamont's satisfaction was not reflected in his face. Instead he glared at the papers spread out on his desk, intentionally ignoring the middle-aged man seated before him. The strategy was simple. The more applicant Bruce Fallens waited, the more he worried. The more he worried, the easier getting the answer would be.

Philippe Lamont flipped the pages, another deliberate ploy. His team already had scrubbed-down the proposal, Philippe reviewing the final details himself. There was no new information. Not that new information was needed. This deal was luscious. A great product, a ready customer; all that was needed was expansion financing. That's where his company came in and come in, they would. The offer was drafted and ready.

Non, the delay had nothing to do with dollars.

Philippe waited a few more minutes, his eyes flicking up quickly to sweep the entrepreneur's face. A trickle of perspiration ran down the man's cheek. This was the one. Philippe could smell the anxiety, and with it, the sweet scent of success.

"It's an intriguing proposition." Philippe closed the file and steepled his long thin index fingers, resting them on his chin. "Well presented." He then asked for what he really wanted. "Who did your business plan?"

Bruce Fallens swallowed, the action bobbing his Adam's apple. "An associate."

Imbecile. Philippe knew that. One dark eyebrow jerked up. "Does this associate have a name?"

"Prefer not to say." Bruce shifted nervously.

Prefer. The other business owners had told him that they would not say and then stuck to their word. Not Bruce; his preferences would be over-ridden.

"Bruce, Bruce, Bruce." Philippe clucked. "If we're to be partners, you must be open with me, share your confidences, *n'est pas*?"

"I can't."

"Then," Philippe shook his head with regret, "if you can't trust me, I can't trust you. *Pur et* simple. And I certainly can't finance your little venture. I don't go into business with people I don't trust." He slid the file across the desk.

It was a bluff. The deal was *fait accompli*, the opportunity too juicy for Philippe to walk away from. He knew that, and his team knew that.

Bruce, however, didn't know. He stared at Philippe in disbelief. "But... but... but... we won't get the contract unless you do."

"Ah, *oui*." A well-defined jaw was clenched to stop the laughter. "I understand that your largest customer insists on my financing and my financing alone." Philippe understood this only too well. It had taken calling in a big favor to have that accomplished.

"I'll give you forty-five percent ownership," Bruce blurted out.

There was a gasp from the row of chairs lined up against the far wall.

Philippe's yearning to meet the business plan coach intensified. "*Merci*, Bruce. A most generous offer and we would be remiss not to take it." Philippe motioned to Gregory, his lawyer, to capture this change. "I still need the name."

Bruce groaned, realizing his mistake.

Sloppy, sloppy. The venture capitalist almost *tsk-tsked*. The business owner had made concessions for nothing. Not that the increase in ownership mattered. Philippe was honest about going into business only with people he trusted. He would buy Bruce out.

They stared at each other, the wall clock ticking loudly. Philippe loved that clock, a constant reminder to guests that his every minute was precious. At exactly 3:54 p.m, the man crumbled.

"Okay." It was barely a whisper, shame etching the desperate entrepreneur's face.

"The contract." Bruce's lawyer piped up from the back row, "There'll be a lawsuit."

At least there was one other true businessman in the mix. The plan preparer was a professional, not trusting on blind faith alone. Philippe had no doubt the contract was leak proof, as polished as the mystery man's business plans. "That's no concern. We'll handle any legal fees or reparations."

"It'll be costly," the lawyer warned.

"It'll be worth it." Philippe brandished his hand dismissively. He had waited too long to let this chance slip by. "So who is it?"

Bruce looked around him nervously. "I'd rather tell you in private."

Oui, betray your confidences with no witnesses, that makes it so much more honorable. Mon Dieu. Philippe waved the others from the room, not bothering to hide his gloating smirk.

Gregory gave him a semi-congratulatory smile as he departed. *Success, finally.*

"So Bruce." Philippe leaned forward eagerly. "Who prepped you for this presentation?"

"She's going to be pissed." Bruce couldn't meet his eyes.

She? Philippe rocked back. *A woman?* All this time he had been pursuing a woman? A woman could sell to him like that? He hadn't even considered. It was an oversight and it angered him. Philippe Lamont didn't make many mistakes.

"The name, Bruce, I need the name. Who is it?" The question came out as a growl.

"Anne James," Bruce's words were scarcely audible over the hum of the office hvac unit.

"Anne James?" Philippe echoed in disbelief. *Anne James. Anne James. Do I know her?* The name sounded familiar but distant, like a childhood memory.

"Missus?"

"Miss," Bruce corrected, his eyes already filled with regret. "I was referred to her. Someone told me that she was the best."

"She is," Philippe confirmed without hesitation. All her plans were bang on, the delivery impeccable, the deals fulfilling needs he wasn't even aware he had. That's why he needed to know. And now he did. *Anne James.* He had a name for his opponent. Did he have a face?

"What does she look like?" Philippe demanded from the downtrodden man.

Bruce shrugged. "Quiet, long brown hair, plain, thin, completely not noteworthy."

Philippe searched through his mental listing of attendees at recent business functions. It was a fairly small crowd that they traveled in, a few hundred people. Not that big of a database.

One image drifted to the forefront. Brunette, head tilted, big brown eyes watching him, like an inquisitive little sparrow. Not unattractive but Bruce was right, not worth noticing. Not worth noticing for personal; Philippe preferred voluptuous blondes. And not for business; he had been told she was merely an accountant.

Merely an accountant. He sniffed in disgust, both with himself and with his sources. All this time, the so-called accountant had been studying him, spying on him. Using his weaknesses, his personal foibles, to manipulate him. *Oui, it must be her, it can be no one else*, but Philippe needed absolute confirmation before taking action.

"Hair tightly pulled back? Always wears black?"

Bruce scrunched up his face in thought. "I suppose so, like I said, she's completely forgettable."

A woman who strived to be forgettable; that was an enigma.

The entrepreneur's eyes narrowed. "Why's her name so important?"

"That you don't need to know." The question should have been asked before the information was given. At this point, Philippe was under no obligation to answer. "And I don't wish Mademoiselle James to know you told me."

"Fine with me. I'd rather no one knew." Bruce breathed a sigh of relief. "She'll sue me for certain. Locked down and tough as beans, that's the way she is."

Oui, that's the way she is. That's the way I am also.

It was done. He had her.

"The contract will be amended for my ownership increase and sent to your office by the end of day tomorrow." The meeting was at an end but as the entrepreneur made no sign to leave, he was coolly dismissed. "You may go."

Philippe left a message for his in-house private investigator, specifying that he needed a file with every minute detail of Mademoiselle James' life, deadline yesterday. *It isn't unethical*, Philippe told his conscience. She already had the advantage, knowing everything about him. This would simply put them on the same level.

"You got the name?" Gregory Myers popped his blond head back in. Philippe's good friend must have been outside, waiting. Philippe nodded, his grin wide and widening.

Gregory temporarily disappeared back into the hallway. Philippe could hear him chatting and laughing with Sylvie, his assistant. Upon his return, his friend carried two glasses and an opened bottle of champagne. It took only one raised eyebrow to get the answer. "We've been saving it for exactly this occasion. The way you were focused, we figured you'd get him eventually."

"Her." Philippe still could not get over it. *A tiny little bird of a woman.* "Mademoiselle Anne James."

"Anne James." Gregory frowned, his forehead creased. "The accountant?"

This got Philippe's full attention. "You know her?"

"No." The lawyer poured the champagne, a tinge of pink across his cheekbones. "We exchanged names once before she dashed back to her corner. Hard girl to nail down."

"You're telling me." It had taken him months.

"The hunt was a blast while it lasted." Gregory handed a full glass to Philippe. "Haven't seen you so passionate in a while."

Philippe sipped at the bubbly. "Been a bit bored lately," he admitted. *"Toujours la meme choix,* you know how it is."

"Both personal and business, no doubt." Gregory's face was knowing as he slipped into the comfy guest chair. "I hear you. Can't play the role of free wheeling bachelor forever, you realize. Gets tired."

"You would know." Gregory had more than his fair share of fleeting relationships.

"I do, I do." Blue eyes crinkled. "I also know that someday, as dreadful as it seems, both you and I may have to settle down."

"*Moi?* Settle down? *Avec* Suzanne *peut-etre?*"

The blond haired man winced. "Or someone."

Gregory was not impressed with Philippe's current *amour*, he drove that point home every chance he could. His worry was that Suzanne wanted Philippe solely for security, or to be more precise, for his money.

That Philippe didn't doubt, but it didn't concern him much either. Theirs ran more along the lines of a commercial exchange. He had the cold hard cash Suzanne hungered for; she had all the core competencies he required. She was the perfect hostess, intelligent and witty, possessed of a quick tongue that Philippe appreciated, and of course, she was physically stunning.

What was there to be unhappy about? Nothing. Their partnering profited both parties. And a business relationship, Philippe understood. It was a comfortable arrangement.

"I suppose I should settle down eventually." He shrugged elegantly clad shoulders. "I'm in no rush however, waiting for you to go first."

"Oh, no." Gregory laughed. "Don't be waiting for me. You're the fearless one, the pioneer. You do the honors."

"Ah, but you see. The problem with pioneers is that a lot of them died in that first harsh drought." Philippe's brown eyes gleamed.

"Indeed, indeed." The lawyer nodded in bemusement and they both chuckled.

Philippe's mind drifted back unaided to a mousy brunette. "Anne James." His mouth turned up at the thought. "I finally got her."

"You did. So now what?" Gregory leaned back in the chair, his arms folded behind his head. Philippe wasn't fooled by his nonchalance. His friend, for some reason, wanted to know the answer. "You've run the tiny Anne James to ground. What do you plan to do with her?"

"Do I detect a bit of interest?" Philippe didn't know where this question came from, a hunch he had.

To his surprise, the question hit the jackpot, causing the man to blush. "Like you said, same ol', same ol'"

Same ol', same ol', my foot. There was something there between Gregory and the business plan coach. Philippe couldn't let it interfere with his revenge.

"She's mine, Gregory." The comment made his stance clear. The lawyer bowed his head in silent concord. "And I'll play her as she has played me. The real fun is only just beginning."

Gregory raised his glass in solemn salute. "Then heaven help the poor woman."

~ * ~

The object of Philippe's contemplations was peering over yet another business plan, this one filled with big dreams, spelling mistakes and some very creative accounting.

"Think, Samantha. Think. Who are your competitors?" Anne's quiet voice implored the perky brunette standing beside her desk.

The teenager thought, blowing out a big pink bubble. When it finally snapped with a wave of strawberry scent, she answered, "Like other vending machines?"

"Yes." Anne nodded encouragingly. "Anyone else?"

"I don't like, think so?" The girl shrugged, her ponytail bobbing.

Telling her would be too easy, Anne knew. She had to get the future business leader thinking, using that brain she was blessed with. "If you were looking to buy candy, where would you buy it from?"

Blue eyes lit up in understanding. "Like, maybe, like the *Minute Mart,* like on the corner?"

"Good." Anne was right about Samantha knowing the answer. "And where else?"

"Like, *Target?* Like... like *Wal-Mart?*"

"You got it, girl. Knowing that takes a good business plan and makes it great," and then Anne's voice rose to reach the entire class, "What have we learned today? Samantha, would you like to share?"

Glossy lips curled. "Do I like have to?" came out as a whine.

"Fearless, Samantha," Anne's tone was kind yet firm. The teen suffered from the typical age-related shyness. "Sales don't go to the meek."

"No guts, no glory. Right Miss J? That's what you always tell us," Dirk, her red headed car-obsessed fifteen-year-old, piped up from the front row.

This earned the boy a nasty glance from Samantha.

"That's right, Dirk." Anne gave him the thumbs up. "So, Samantha, be fearless. You know the answer."

"Okay, okay. Like, if I have to?"

"You have to," Anne reinforced yet again. Sometimes getting a simple statement from Samantha was as difficult as reprogramming her cell phone.

"Blah." Blue eyes rolled. "We like, learned that, like, competition is bigger than, like, just who you, like, first think?" Samantha's voice lifted in perpetual question.

"Absolutely." Anne stood up and strode to the black board to capture the thought. "If you're to build a successful business, you need to watch all the players, everyone who might steal a customer from you. You need a point of differentiation from each of them."

The buzz of the clock signaled the end of the Tuesday session. Anne watched contentedly as her *Young C.E.O.'s* class continued to hang around, talking amongst themselves, exchanging ideas.

"Miss James, there's someone at the door for you," Tanya, her chubby cheeked future restaurateur, lilted in a singsong voice.

Anne glanced up at the door and inwardly groaned. She kept her face serene, her voice pleasant. "Thank you, Tanya."

"Remember next week, we're reviewing pricing. I need competitive pricing; your own pricing and the rationalization behind it. Be prepared to talk about it and that includes you, Samantha," Anne called out as she gathered up her papers, sliding them into the black leather briefcase. Her laptop, unneeded today, already was packed up.

Dirk jumped up from his seat to open the door for her. "Thank you." Anne's face mirrored her gratitude.

"No prob, Miss J." The boy beamed back. "That laptop looks kind of heavy. I could carry it to the car for you if you want."

Both of Dirk's parents worked multiple jobs, struggling to keep a roof over their heads, yet they managed to teach their children manners. It never ceased to impress Anne.

"That would…"

"Not be necessary. I'll help Miss James." Glenn Howard, Wilson High's Principal, wrested the laptop out of her hand.

The two males glared at each other, shoulders squared, the boy not backing down.

Oh, no, not this again. Anne didn't know what the problem was between the two. She just knew that there was one.

"Miss J?" Dirk's eyes stayed fixed on Glenn.

"It's okay, Dirk. I have to talk to Mister Howard anyway." It was only a half fib. Anne didn't want to talk to Glenn but she got the feeling that he wanted to talk to her, likely about that blasted fall class schedule. Though it could be something else entirely. There always seemed to be some trivial issue popping up after each and every session.

"Okay then, I'll see you next week, Miss J." The fifteen year old's smile for Anne morphed into a scowl for his Principal.

"That Dirk," the former football player muttered as the door closed.

"Is a good kid and a good student," Anne finished.

"Yes, er …on that subject, we should have a talk about your students and your class." Glenn used the *Kleenex* scrunched in his spare hand to mop his moist forehead. "Would you, that is, maybe we should go for a coffee, or a tea or whatever you wish to drink."

Anne suppressed a sigh. A monster shot, that's what she wished to drink. Admin work was so deadly, the only dark part of teaching. She couldn't even delegate it like she did at her own office.

She checked her watch; it was getting late and she had an early morning meeting to prepare for. "Tonight's not good, could I come in a bit early next week instead?"

Anne didn't quite catch Glenn's answer as she spotted a familiar figure traipsing down the hallway, her *Gucci* handbag swinging. "Ginny." Anne strode up to hug her younger sister, breathing in her fresh floral scent. "I didn't know you were coming."

Her sister's face was radiant even under the dreadful fluorescent lights. "I didn't know either but I was in the neighborhood. Mom forwarded me some of my mail and asked me to give you this coupon for," she threw Glenn a look and whispered in Anne's ear, "*Victoria's Secret*," continuing louder, "so I thought I'd drop by."

"I'm glad you did." Anne grabbed her arm, bringing Ginny closer to the Principal. "Glenn Howard, I'd like you to meet my baby sister, Ginny. She runs a very successful party planning business. Ginny, Glenn Howard is the Principal here."

"My sister exaggerates. A not yet successful business, Mister Howard." The big man blushed under Ginny's blatant perusal. "Do you work closely with Anne?"

"Not as closely as I'd like," he mumbled.

Anne almost rolled her eyes but caught herself in time. Glenn could be a real pain in the ass when he wanted something and what he wanted, she guessed, was that fall schedule. She had to get it done.

"I find it hard to believe that you're sisters." Glenn looked between the two of them.

"We are." Anne laughed, as did Ginny, but the innocent comment rankled.

They were as different as two women could be. Ginny was all golden hair, golden tan, and generous curves. Anne—well, Anne was brown. There was no other word for it. Brown hair, brown eyes, brown skin. Brown, brown, brown. And no boobs to speak of; flat as a fresh piece of paper.

Anne was saved from responding, by her phone humming against her hip. "Sorry but I have to get this," she apologized, taking a few steps away before flipping her phone on.

Anne didn't bother checking the number. The call was expected and was answered with a curt, "Anne James."

"He got it," her friend and partner Nancy squealed into her ear, nearly causing Anne to drop the phone.

"Awesome." Anne smiled reassuringly at Glenn from a distance. He looked sad and a bit lost standing there. Ginny would soon put him at ease. "Good for Bruce. I'm so relieved."

"Come on, Annie." Nancy snorted. "You couldn't have been that worried. The deal was a shoo-in."

"Yeah, it was pretty foolproof; a fast, easy return," Anne admitted as she paced the hallway. Glancing back, she relaxed. Glenn was even now laughing at something her sister was saying. "But you never know. So what's the hit to equity?"

"Forty-Five percent."

"Whoa," she whistled. "That's high for first round. Bruce must have been ticked."

"He didn't have much choice."

"No, he didn't." Anne had heard about the key customer sticking their nose into the financing. It severely limited their sourcing. "And Lamont knew it. What a ruthless bastard." This was said with admiration. When it came to business, the venture capitalist showed no softness. That's what made the business plans presented to him so challenging.

"A good-looking bastard."

Anne didn't argue. Philippe Lamont was a good-looking bastard.

"I doubt Bruce cares about that. He just cares about getting screwed over." Anne shrugged. It couldn't be helped. "Well, a piece of something is better than all of nothing."

"True, true." Nancy's agreement was quick in coming, as she took Anne's lead on strategy. "He's having a do next Friday to celebrate the financing and the customer deal. Black tie affair, cocktail wienies and bubbles. We're invited, the usual cover story, of course."

Accountants, as glamorous as it got. "Are we going?"

"You know you wanna." Nancy, after years of working together, knew Anne too well. "If only to observe your favorite money man interacting naturally with his glam bunny compatriots."

My favorite moneyman, Anne's eyes glowed, *the dynamic Monsieur Philippe Lamont, venture capitalist extraordinaire. Hmmm, in his tux too. Yummy.*

"Our job is so rough, hey, Nance?" Anne sighed with exaggeration. "Forced to go to fancy parties, toss back free drinks, and spend the evening watching a handsome playboy flirt with tall blondes."

"The roughest," her friend concurred with a laugh. "So I take it that's a yes. I'll dust off the uniform then, gotta swoop by the dry cleaners. Do you need a pick up?"

"Nah, mine's ready and waiting." The uniform, the standard little black dress, so standard that it would garner no interest. They could slip in and slip out and no one would be the wiser. Invisible.

"You're going to a party?" Ginny asked, as Anne rejoined them. Anne's voice must have carried in the narrow school hallway.

Her sister loved parties, so much so that it was her business now. "Just work, Ginny. A small client thing."

"Oh." The blonde's face fell in disappointment.

Silence stretched. The sisters both looked at Glenn pointedly, expecting him to take his leave so they could talk in private.

"I'm thinking about having a party," Glenn burst out.

Yeah, right, he was. This was the first Anne had heard of that.

"Really?" Her sister's spirits rebounded. "Do you need help planning?"

"I might." Glenn didn't have the guts to meet Anne's eyes.

"Well, then I'll give you my number." Ginny tucked her business card in Glenn's meaty right hand, her fingers lingering a moment longer than necessary. "Call me if you need help."

The older man looked at Ginny like he had been given the world rather than her blasted digits.

Chalk up one more admirer for Ginny. *What was the score? Hmmm, let's see, Ginny, one zillion, Anne, a big fat zero.*

It was on days like this that Anne was tempted to give herself up to her friend Stanley's not so gentle ministrations. Her make-up-artist buddy was a genius at creating illusions of beauty. With his talents, Anne could easily smite some poor unsuspecting man.

But what would happen when she stripped off the make up? When her brunette roots grew back? When she removed the bust-building water bra? When she went back to plain ol' Anne? Nope, Anne shuddered at the thought, deceptions were always found out sooner or later. And when they were, well, let's just say

that being ignored was preferable over outright rejection.

Two

The next Friday night, Anne studied the busy scene before her, frowning. "Nance, something's wrong. I can feel it."

To the average person, it looked like business as usual at one of these appreciation events. The speeches were standard, thanking the tireless support of staff, welcoming Lamont's company to the team, discussing goals and recent wins. The setup was also the same. Finger food and champagne circulating by wait staff. A bar in the corner. Men in tuxes and women in black evening wear swirling around them, crystal flutes in hand, their chatter a constant drone over the classical music being played. Yes, to an outside observer, everything looked fine.

However, Anne was no outside observer. She had attended hundreds of these parties and her entire career revolved around capturing nuances. Something was off; something didn't feel quite right, like the faint whiff of floral perfume in an all male office. What was the source? What would be the effect? That Anne couldn't yet put her finger on.

"What possibly could be wrong?" Her business partner and close friend sipped at her own champagne, blissfully unaware. "There hasn't been as much as a speed bump since last week. Bruce has his financing, and the orders are starting to ship. Your *M'sieur* Lamont should be looking at a return already."

"He's not mine." Anne murmured, "He doesn't know I even exist."

That was the absolute truth. All these years of following Lamont and he didn't know who she was. Sure, she would prefer that he not know what she did. That made the job easier, but he didn't even know her name.

Why did that rub Anne the wrong way?

Maybe because she was always so aware of him, Anne felt Lamont should be aware of her, at least slightly. Even now, her eyes drifted on their own accord to the dynamic venture capitalist. *Nope,* he certainly wasn't aware of plain, little Anne James. Philippe Lamont, not the tallest man himself, was busy charming some leggy blonde towering over him.

At least that was in character, Anne's lips twisted in disgust. He never could resist the tall blondes.

"Maybe if you actually talked to the man, he'd know who you are." Nancy nudged her forward.

Anne resisted, her bottom lip curling. "Oh, what's the point?

Jumping through hoops to make Lamont notice me couldn't help the business, and might even harm it."

"Annie, were we talking about business? *Geez,* when I said talk, I meant talk, not give him a sales pitch covering what you do for a living." Her friend shook her pretty auburn head. "Small talk like, 'Boy, summer sure has been hot,' or 'Hey, did you see the ball game last night.'"

"He's not interested in sports," Anne murmured, distracted.

Nancy's patient smile also was ignored. "So talk to him about something he is interested in. That you should know, Annie. You know everything about the man."

"Exactly," Anne agreed, her keen ears picked up Philippe's laughter over the buzz of the crowd. "That is why..." She tapped her pointed chin with her index finger.

"Why what?" Nancy finally gave into her friend's musings.

"Why I know that Philippe Lamont's acting strangely. His normally languid movements are a bit too fast, his voice a little too loud," Anne outlined, "like he's jumpy, eager, overly happy."

"Of course he's happy. He's getting a good return. I'd be thrilled with those dollars also."

"But he wouldn't be. This little deal wouldn't do it." She studied him. *Nope, it was something else,* she was sure of that. "He's acting like one of his babies has gone public."

"Maybe they have." Nancy turned to peer at the venture capitalist.

Anne shifted so her back was to Philippe. She didn't want their interest in him too apparent. "Nope, I would have known."

"Yes, you would have." There was a pause. "Maybe it's personal. Maybe he finally has succumbed to the fabulous Suzanne."

This last maybe caused the tinge in Anne's heart. She didn't know what that tinge was but it sure wasn't jealousy. That wouldn't make sense, to be possessive of a man who didn't even know her name. And above all, Anne was sensible.

"He wouldn't be flirting with the other blonde if he had. He's not a complete ass." Anne moved away from those dangerous thoughts. "What about Bruce? He isn't acting like himself either."

"Do you expect him to? Here? He's uncomfortable. Bruce is our typical entrepreneur. The social scene isn't his thing," Nancy rationalized.

"He wouldn't meet my eyes."

"Bruce isn't supposed to know you. You're a faceless accountant, remember? He's not the fastest thinker either. That's why we had to prep him so much before pitching to Lamont."

All good reasoning, but it didn't ease Anne's trepidation. Nancy could explain away until she was blue in the face, but she wouldn't convince Anne that nothing was wrong.

"Relax, Anne." Nancy gave her a side hug. "Everything's okay. Enjoy the night. Mix it up a bit. Have a drink."

Anne glanced down at her empty glass and then placed it on the tray of a passing busboy. The refill would have to wait. Before she could truly relax, she wanted to lay her suspicions to rest. The best way to do that was to get close to one of the players.

Hmmm. Preferably someone tall, gorgeous, and chatty. The fabulous Suzanne headed to the powder room, two equally beautiful girlfriends in tow. Anne followed at a safe distance. Yeah, Suzanne would know what was going on. She might let something slip in the intimacy of an all female tête-à-tête.

When Anne entered, the women were huddled around the mirrors, powdering their faces down and reapplying lipstick. Perfume hung in a stifling cloud around them. Anne didn't even warrant an acknowledgement as she slipped into an empty stall under the pretense of adjusting her black silk stockings. It was a pretense. The garter belt had them securely fastened. Pretty undergarments being her secret indulgence, she liked the very best.

"Is that a *Chanel*, Suze?" Deidre asked.

"Yes." Anne heard the rustle of skirts. "I thought such a tediously proper outfit was well matched to this sleeper of a party," the husky tones of Suzanne filled the room, "I swear if Philippe drags me to another…"

"But he will, and isn't that what you want, Suze? I thought you said that Philippe was a keeper." Her other friend twittered. *Must be Annabelle.* The grown woman ended every sentence in an adolescent giggle.

"Oh, he is, Belle, he is." This comment was flat and there was a pause. "But once I have the ring on my finger, I won't be going to these boring work functions anymore. No more consulting work for me either. With the wedding, I'll only have time for me."

There was a sharp intake of breath through perfect teeth.

"Okay, time for my girls too," Suzanne amended, and Deidre murmured something Anne couldn't make out.

"And it'll be easier planning the wedding this time. We'll be in the same city," Annabelle giggled.

"First things first. Focus on the ring. I just saw Philippe flirting with that chesty trollop Tiffany. Déjà vu all over again, Suze, shades of Michael."

"You know that we're never to discuss that," Suzanne hushed, and there was silence in the room.

"I think the ring will come soon," Annabelle soothed, "No one can resist Suze, the new and improved Suzanne, not even Philippe. Maybe tonight will be the night? I haven't seen him this excited since the two of you first started dating."

"God no. Get a grip, Belle. That isn't why," the girlfriend sighed, "Philippe's excited because of some information he received, or what not.

Said he was waiting for this for a while. I don't know, it really has nothing to do with me."

And as such, Anne concluded, Suzanne wasn't interested.

"Waiting for it for a while, huh?" The horsey laugh came from Deidre. "Sounds like you and the ring."

"Like you have one coming, Dee." The door opened. "You would be so lucky especially with that thing you're wearing." That spurred on a fresh round of fashion commentary until the voices finally drifted away.

Anne's instincts hadn't been wrong. Something was up but what? And how could she and her clients take advantage of it? Hoping to overhear more, Anne drifted to the crowded bar area and pushed herself to the front. The gossip mill was running overtime. Such and such deal had closed. A company was rumored to be for sale. A senior exec left. But nothing she didn't already know.

While Anne waited for her *Perrier*, she was jostled a bit, thrown off balance. That blond lawyer friend of Lamont's threw a thoughtless apology over his shoulder.

Gregory Myers. They had been introduced briefly once before though he probably wouldn't remember her. Why would he? No one else did. But where Myers was, usually Philippe Lamont wasn't that far off. The two friends, one light, one dark, worked the room as a devastatingly handsome duo. Women didn't stand a chance.

Even as that thought percolated, Anne was pushed once more. This time, her waist was grasped, anchoring her, her slight body pressed to hard muscle. "*Ne bougez pas*," an achingly familiar voice buzzed in her left ear.

"Thank you." An auto-reply. It was his hand on her waist. His body against hers.

"What a pleasant surprise, Mademoiselle Anne James." Hot breath caressed her cheek. "I had been wondering when my little brown sparrow would finally surrender to thirst, bless the water hole with her presence. Now here you are, in my arms."

She looked up into laughing brown eyes and swallowed. Hard. *No*, it hadn't been her overactive imagination. It was the man himself. Even more handsome up close, his chin etched and defined, his eyelashes obscenely long for a male. He had his arm around her like she was his to handle. And he knew her name.

"What, not even a chirp, Mademoiselle?" Philippe Lamont's mouth quirked upwards in a challenge.

She had to get a grip. This was a challenge, classic Lamont. He was playing one of those games he played with unwitting people when he was bored. Well, he wouldn't play with her. She eyed him warily and tried to step away. His fingers splayed across her hipbone wouldn't allow her.

"Chirp? Chirp?"

And now he ridiculed her like she was one of those brainless twits that fawned over him? Insulting. Her response was cool and steady.

"*M'sieur* Lamont, why should I bother to speak? My common sparrow song pales with that of the canaries you normally listen to. To try to compete would be foolish and I'm not a foolish woman."

"Indeed." His eyes sparkled with appreciation. "You're not a foolish woman and I have been listening to a canary. You're quite correct, *mon Cherie*, although not the type you were thinking of. He told me all sorts of things, interesting things about you and I."

You and I, that sent a quiver down her spine. It was business then. *How had he…*

"Who?" Anne stopped in mid question, her *Perrier* arriving.

Philippe picked it up with his spare hand, waving the glass underneath his slightly hooked nose. "No alcohol?"

Anne shook her head, bringing his attention to her hair. Before she was aware of what he was about, Philippe reached up and slid off the barrette holding it back. Her long straight brown tresses cascaded over his fingers.

"Much better," he murmured, "so soft, like a bolt of honey brown silk." His eyes warmed for only a moment before returning to their usual cold brilliance. "Yes, no alcohol for my Anne. *Ahh*, but then you are working tonight, *non?*"

"Working? Do I look like the wait staff?" Anne's answer was as dry as she could manage, trying to put him on the defensive. This tactic backfired.

"Do you look like the wait staff?" his voice lowered. He held her at arm's length and let his lazy appreciative eyes rove over her body, his glance as intimate as a touch. He was good, she had to give him that. Anne found herself responding before remembering that this was part of his strategy. "With your hair up, you looked like a woman who didn't want to be noticed. Now you look like a woman a man already has noticed."

"*Hmmm*, so what you are saying is that I look used up and tired." She couldn't take the nonsense he was spurting seriously. It meant nothing, flirting second to Lamont's nature.

Knowing that, his amused smile still managed to light something deep within her. "Ah, *mon Cherie*." His fingertips caressed her cheek. "You were worth the effort."

Anne was bumped again, pushed against Philippe's body. She tried to step back but his arm was around her waist, her hips squashed against his.

"What do you want from me, *M'sieur* Lamont?" came out as a strangled question.

"*Tout a coup*, I don't know." His eyes were on her lips and he leaned forward. Anne thought for one wild moment that he was going to kiss her and it was a struggle to keep her features serene.

But then Philippe stepped aside, his face knowing as though, despite her best efforts at concealing them, he had read her fanciful thoughts. He slid her hand through the crook of his arm; she could feel his lean muscles ripple under her palm, and he starting moving her toward the center of the room. Anne didn't know what he was planning. She knew only that there was a plan and she needed to put a stop to it. Pronto.

"How do you know my name?" Her question was deceivingly light and careless.

"How do you know mine?" Philippe asked back.

"Everyone here knows yours." Anne looked around. People were glancing at her curiously. "Not everyone knows mine."

"Not many people know yours." His long fingers drifted over the back of her hand. "It took me a while to uncover it."

"Why would you bother?"

"Why? I've been hunting you, *mon Cherie*. I know your business plans, they have the smell of you." He sniffed by her ear and she shivered. "The Bernstein was yours?"

"Yes." Anne's backbone straightened.

"Ace?"

"Yes"

"D-F-T? Promagic? Chinklette?"

"All mine," Anne admitted proudly. They were excellent offerings, most proved lucrative for Lamont. "But how did you…?"

"With each, I threatened to withhold funding if they didn't tell me who did their plans. Who coached them to sell to me. Who told them my preferences, my weaknesses. My secrets. You do know my secrets, don't you Anne?"

Anne ignored his question. "They were good deals. You wouldn't have walked away from them."

"Ahhh, my little sparrow, you know that. I know that. The entrepreneurs, they weren't so sure. But to your credit, none of them caved. Quite loyal to you."

Anne's stomach fell. She knew where this was heading. "Until Bruce."

"Mais oui." He grinned. "Bruce needed the financing too badly and he is weak. Under my questioning."

"Interrogation, more likely," Anne amended coolly.

"D'accord, interrogation, you are correct." Philippe nodded, his brown curls springing to life upon that high forehead. "He fell apart like a business with no sales force. He told me all about you, little one. I even know where you live."

"I'm in the book. You could have just looked me up," Anne used flippancy to hide her growing anxiety. "So what? You now know I did the business plans. Did you track me down to thank me?"

"Thank you?" Philippe sounded entertained.

"For making you a lot of money over the years." Her chin lifted in defiance. "You should be thanking me."

"Sorry to disillusion you, *mon Cherie*, but you didn't do me any favors. No, I would have found the deals eventually," he dismissed, "and at a greater discount, nests fallen from trees, rather than polished plums. You merely increased the price and cost me money."

"Ungrateful bastard." Anne dropped her head, her voice barely detectable.

But loud enough for Lamont's sharp ears to pick up.

"My sweet little sparrow, you call me a bastard in front of my sister?" Philippe repeated the insult clearly, nodding to the sophisticated older woman now beside them. Anne recognized her immediately. "Not nice."

"Your brother is a bastard." Anne didn't hesitate to announce, her voice flat and matter of fact.

"Child, in that, you're correct. Philippe is a bastard. However, he's not my brother." The perfectly coiffured woman's tone was slightly amused, her blue eyes flashing in interest.

"I know that, Ms. McKenzie."

This widened those eyes. "How do you know me?"

Sixty-three, twice divorced, ten year old Siamese cat named Fluff. Anne did her research. Plus everyone in the start-up financing business knew of Ms. McKenzie, angel of the angels. She had been one of the first local female financiers, blazing a trail for others. To repeat that would be viewed as sucking up and Anne had no reason to do that. Regardless of what Philippe said, she brought deals to them, not the other way around.

She simply said, "It's my job."

"And that job is?" Anne was looked up and down, it was no *Chanel* she was wearing but she knew that the slim black dress was simple and elegant. Ms. McKenzie would not find fault with it. "I'm sorry but I don't know you."

Anne wasn't about to leak her identity to another funding source. "That also is my job."

Two sets of white teeth gleamed their appreciation.

"She's not a fountain of information, is she, Philippe?" The angel investor spoke as if Anne were absent. Or deaf.

She was neither, but ignored them all the same, her teeth gritted. She would not lose her temper. This was business and emotion had no place in it.

"*Au contraire, mon ange*, she knows more than you and I would wish."

His eyes danced merrily. "Don't you, Anne?"

Anne smiled sweetly, trying to slip her hand out from under his. Philippe held on tight.

"Anne, doesn't ring a bell. She must know more, I suppose, if she interests you, naughty man." Ms. McKenzie patted Philippe's shoulder. "Will I be seeing more of her?"

"Much more. Anne will be working with me closely," Philippe explained cheerfully.

Anne swallowed back a nasty retort, counted to three and said lightly, "Our dear, dear Philippe is laboring under some misconceptions, I'm afraid."

"Don't be afraid, *Cherie*. You know that I don't believe in labor and you will be working with me." He winked at her. "That's already decided, or are you too busy doing… what is it that you do again?"

Brown eyes met brown. Anne didn't say a word. There was no misunderstanding the veiled threat. He would expose her here and now if pushed.

"Sounds like details are dangling," Ms. McKenzie cooed. "Wrapping them up does interest me but that's your responsibility, Philippe, and of course, best done in private. May I suggest the two of you take a stroll in the hallway? It is more conducive to such things."

And with that, the Angel drifted off to another nearby group, dragging their interest away from the sight of Philippe playing with the sweet little sparrow as he so aptly called her.

"We have been told, *mon Cherie*." Philippe's dark head bowed. "*L'Ange* is always so correct about these things. There are ears all around us and what we have to discuss should be done in private."

"I don't have anything to discuss with you," Anne proclaimed airily, but they were already headed toward the door.

Although the corridor was several degrees cooler, Anne didn't feel it. She was irritated and flustered. How could she not be? Philippe was a typical power demon and now that he had dirt on her and her company, he wouldn't shy away from leveraging it to gain control over her. She had to discuss it with Nancy first, Anne fumed, but she wasn't about to let that happen. She'd send out a press release before she let him call the shots.

Anne walked only so far before stopping. "So *M'sieur* Lamont, you wished to discuss something. Let's be professional, and discuss it."

Philippe looked down at the brunette and grinned. Anne James appeared to be pure business, her actions devoid of emotion, her words cool and collected, but he knew that he had to be getting to her. She was intelligent enough to realize that she was being maneuvered, proud enough to dislike it. He had a few weapons in his arsenal, one being the ability to draw a physical response from the opposite sex. Philippe slid an arm around her slight form, running his fingers up her backbone. Anne straightened so abruptly that he thought she would clear the ground.

The sparrow had passion, she couldn't disguise it, no matter how hard she tried.

Her pride was also a tool to be used against her. She couldn't tell him to shove off without admitting that he affected her. She'd never do that.

Anne turned from him, a subtle attempt to dislodge his hand. He moved with her. "Nothing to discuss? Then I'll go."

Philippe wasn't about to let her go anywhere. "Not so fast, *Cherie*. We do have some things to talk about."

"Like what?" Anne looked at him doubtfully.

"Like your starting date, for example, and your title."

"*M'sieur* Lamont?"

"Philippe, please," he murmured. "We know each other well enough to be on first names, wouldn't you say?" His hand drifted down her back to the soft round of her buttocks. She tried to shrug him away but he grasped on more securely.

Philippe had expected the smoothness of tights under the fabric of her skirt. Instead he could feel the ridges of her undergarments, straps running down her thighs, like, he didn't quite know. Yet another mystery to be solved.

"Philippe." She sighed. "I have my own business to manage. We've a backlog as it is, I can't give that up to work for you."

"Only temporarily." He studied her serious pixie face, those big brown eyes. No she wasn't so plain, not beautiful, but not so plain either. "It should take you three months, tops."

"Irrelevant. Why would I work for you?"

Because I can teach you things, some wicked, wicked things. But no, he couldn't say that; it would scare her. Besides, he had to stay focused, revenge first. "Because then we'll be even."

Brown eyes rolled. "I don't owe you anything. You owe me."

"Ah, that we can argue about all day."

"I don't have all day." She tapped one high-heeled shoe in impatience. Was it a trial for Anne to talk to him? Didn't she know how many women would kill to be in her place?

"Me neither, *Cherie*." That was incorrect. For her, he had all day or at least until she no longer intrigued him. "If you do this, I'll keep quiet as to who you are."

One delicate eyebrow rose. Anne didn't believe him.

"I promise you." He brought her hand to his heart. Philippe could feel her fingers tremble under his.

She opened her mouth and he knew then that she was going to

question his word. He wouldn't tolerate the insult, his dark look nipping her comment in the bud. His word was his bond.

"Three months and you'll stay silent?" Anne bit her full bottom lip, drawing Philippe's eyes there.

"Yes." He brought her hand to his own lips and pressed a kiss to her palm, his tongue darting out to taste her skin. Salty. Soft.

Anne's eyes flashed, and she pulled her hand away, bristling with suspicion. "What will I be doing?"

Whatever I like, Philippe's eyes roved over her body. "We can discuss that on Monday."

"I don't know about this," she stonewalled. "I'll have to discuss it with my partner."

"Nancy Sherbourne," he interjected, and Anne stiffened in surprise. *Ah, little sparrow, you're not the only one doing your homework.*

"Yes, I..." Whatever she was going to say was interrupted by Suzanne.

"Philippe, darling, there you are." Anne watched as the blonde's perfectly manicured hand wrapped around his arm. Philippe immediately dropped his arms from around Anne, leaving her with no doubt that he knew his behavior had been improper.

"Suzanne, this is business," the venture capitalist rumbled.

The scornful look Suzanne gave Anne dismissed her as possibly being any threat. "Of course it is; it couldn't be anything but."

Anne's lips twisted.

"Whatever it is can wait until later," glossy lips cooed, "Gregory's looking for you, said it was urgent, some deal gone south, or some other."

Business. This got Lamont's attention. "Anne, we'll discuss this further on Monday."

"I'm busy Monday," Anne murmured, secure in the fact that he didn't have time to delay.

"Monday." Philippe shot one last look over his shoulder as he strolled away. "I'm expecting you."

Three

Anne did not make her Monday meeting with Lamont. Why? For no reason other than stubbornness. Was she busy? Not at all.

The day started with her nine o'clock calling in sick with the flu. It had been going around, or so the *CNBC*-watching Nancy informed Anne. Then her ten o'clock hadn't received the necessary paperwork. It didn't make much sense to meet without it, did it? Anne supposed not. And so it went all day. Appointment after appointment cancelled or rescheduled.

It could happen, Anne told herself. The odds were very, very low but it could happen. Those already impossible odds dwindled down to nothing by end of day Tuesday. Not a single client made their way into the office, their explanations, pathetically weak, and in the case of one poor CEO suffering from smallpox, improbable.

If that wasn't suspicious enough, there had been no word from Lamont. On Wednesday morning, the matter had to be addressed.

Nancy burst into her office and flopped down on the guest chair. "Cancelled." she proclaimed in a huff, "Our ten o'clock cancelled."

"Again." Anne groaned. "What was the excuse this time?"

"Said production went down." Her friend made a face. "I don't believe him. He's not a good liar."

Making her clients lie. "That, that…" Anne rose from her seat and strolled over to the window, watching the traffic crawl like ants twelve stories below. She clenched and unclenched her fists. *Of all the controlling…*

"Annie, do you think it's…?"

"That cold hearted bastard, yes." Anne nodded. "I gave being busy as an excuse and then surprise, surprise, my days magically free up."

Nancy didn't have to ask which cold-hearted bastard, Anne was referring to. She knew the story. The blackmail, the threats, the feel of his body snug against hers. Correction, Nancy knew most of the story.

"Amazing how that happened." Her friend sounded slightly bemused.

"No, not amazing at all. Blasted aggravating. He's trying to force me to do what he wants. I just know it." *If he thinks he can control me, he has another think coming.*

"It does sounds like Lamont. It has his finesse. But Annie, think, how would he know about our appointments?"

She glanced at Nancy. Anne was not as naïve about the accessibility of corporate information. "He, unofficially, has hackers on staff." Lamont skirted the borders of legality, whatever got the job done. "A throw back to his programming roots. I suppose he just lifted the information."

There was silence as Nancy absorbed this, then she started moaning over and over. "Oh my Lord, oh my Lord."

"Oh my Lord, what?" What was Nancy hyperventilating about?

"I'm so sorry, Annie, he might not have had to. Lamont has partial ownership in the IT company we outsource to."

"Nance!" Anne's mouth dropped open. Office management was her friend's domain. Anne assumed there was separation between vendors and end users. "What were you thinking?"

"That they were the best value," Nancy said in way of an explanation. "How was I to know Lamont would play hardball?"

"He doesn't play anything but." *Focus on the issues.* It didn't matter how they got into this predicament, only that they got back out again.

Anne glared at the nearby office tower blocking her morning sun as she rolled the options over in her mind. Only two presented themselves. Stubbornly hold out, harming the business in the process, or swallow her pride and meet with him. Swallow her pride? Cave in? Not if it was up to her.

But it wasn't up to her. They were a team, she and Nancy. And Nancy had her own issues. "What are we going to do? We can't have that many down days, it'll drain our cash flow and I really, really, really need this month's distributions, Annie." The desperate plea took the decision out of Anne's hands.

"There isn't much else to do." Anne would do what was best for the business and what was best for her friend. "I'll go see Lamont."

"Are you sure?" was Nancy's attempt to sound sympathetic. Anne heard only relief in her voice.

Was she sure? The only sure thing was that she was walking into a trap. "Might as well hear what the man has to say. He won't let up 'til I do."

"What do you think he wants?" Her friend came to stand supportively beside her.

"He said three months of my time."

"Doing what?"

Anne shrugged, not willing to waste energy assigning words to her worry.

Nance had the energy. "Three months is a long time, Annie. A lot could happen."

Yep, a lot could happen and none of it good. What had Lamont said? He had been hunting her. That was it. The goal of hunting was to kill.

Anne's bleak outlook must have reflected in her face. "It'll be okay," Nancy soothed, hugging Anne's shoulder. "You know Lamont. If anyone can get out of this unscathed, it would be you. You know how to sell to him."

Nancy was right. It was selling, like pitching a business plan, a task she did every day. But with Philippe Lamont, could Anne keep herself emotionally detached? Somehow the man got to her.

"And treat it like selling." Nancy read her thoughts. "Business, nothing else. You can do that, can't you Annie?
Your feelings for Lamont won't get in the way?"

Anne's head shot up. "What feelings?" What was Nance talking about now?

"You know." Her partner couldn't hold her level-eyed gaze. Head down, she fiddled with the papers on Anne's tidy desk. "That you have a bit of a crush on the man."

"Crush?" Anne snorted. "I don't think so. This is business Nance. Sure I might admire him…"

The redhead gave her an arched eyebrow look.

"But that's all," Anne insisted, her gut telling her that wasn't exactly true. It should be true, if she was thinking straight, it would be true, but it wasn't quite. Did she let just any power monger grab her ass at a party? Well, no …

"If you say so." Nancy didn't believe her either.

"I say so," Anne said firmly, as if saying so made it true.

"Good. Then we'll have no issues, Annie. You'll talk us out of this mess and it'll be back to business as usual." Nancy made it sound so easy.

Easy, it wouldn't be, but nothing Anne couldn't handle. She straightened, rolling her rounded shoulders back. "That's the plan."

~ * ~

Less than three hours later, Anne was seated in Lamont Ventures' luxurious reception area, cooling her favorite navy blue heels on the dark hardwood floor. He was purposely making her wait, showing her he was the boss. *Bloody control freak.*

It didn't matter. Anne was prepared. Seated in the black leather chair, she glanced through the colorful papers in her lap. This was the baby business plan for a hip, new club, belonging to Rochelle, one of her *Young C.E.O.*s students. She scanned it with the critical eye of experience. Where was the college radio marketing? Yes, the Internet stuff was good, but club kids also listened to music, their own music. Anne jotted these thoughts into the margins.

That wasn't her sole diversion. Her eyes and ears were open, mentally recording names funneling through the switchboard, watching guests flow in and out of the active office. Anything she might be able to use in the future, Anne made a note of. There wasn't much. One strange instance when she was on the receiving end of a nasty glare. A tall and distinguished silver haired management type blew through the lobby. His face dark with fury, he shot Anne a hate filled glower.

Why? She didn't know him. So who was he? Could be no one, could be one of the new executives she hadn't yet met. Careful about who faced the public, Philippe kept his untried henchmen under tight wraps.

The man's identity was still in the top of her mind when the solid mahogany door swung open, revealing an older lady, only a few inches taller than Anne. "Miss James, I'm Missus Depeche, Mister Lamont's executive assistant." One soft lined hand grasped hers as Anne rose. "He will see you now," her pleasant voice matching her smile, "if you'll follow me."

He will see me now. Well, jolly good for him. I am not ready to see him. Anne took her time, lining the papers up carefully before putting them back in her briefcase, working in deliberate slow mo. *Lamont could dang well wait.*

Finally, fresh out of ideas to stretch the turnaround time, she straightened. Was that a glimmer of amusement in Mrs. Depeche's eyes? That is, before her face smoothed serenely into business. Anne thought so. The lady was on the ball, didn't miss a thing; probably knew everything about everyone that shared the same air as her boss. That meant...

"Missus Depeche, I saw a man while I was waiting. He looked familiar and I'm certain that we've met before but try as I might, I can't place him."

The older woman eyed Anne suspiciously. Seconds stretched before the woman finally broke down. "Maybe I can help. What did he look like?"

"Tall, gray hair, trim, dark suit..."

"Green tie?" Mrs. Depeche relaxed a bit.

Anne nodded.

"Must be Kevin Maple, our vice-president of new business development," Lamont's executive assistant explained. "He joined us last week but some of your clients have been working with him closely."

"Oh, yes, that's it." Anne was now certain she hadn't met him before. Maybe his dirty look hadn't been directed at her but at the world in general.

"Have you been working with *M'sieur* Lamont long, Missus Depeche?" Anne switched gears, making small talk as they clipped along the hallway.

"Since the *L-W-H* days." The woman smiled. That was Lamont's start up, *Lamont, Westfield and Hartford*, or "Lamont's Working Hell" as it was nicknamed due to the grueling hours worked. The hard work had paid off. Lamont and team took the company public, giving him his venture-capital seed money, Lamont eventually selling *LWH* completely. "But then you knew that, didn't you, Miss James?"

Anne did. The story was that fiercely loyal, Mrs. Depeche had stuck with Lamont through the lean times, times with no reliable salary. In return, he trusted her completely. "You know why I'm here?"

"Of course. I'm his executive assistant, dear."

Anne knew how that went. Mrs. Depeche was the gatekeeper. She saw and heard all flowing through his office. Including any plans for revenge. *What dreadful task does Lamont have lined up for me*, she wondered. Had to be especially horrid, for him to blackmail her.

Anne took a ragged breath and crinkled eyes darted to her face in sympathy. "Don't fret too much, Miss James. From what I understand, you'll manage," the older woman assured her as she opened the corner office door.

"*Merci*, Sylvie. Close the door when you leave, *s'il vous plaît*." Philippe sat behind a large wooden desk, flipping through a file. He didn't glance up as Anne entered but she couldn't ignore him as easily. *Blast it, the man is striking to look at. He oozes power, strength, control.* A loud click signaled her escape route blocked off. *Complete control.*

"Sit." He gestured to the chair in front of him, frowning at a paper in his hand.

Sit. One word. Sit. Like I'm a dog, a stray dog, full of fleas, about to be put out of my misery.

"I'd rather stand. I doubt that this will take long."

"It will." He flicked cold brown eyes over her serviceable navy blue suit. It fit her like a glove, the pencil line skirt ending just below the knee. "Sit."

She didn't. Even if she had to stand for hours, she wouldn't sit.

Philippe took out an eight by ten white square, holding it up as if to compare against her face. "I prefer you with your hair down." His lips twisted disapprovingly at the tight chignon she was sporting. He tossed the glossy piece of paper, print side up, across the desk.

Before her brain told her hands to resist, Anne clasped the photo. *Mistake.* That was exactly what he wanted. *Why would he want that? To shock me.* It was a shot of her face, her hair tumbling down all around, the fitted tee shirt, she recognized as the one she wore on Saturday, grocery shopping. *Shock me?* Consider it mission accomplished. Anne sat down with a thump.

"Why do you have a photo of me?" she asked, her voice not betraying any of her wonderment. Later, she would be proud of how calm she sounded.

"Not a photo, photos." Philippe dropped a couple more in front of her. "I like this one." It was of her laughing, out walking her elderly neighbor's energetic Jack Russell terrier, the lease tangled around her legs.

"But this." He tilted the photo up so she couldn't peak. "This one is my favorite." He looked at her, thoroughly entertained, the devil dancing in his eyes.

Yep, entertained. The man was having fun at her expense. Playing another game, trying to throw her cool demeanor off. It wouldn't work. She wouldn't let him see her squirm. Anne waited patiently, her hands folded ladylike on her lap. *Breathing in. Breathing out.*

Philippe paused. Should he wait? Make her beg to see it? *Non,* chilly Mademoiselle James wouldn't beg, she wouldn't even ask, and hesitating would only punish him, not her. He'd bet his last billion this would get the reaction he wanted. Philippe slid the photo across the table, watching her closely. Although she didn't make a sound, a vivid red crept up that long neck and flushed her cheeks. *Success. Finally, a human response.*

He knew exactly what she was looking at. According to the investigator, Anne had been grabbing a newspaper from the box outside her condo building as she did every morning. She was a creature of habit, this Anne, and just when she bent over, a lucky gust of wind lifted her knee length black pleated skirt.

Ahhhh... and what it exposed, neither man would have guessed. Not in a thousand years. The prim and proper, oh so serious, Anne was wearing silk stockings and a garter belt. Who wore garter belts nowadays? Especially as everyday wear? Most especially since as far as he and the investigator knew, she had no current *amours?*

Only the woman before him would. And those legs, *merde,* those legs, she really was hiding something wonderful. He could feel his body responding, hardening, and shifted in his chair, uncomfortable, grateful for the concealing desk. A delicious dessert in lackluster packaging, this Anne was. Philippe liked that.

Back in France, when he was a child, his mama would, on special occasions, bring home pastries from the corner bakery. The box would be plain, brown cardboard tied with string but inside, well, inside was a treat for the eyes and for the mouth. That was Anne, a treat for the eyes and likely for the mouth too. As long as one looked past the wrapping.

She didn't wish for that to happen. Mademoiselle James, as his fanciful thoughts swirled, had slipped the photo into the side of her briefcase and refolded her hands calmly.

Damn, she is a cold one. Any other woman would have been hopping mad.

"*Oui,* you take that one, *mon Cherie,*" he purred, the challenge to crack her professional demeanor too tempting to resist. "I have copies. In fact, I'm thinking of loading it as a screensaver."

"You, *M'sieur* Lamont, are a bastard," her gentle tone took the edge off her harsh words.

"You keep calling me that, *Cherie.*" Philippe smiled condescendingly at her. "I'm not one, you know. My parents were well married, had two daughters, by the time their only son came along."

He watched as her eyes closed, dark lashes fanned against pale cheeks. It looked like she was counting. Calming herself back down, no doubt. He was impressed with her control.

Steady brown eyes opened, holding his. "You wished to discuss something, *M'sieur* Lamont?"

Ah, business, he supposed they should complete that. What was the phrase? Business before pleasure.

"I'll need you for three months maximum." She crossed her legs and Philippe could hear the whisper of silk on silk. *Merde, I need her here and now.* How had that happened? How had such a quiet brown sparrow managed to stir his desire so?

"So you've said. Three months of my time in exchange for your silence." Anne summed up the deal in one sentence. "Why me?"

Was that slight eyebrow twitch curiosity? Philippe thought so. Anne had a good poker face, *oui*, but there were subtle clues that he was starting to pick up on. "You know me, *Cherie*, you know what I like, you know what I look for in a company."

"That irritates you," she read him as he was reading her. He had to work on his own tells.

Et oui, it irritated the hell out of him, he preferred his thoughts to remain shielded, a mystery. And it wasn't just that she knew his thoughts, she knew his next moves, his intentions.

"It is… unnerving, that you are a woman too and know that I think." Philippe shrugged. He couldn't understand it, usually women and men were so different, the Venus and Mars thing.

"Let's forget for a moment that I'm a woman," Anne suggested.

Come again? The image of shapely legs wrapped in black flimsy fabric filled his mind.

"Impossible," was his only comment.

"It isn't relevant to the discussion." She stacked the photos into one neat pile. "So I know you. Why's that important?"

"I need someone who knows me to evaluate some companies I'm considering."

"Why can't you do that yourself? Why do you need me?"

"I am not, how can I say it… impartial." Philippe watched fascinated as a faint trace of expressions swept across her face, starting with disbelief and ending with understanding. *Zut, she holds her emotions close.* If he hadn't been paying attention, they would have been missed.

"You slept with them," was her blunt conclusion.

The woman didn't mince words. And the fact that she saw him as some sex-obsessed Romeo didn't please him. He was more discriminating than that. Philippe wanted to say no, he had slept with none. However, that was not possible. Mademoiselle James was the type to dig, dig into an investigation, and Denise, to add fuel to the fire, was not shy about their former relationship.

"Only one," he was forced to admit, "the others are family. None I can look at without emotion."

"So you wish me, a complete outsider, to evaluate them? Why not one of your staffers?"

"An outsider is ideal and I wish for you to both evaluate and pass judgment."

"You mean turn them down," she guessed. "You think their proposals are weak and want me to do your dirty work."

She was a smart one, this Anne. "I don't know that. They could be brilliant."

The sparrow tilted her head in clear question.

"*D'accord, d'accord*, you're correct. They are most likely sub-par. You and I know how hard it is to find a gem."

"I do. So I'm to turn them down. You couldn't ask your team because you're too professional to place any of them in that position." Her brain was ticking along, putting all her concerns to rest. She liked everything nice and tidy. "Whereas, I'm disposable."

"It shouldn't be that difficult for you. You turn down clients also," Philippe pointed out.

She did, she did indeed. Anne had to, to ensure that she represented only quality offers. She didn't like it though, and she had a feeling that turning down companies for life-extending financing would be much more difficult.

Is that his plan? Anne studied Philippe. *To emphasize that his job is more difficult than I imagined?* Plausible, but she didn't think it enough. He had some larger goal to justify her involvement in his business. Anne wouldn't feel comfortable until she figured out what it was.

She left her seat and strode around the office, slowing only at the window, giving the executive toy telescope positioned there a quick peek into. He had a nice view of the city; better real estate than her little office but it didn't tell her much about the man. No, where she stopped was at a framed photo hanging on the dark walls. It was a group shot, faded, the fashions from over a decade back. Anne searched the photo for a familiar face. Yes, there he was, much younger, innocent almost, his arms around a gorgeous, generously endowed blonde, many inches taller than himself.

What to do with this man? Three months of working with Lamont and he promised to keep her anonymity intact. Anne didn't fool herself that it would go back to status quo afterwards but perhaps the hands-on learning she gained would offset any fallout. It was manageable, running her business and assisting Lamont. She could meet with her own clients outside of the nine-to-five. Entrepreneurs tended to work all hours and the ones she worked with were especially motivated. It would mean long days and a pull back in some revenue, *Nance wouldn't make her numbers, unless, hmmm, that was a thought.*

"It was taken less than a week before we went public." She looked up to find Philippe standing beside her. He was taller than her, most people, male or female were, but his height differential wasn't that significant. Looking into his eyes didn't cause a severe crick in her neck.

"I like your hair" was all she said.

"Mais oui." Philippe chuckled, running a hand over his close cropped curls. "It was much longer then and less gray."

"A long time ago."

"It was. But not so long that I've forgotten how nervous I was. So many of my employees were counting on the I-P-O to pay their bills. Not much room for failure. I couldn't sleep the entire week."

Nervous? Lamont? That must have been a long time ago. Anne couldn't picture him less than one hundred percent confident. Not now, not ever.

They stood in silence, both peering at the photo, lost in their thoughts.

Why would the invincible Philippe Lamont share what could be seen by many as weakness? It wasn't a random confession. It had a purpose. What that was, Anne didn't know.

She did know that his every word, his every action was a part of a bigger strategy. That's the type of game he played, tight. Could she match him? Could she go head-to-head with Lamont on his own turf, and win? Then again, did she have much of a choice? She doubted that. Even if she said no, Lamont would have alternative plans for her. His first offer was usually his best.

"It'll cut into business. To offset, I'll require compensation."

"One hundred grand for the three months," he offered, and her eyes darted up to meet his. That was exactly the figure she had been thinking of.

"One twenty-five," she countered, regardless.

"One hundred, and that's final," Philippe repeated, "I'm not haggling with you, *Cherie.*"

"If, and that's a big if, we're to work together, I'd prefer Anne." She wanted to be taken seriously in his organization, by him, by his staff. The endearments had to stop.

"I'll call you Anne," he agreed, "in public." Since she wasn't about to entertain him privately, that would suffice. "I've delayed the entrepreneurs long enough. I'd rather not waste more of their time. Start date tomorrow?"

Too soon. She had to wrap her head around the situation. "I need at least the rest of the week to rearrange my schedule."

"I thought it was clear." Confirmation that he was the person messing with it.

"Yeah, that was convenient." Anne didn't bother to say more. "I still need the time. I'll start Monday and work nine to five, no overtime. Take it or leave it."

"Take it or leave it? You forget, *Cherie*," Philippe stepped closer. "that I hold all the cards."

"And you forget," she didn't back down, "that holding all the cards leaves me with nothing, nothing to play with, nothing to even bluff with. To win, I'll be forced to cheat."

"You can't touch me." Philippe stroked under her raised chin, causing shivers on her skin.

"No one is untouchable, *M'sieur* Lamont." Anne resisted the urge to move away. "Even you. Mess with me or my reputation and I'll take you out."

"Is that a threat, Mademoiselle James?" His voice was deathly quiet, matching her own.

"That's a guarantee."

They stood chest to chest, neither relenting. Then a wicked grin spread across Philippe's handsome face and he started to chuckle. Anne almost returned the smile, catching herself in time.

"We are too stubborn, you and I," Philippe admitted, "Can we declare this match a draw, *Cherie*?" He held out his hand in a gesture of peace.

She hesitated only a second before slipping her hand in his. Instead of grasping and releasing, he held on, his hands warm, firm.

"You understand that I'll have to sue our friend Bruce." Anne felt obliged to be open. Much as she regretted filing the lawsuit, she was forced to, to set an example for others. To do anything but would be a sign of weakness, and weakness killed companies.

"I expect no less. Gregory is already preparing the defense." Philippe nodded, his fingertips caressing her wrist. "It won't affect our relationship."

"Our working relationship," she clarified.

"*Oui*, that too." His eyes twinkled and she decided to take his words as a jest. Lamont flirted with every woman, young or old, attractive or plain. It wouldn't progress further.

But when he looked down at her, and his eyes glowed with that amber undertone, remembering that was difficult. Her breath caught as he brought her close, his arms slipped around her and his hands drifted down past her waist to her buttocks.

"Philippe," she squeaked out a protest, trying to twist away. He held her securely, his lack of height not translating to lack of strength.

"Anne, I'm disappointed," he murmured, "no stockings today?"

Blasted man, he was feeling for a garter belt. There wasn't any. Of course she was wearing stockings, she hated tights with a passion, but today, hold-ups. The stockings didn't require any assistance and provided a smoother line under her slim skirt.

He was watching her, reading her, and the gold in those brown eyes burned brighter. "Interesting, *mon Cherie*. I see I must look into this more closely." His hand passed over her rear again, squeezing softly.

It wasn't a good situation. Sure, her traitorous body was having a field day but indulging her baser needs would put her at a further disadvantage. She couldn't allow that. *No*, Anne had to resist, but prudently. She knew Lamont. If she simply pulled away, Philippe would pursue her. He was a hunter to his soul.

So Anne tried another tactic. She leaned towards the heat, letting her body go limber, her eyelids lower, resting her hands on his shoulders. It drew an immediate response, his grip loosened while his body hardened. She could feel him pressing against her.

As her own body temperature rose, as his musky male scent reached out to ensnare her, Anne looked up. What she read in his eyes brought her back to earth with a bone-jarring thump. There was emotion there; yes, but it wasn't passion. It sure wasn't love. Nope, it was pure unmistakable triumph. Like this was some battle he had won.

The bastard. Anne pushed him away, disgusted with both him and herself. She should have known better. She knew Lamont. She knew how he operated. Anne scrubbed all emotion from her voice until her breathlessness was barely detectable.

"I'd appreciate not being manhandled during my three months here, *M'sieur* Lamont. I trust you can control yourself."

Yet another emotion colored Philippe's eyes dead black, anger. "I'll manage, mademoiselle," he growled, "Since we're clearly done here, please leave. Forgive me if I don't walk you out."

She understood this lack of courtesy only too well, his arousal outlined against his navy blue dress pants. His brain might have been experiencing triumph but his body told a more primitive story. Philippe Lamont wanted her. Her, Anne James, plain brown Anne. It was almost beyond comprehension.

She scurried from the room, eyes forward, avoiding Mrs. Depeche's curious gaze. It wasn't a pure physical wanting, Anne knew that. It had purpose, an ulterior motive.

But under all those layers, it was still desire at the core. That was something, wasn't it?

Four

For the past three weeks, Philippe hadn't touched Anne. That wasn't exactly true. He had touched her, a fleeting hand on her wrist, a circling of her waist, a gentle squeeze of her shoulders. Once he had been unable to resist running the back of his finger over the softness of her cheek.

But he hadn't explored any forbidden places, not one curve of that perky rear, not one plum sized breast. Not that he hadn't wanted to; he had, with every essence of his being. Even now his hands itched to travel along her jawbone, down that long neck of hers and disappear into the gentle valley below. She was driving him absolutely mad, this little brown sparrow, and she seemed unaware of that fact.

These afternoon meetings were a special kind of torture, designed especially for him. It was the two of them, alone in his office, Anne so close he smelled the fruity fragrance of her hair. He should stop holding the meetings, *oui*, he really should, but he couldn't help himself.

Right now, she frowned down at a contract he gave her to peruse. A feather-light sigh escaped those full lips, rippling her sleeveless beige shirt, her chocolate brown jacket hanging on the chair back behind her.

"I'm not being too hard on you, am I, *Cherie*?" Philippe had to touch that exposed bare arm, stroking it with his fingertips, her skin humming.

"Hard on me? I've done nothing for the past two weeks." Anne knew not to glance up. Philippe would be watching her, his brown eyes glowing gold, not bothering to hide his need.

"You will." Anne also ignored his touch or at least tried to. It was as light as a breath upon her and did funny things to her mind, over-riding rational thought with pure sensory reaction. "I intend to get my money's worth, my pound of flesh so to speak."

His pound of flesh, figuratively and literally. There was a promise in those words, a promise of more than business. And she would give in, her resistance, pitifully weak to begin with, cracking. But not yet. Anne had no delusions that Philippe's attraction to her was purely physical. There were a million more desirable women he could vent his lust on, and she'd prefer to know his reasoning before taking it to the next level.

"Why are you introducing me to everyone, Philippe?" Anne's eyes met his, watching his reaction.

One dark eyebrow merely raised. "You don't want to know your co-workers?"

"They're not the issue as you well know. Why introduce me to your clients? Your business associates?" She was getting recognized outside the office, receiving invitations to luncheons, becoming part of the networking loop. It made Anne nervous.

"You knew most of them already."

"But they didn't know me," she pointed out. The same people she used to watch were now watching her every move, listening to her comments. It couldn't be a good thing.

"Ah, *Cherie*," he murmured in understanding, "your business will never grow big, big if you shun publicity, if you don't make connections." Philippe moved around the desk to the mini fridge in the far corner of his office.

"Water?" He held out a plastic bottle.

A trap. Say no, walk away, her mind did its best to warn her. The warnings were blithely ignored. "Yes, thank you." Anne reached for the bottle. Philippe didn't let go, hanging onto it, until he could grab her other wrist, his long fingers cool and wet with condensation.

Yet again, her mind had been right. She was trapped. Part of her was appalled. Part of her didn't care. All of her knew it was too soon.

Anne distracted him. "I don't need to grow the company. I like it the size it is."

"But when you retire, the income will stop," Philippe pointed out, "Right now, your business is based on your personal touch with the plans, and doesn't have enough volume to support a full management team. It isn't self sustaining; it isn't a true business."

"That doesn't concern me, Philippe." She licked her lips nervously, inadvertently drawing his eyes there. "If it stops, it stops. Even if that happens tomorrow, I'll be okay. I'm taking care of myself."

"Are you?" He took the bottle of water back from her and placed it on the nearby table. "Are you, *vraiment?*" and she knew exactly what he was going to do.

Anne put up one last feeble attempt at resistance. "Missus Depeche will be in any minute."

"Sylvie doesn't gossip." With what little consolation that offered, Philippe pulled Anne to him, his hands running over top her trousers, scooping her buttocks. "I prefer you in skirts."

"I don't dress to please you. I dress to please myself." That was the half-truth. She intentionally wore slacks this week, trying to damper his unrelenting fascination with her undergarments.

"And the stockings, *Cherie*, are they to please yourself?"

"Yes." Her hands pressed against his dress shirt, a solid wall of muscle under her palms. "I get hot."

"You do, *mais oui, Cherie*, you do." He brushed his cheek against hers.

Before the sharp tap at the door registered in Anne's brain, Mrs. Depeche entered. Their shared assistant blinked at their close proximity before baldly stating, "Miss James, your four o'clock will be here shortly. I assume you'll be seeing him in your own office."

"Yes, thank you." Mortified, Anne managed a calm response. "I'll be there momentarily."

Anne waited until Mrs. Depeche left to slide on her jacket. "I have to go."

"We're not finished, *Cherie*. This will continue after your meeting." Philippe didn't ask. He told.

"Maybe. If it doesn't go long." She wouldn't be bossed around, "I need to be somewhere right after work." Tonight was her *Young C.E.O.s* class and nothing, not even a temptingly handsome man, would make her miss it. Lamont would have to learn patience.

He wasn't a quick learner. "I need to hear your thoughts on Henri's business."

"It'll wait 'til the morning."

"*Cherie!*" came out as a growl.

"There's no need for you to be involved, Philippe. It's my call to make, and I won't have you looking over my shoulder, second-guessing my decisions. I do have total control over accepting, don't I?" Anne verified. Those were her terms.

"You do." He nodded. "But he's my cousin. I'll need to know our answer, *oui ou non*."

Anne didn't reply as she gathered up the papers. Philippe's lips twisted. "Try not to be too hard on Henri, will you? I like the man."

"I can't promise anything." Anne threw over her shoulder while she exited the office. *Was that deep throated rumble a chuckle? Sounded like one. Fine for him to laugh. He isn't the one turning down an entrepreneur for funding. And not any entrepreneur, one of Philippe's beloved relatives.*

~ * ~

Philippe's cousin, Henri Lamont, headed up a hot sauce company requiring financing for a marketing campaign. He was in the awkward stage between being a small business, creating hot sauce in his certified home kitchen, and having enough volume to fill a complete co-packer production run. To mitigate losses, he had to ramp up sales quickly. To ramp up sales, he needed the marketing funds.

There was another tap, this time at her own office door. Mrs. Depeche, exercising more caution, waited for Anne's acknowledgement before showing her entrepreneur in.

"Hello, Henri." Anne walked over to the rotund man, stretching out her hand. "Thank you for meeting with me. I'm Anne."

"*Enchante.*" Henri's jovial smile lit up his round face. Instead of shaking her hand, he pulled her forward to kiss her cheek.

And that's not where his similarity to Philippe ended. As they seated, Anne studied the cousin. An older version of Philippe, a little more plump, more gray hair, wrinkles around the same laughing brown eyes. *Still attractive. Still charming.*

Henri, not trying to hide his own curiosity, was examining her as thoroughly. "Have you been working with Philippe long, Miss James?" His voice lacked his cousin's heavier accent. "He never mentioned your name."

Why would Philippe mention her? And why would it bother her that he hadn't?

"Please call me Anne, and this is my third week. I have years of experience evaluating business plans, however," she added, anxious that he not think her an outright amateur.

"I'm sure you do and even if you didn't, I'd have no reservations. Philippe hires only the best." Henri was in no great rush to get to the topic at hand. "You're not what I expected."

Oh, lordy, not a male chauvinist. "A woman?"

"No, no." The man laughed. "Your name gave that away. I guess I expected someone like Suzanne or Denise."

Suzanne, she knew. Denise, Anne gathered from office gossip, was an ex-girlfriend. Supposedly even more gorgeous than Suzanne. "Well, I'm not." And that irritated her also.

"Well, I'm pleased." This sounded sincere. "I love Philippe like he's the younger brother I never had. He stayed at my parents' house when he first came to America for school. It was tough, his being away from his family, but selfish boy that I was, I loved it. Didn't have any siblings myself."

What was Henri doing? Building sympathy for his cause? Pulling at her heartstrings? Not going to work. This was a business decision.

"So you make hot sauce?" Anne put the conversation back on track.

"Yep." The man had the audacity to wink at her. "I adore the stuff; put it on everything."

Not Anne. She didn't like hot sauce to start with. After all week sampling competitive product and more than one stomach ache, she hated the condiment now.

"Is that why you got into the business?" Henri hadn't swung into the usual entrepreneur hard sell razzle-dazzle. *Must be nerves.*

She never received an answer. The door opened, and Kevin Maple, the V-P of new business development, sauntered in, a smirk on his insolent face.

This interruption had been planned. Why Maple was gunning for her, she didn't know, but he had from day one. "Can I help you, Kevin? I'm with a prospective partner." She smiled to offset the irritation in her voice.

"Then allow me to help you."

Help me? Yikes, this is going to be trouble.

"I pulled the *Nielsen* numbers." Kevin rushed on. "Even a junior analyst knows you can't make a decision without them."

Junior analyst? He's calling me a junior analyst?

The exec continued, turning to Henri. "She's new." Like that explained everything.

"Thank you. I sourced the numbers elsewhere." Anne placed the pages on top of the file as proof. Nancy ran them for her this morning, the request for information Anne placed with Maple's group last week ignored, purposely she suspected.

"Confidentiality, Miss James," implied that she spilled start up secrets while gathering simple statistics. "Henri." Maple settled into the other guest chair, signaling that he planned to remain for the duration.

"Maple."

Great, the cousin knows him. Anne fumed in silence as the two gabbed about last night's football game and barbeque and every other boy skewed topic under the sun. Except Henri's hot sauce. That wasn't mentioned once. Not once. Peculiar, for an entrepreneur. His sort tended to live and breathe their companies.

Anne let the male bonding go as long as she could. Finally she had to say something. "Kevin, I appreciate your assistance," her tone perfectly cordial, "but I can take it from here."

"I'm not certain that you…"

Anne wouldn't let him finish. "I'm certain." She held the door open pointedly.

Maple was leaving, "Henri, you have my card," but not going quietly, "Call me if you have any questions."

"I'm perfectly capable of handling *my* entrepreneur's questions." *Enough with this power play.*

"Sure you are."

Sarcastic jerk. She was happy to close the door behind him. Now where were they?

"Do you have a sample of the product?"

"Of course." Henri didn't comment on the rough transition, flipping open his square black leather case, rummaging through the mess inside. No organization, everything tossed in.

Who could work that way? And what businessman didn't have a sample of the product right at the top of the bag? None that she knew.

While Anne was contemplating this, she set out some plain crackers, paper napkins, *Dixie* cups and a bottle of water on her now clear desk. Standard taste testing supplies.

She picked up the bottle finally found, rotating it in her hands. "We'll have to change the label."

"Why?" Henri demanded, defensively. "I like the label."

Anne stood up, her fingers flying over her recently acquired hot sauce collection, pulling a bottle from the back row. She plopped it on the desk, a solid clunk as the glass hit the wood surface.

"That's why." She slid the two bottles so they were side by side. The packaging was almost identical and left Anne questioning Henri's development process. No competitive research done. No knowledge of the market. Her teens could do better. But she kept an open mind. Package re-design was simple. A superior taste could be enough to work with.

She sipped water to clear her palette and then dapped a drop of hot sauce on a cracker. Anne sniffed it first, a pleasing aroma for what it was, and then put the cracker in her mouth. *Blast it, it would have to be an extremely hot one. Chile,* habanero *chile. Wait a minute! This mix tastes familiar.* Again she stood up, looking over her collection, pulling another bottle.

She reset her taste buds and tried the competitor's sauce. Anne almost groaned out loud. It was identical. A rip-off product in a rip-off package.

Maybe he doesn't know. Anne dabbed the competitor product on another cracker and handed it over. "Henri, taste this one."

He took a swig of water and then a bite of the cracker. His face fell.

Nope, he didn't. His reaction cleared up that key point for Anne. The surprise was genuine, the theft unintentional.

"What do you think?" *Come on, Henri,* she silently urged, *you seem like a nice guy, tell me what's going on. How can you, as the sole owner, be so uninvolved?*

"It's good," Henri admitted that much. "Really good."

It should be good. It was the product his company decided to copy. "I'm curious. How did you come to your formulation?"

The man wiped his forehead with a napkin, the hot sauce heating him up. Or maybe it was guilt causing him to sweat.

"Makes your mouth zing, doesn't it?" Henri puffed.

Anne noticed that he didn't answer her question, didn't meet her eyes. "I'd be interested on hearing how you came to this specific mix of jalapeno and chili peppers."

He started peeling the label off his beloved bottle. "It took a bit of trial and error. Some versions were heavier on the jalapeno and some on the chile. I thought this balance was just right, hot but not too in your face."

"Except that there are no jalapeno peppers in your product," Anne pointed out quietly. A man who went through the tedious back and forth of formulation would know the recipe better than he knew his own name.

Henri gulped, speechless which was fine for Anne. She didn't need to hear more.

Anne slid his business plan across the desk. "Henri, I appreciate the work you've put into your business plan. However, Lamont Ventures prefers to deal with unique propositions. As your package is similar to a competitor's and the product itself is identical to yet another established brand, we're turning down your request for funding."

"But… but." The man's eyes blinked rapidly. "But, I've invested all my personal money into this company. I have a wife and kids to support. What am I going to tell them? How am I going to pay my bills? What am I going to do?"

Though not relevant to the business, it was sad all the same. "It's for the best, Henri, believe me. You're setting yourself up for a nasty lawsuit from not one, but two companies. And as you are a sole proprietorship, even a single lawsuit could wipe out more money than what you have put into the business. They could take everything, including your home."

"If I talked to Philippe…" Henri tried.

"The answer would be the same," Anne told him firmly. She couldn't have him running to Philippe, not after she told her new boss she could handle it. "I assure you that I speak for Mister Lamont on this."

Henri's face drooped with merely mild disappointment. Interesting, considering his financial future was supposedly at stake. "Anne, I didn't know about it being the same, I swear. I relied on a third party to supply me with the product." This, she believed, was closer to the truth. "I wouldn't have done that. It's not right."

"A learned lesson for your next venture." Anne used this experience as a teaching tool. "Advisors can make or break a business. Do your research, be more careful with your choices." She stood up to walk him out.

"Thank you, Anne." Henri gave Anne an impromptu hug, surprising her. "Philippe was right about you being one smart woman."

Philippe was right? Anne stiffened. But Henri previously said Philippe never mentioned her name. That meant…

"That bastard."

"I blew it, didn't I?" Henri laughed, not at all distressed about his slip.

"From the start, you were a little off, not talking up the business enough. Entrepreneurs are usually stressed out and determined to hard sell."

"Told Philippe I wouldn't pull it off." Henri sat back down again. "He insisted I try."

Anne glanced at the clock. She had to leave soon if she was going to make class. "You couldn't have mixed a couple hot sauces together to get a different formula?"

"I didn't know about that, I swear. Philippe's formula, and I guess he thought you wouldn't taste the competition. You do your research."

Henri nodded, impressed.

She did do her research, a lot of blasted research. Resentment built as Anne thought of all the time she put into this project. She worked two full-time jobs plus her *Young C.E.O.s* coaching. She didn't have a minute to waste.

"Well, that was a great allocation of time, wasn't it?" Anne moved to the door.

"Hey." Henri held up his hands in defense. "Don't get upset with me. I did Philippe a favor."

"Oh, I realize that." Anne sucked back her anger, reserving the few choice words for *Monsieur* Philippe Lamont. "It was nice meeting you despite everything."

The older man reached for her hand and brought it up to his lips in a brief salute. "Likewise, Anne. We'll meet again, I'm sure of that now."

Anne didn't know what that meant and she didn't care. She didn't have time to think about anything. She was late. After leaving Henri happily chatting with Mrs. Depeche, Anne closed her door to vent her irritation on the office furniture. She packed up, furiously stuffing the loose papers into her desk, slamming each drawer with satisfaction.

Before she could successfully make her escape, the internal phone line rang. She debated answering it, finally deciding that she didn't have time; she'd return the voicemail first thing tomorrow. But as the phone rang and rang, Anne gave into curiosity and checked the call display. Instant regret. It was Mrs. Depeche, impossible to sneak past and not pleased with her as it was for some reason. With a sigh, Anne pressed the speakerphone. Another mistake. Philippe wanted to see her in his office. Now.

Well, screw that. He wasted enough of her time today.

"I'm sorry, Missus Depeche," Anne told the assistant, her voice overly perky, "I can't meet with him today. Schedule something for early tomorrow morning. If *M'sieur* Lamont protests, please tell your boss that I'm working on real business plans. He'll understand."

He did. Minutes later as she waited for the elevator, Philippe came to stand beside her, his eyes wary, his own briefcase and laptop in hand.

"I wanted to talk to you before you left," his voice deceptively quiet.

Anne didn't care about what he wanted. She wanted him to stop playing games and that wasn't about to happen, was it? "It's past five o'clock, Lamont. We agreed—no overtime, remember? Take it or leave it."

"*Je comprends.* Then we'll talk in the car." Philippe entered the elevator with her, pressing the button for the parking garage. "While I drive you to your office."

"I'm not going to the office." She stared straight ahead at the blink of the descending floor numbers. 22—21—20

"It doesn't matter. I'll drive you wherever you are going," Philippe insisted.

"And what will happen with my car?" Anne pointed out the error in his plan.

He had an answer for that too. *The quick thinking ass.* "I'll drive you back again, after dinner."

"I'll be hours." 14—13—12

"I'll wait."

Anne checked the time again. If she arrived late—she was never late—the students would assume she wasn't coming, and leave. With traffic, getting there on time would be close as it was.

6—5—4

Arguing with the stubborn, stubborn man would take even more time. She didn't have a choice, not if she wanted to make the class.

2—1—P-1, the doors opened. Decision time.

"We'll be on my schedule, Lamont," was her not-so-gracious acceptance.

Philippe held the doors open for her to exit first, his satisfied smile making Anne want to scream. If he thought he had her at his mercy, he had another think coming.

He offered to play chauffeur, then fine; a chauffeur would come in handy. Anne would recoup some of her precious time and correct business plans while riding in the back seat.

That should tick the man off.

Five

Philippe was more amused than ticked. Not that he misunderstood the situation. It couldn't be more clear. The sparrow's feathers were ruffled but good. Had she finished telling him off? Not even close.

The timing of the confrontation was key. If Anne lost her temper too soon, she simply would walk away from him and he would end up eating alone. That Philippe didn't want to happen. So it was worth forgoing the wise-ass comments. He kept his mouth shut. Even as Anne loaded him up with a box from the trunk of her Volvo. Even as she slipped into his own car's backseat, leaving him up front alone to drive. *Et oui,* even as she barked out directions like some power-obsessed line manager. Philippe bit his tongue and eased the Maybach out of the parking garage.

Non, he was not giving her a reason to change her mind. Not until they were well on their way. Not until there was no escape for her.

Was all of it a sacrifice? *Non, non, non.* Little did Anne know, but he had a better view of her in his rearview mirror than if she sat beside him. Philippe covertly watched her as she took her jacket off, and let her hair down. It fell in waves of brown satin around her face. Every once in a while, she ran a hand through that luscious mane of hair, the honey brown strands picking up the light.

As they moved onto the freeway, Philippe knew it to be time. "How did the meeting with Henri go?" his words penetrated the suffocating silence filling the vehicle.

Anne looked up from the papers in her lap, frowning slightly. "Philippe, can it wait until tomorrow? I'm off the clock."

His mouth turned upwards. *Can it wait? Ah, non, it can not.* He preferred to control the situation. "That poorly, *Cherie*? Let me know if you need any assistance with the evaluation."

As designed, his offer set Anne off. "Assistance with the evaluation?" She slammed the papers down on the black leather seat beside her. "What evaluation? None was needed, a complete waste of my time. I'm busy, Philippe, I don't have time for your stupid games."

Mon Dieu, she was magnificent, her whole body vibrating with anger. "Stupid games?" Philippe played the innocent.

"Cut the crap, there isn't any *Henri's Hot Sauce*. It was all a ruse, to mess with my mind. Do you know that I spent the week drenching every meal with hot sauces? I hate hot sauce."

That was his buttoned down sparrow, throwing herself heart and soul into every job. Did she put so much passion into her lovemaking? Philippe was determined to find out.

"I couldn't let you loose amongst the legitimate offerings without testing you first. I have to count on you to make the tough calls, *Cherie*, to not wimp out on me. You understand that, don't you?"

Anne rolled those soulful brown eyes of hers. "I'll have you know I don't wimp out, not ever."

"Noted, *Cherie*. The next one is the real thing, promise. If it makes you happy, you really will be squashing people's dreams."

"It had better be, and no more hot sauce." She groaned, rubbing her flat stomach as in remembered distress.

Poor little sparrow, she punished herself to get the job done. He would make it up to her. Tonight, with any luck. "Nothing food related, something completely different, a different industry, something new, something fresh." He watched as her eyes lit up with interest. "But we'll talk about this tomorrow. You're off the clock, remember?"

Philippe waited for her to ask what the next offering was. He should have known she wouldn't be baited. Anne went back to her papers, nibbling on the end of her red pen.

Philippe kept one eye on the road and the other on Anne, watching as she circled a paragraph. "So I guess no Indian food tonight." He thought of their dinner options. What would a woman like Anne like? And why did he care? He felt nervous like this was their first date and if he wanted a second, he had to get it right. Was that what he wanted? A second? *Non*, a second wouldn't be needed. A one-night stand and she'd be out of his system.

"Indian?" She looked up puzzled.

"Or Mexican. That can be spicy too," Philippe added.

Her forehead wrinkled, a picture of confusion.

"For dinner," he clarified. Had she forgotten? They were going for dinner after her class. That was the plan. Wine her, dine her, bed her and then back to business. No more daydreaming about underwear.

"I don't know, Philippe, I don't have the time." Anne put her papers aside again. "I should drop in at my own office."

She was trying to wiggle out of dinner, damn difficult woman. "You have to eat."

"I'll probably pick something up and eat at my desk."

He wasn't going to let her succeed. "I'll keep you company, *Cherie*."

Anne grumbled something very uncomplimentary under her breath. It was a new experience for him, a woman trying to avoid his company. Avoiding his company and blocking his physical attentions semi-effectively all week. What was Anne doing? Trying to stop the unstoppable? Keeping it platonic?

Wouldn't work. She could delay as long as she wanted, it would happen. After this afternoon's meeting, Philippe was sure. He wouldn't be satisfied until he tasted her fully, all of her, every soft inch. She intrigued him too much. It would cost him money. He wouldn't be able to look at one of her business plans logically afterwards. Likely he couldn't do that even now. All he'd see would be black stockings covering shapely legs.

And revenge? His plans for that were gone. Even one night of passion took Anne off his hit list. He might be a bastard but he played fair. It'd be worth all that to hear her moan his name, her voice throaty with desire. He'd do that to her. Make her moan.

Philippe grinned as he walked down the school hallway, his arms full. *Oui*, he was her little pack mule now. Later, *ahhh*, later they'd both be working even harder. He'd see to that.

The door was held open by a freckled faced teenager.

"Thank you, Dirk." Anne smiled.

"No prob, Miss J." The boy beamed at his teacher, his whole face lighting up. Then he glared at the following Philippe. Someone had a big crush.

She's mine, kid. Philippe's face conveyed the message.

"I'll take that box for Miss. J." The boy's voice broke a little.

Philippe made his position even more clear. "I'm taking **care of Anne now.**" *Today and maybe even tomorrow if the afterglow lasts, so get used to it.*

The boy, Dirk, Anne called him, had guts. He didn't back down, staring at Philippe, shoulders thrown back, feet planted solidly apart. Philippe kept cool and steady eye contact, his one raised eyebrow daring the taller kid to dispute his claim. Finally the boy gave a curt nod, conceding Philippe's win. Without another word, he turned on his running-shoe heels and strutted to the front row.

"Do we have a guest speaker today, Miss James?" a baby faced goth-like creature piped up from the back of the classroom.

Anne turned to Philippe with more of a dare than a question in her eyes. He nodded. Might as well volunteer. His speaking was going to happen.

"Very observant, Rochelle." Anne looked out at the class like she was a proud new mother and they were, every scruffy last one of them, her children. "As you all know, starting up a business often requires financing, sometimes a lot of financing. That's one reason we prepare business plans. What types of financing are there?"

Several suggestions were thrown at Anne. She probed until she got exactly what she wanted, Anne's love of teaching reflected in her animated face. From the rapt attention of this straggly group of teenagers, she was good at it.

"That's the answer I was looking for, Denny, venture capital." Philippe stood up; this was his cue. "Today, we have the honor of having Philippe Lamont of Lamont Ventures, one of the country's top venture capital houses, here to talk to us about the process. He'll give you an overview of what he and his company does."

I will, will I?

"I'd like you to pay close attention and think of questions. Take this opportunity to find out how a real venture capitalist thinks."

Philippe easily won the rowdy group of teenagers over, smoothly mimicking her style of teaching with questions and informal discussions. They were a tough crowd, cynical of authority and bored too easily but he, with his use of juicy real life examples, held their interest. When the bell rang, the students didn't want to leave but they didn't have a choice.

Anne could see Glenn through the door window pointing at his watch. The Principal had a stick up his butt since her sister shot him down. Anne felt bad but not too bad. At least now, Glenn no longer bothered her about paperwork.

"Miss James." Tanya's round face was flushed. "A bunch of us are going to my *In-N-Out Burger*, you know the one on the corner. We'd really like it if you came." Her shy eyes slid to Philippe. "And maybe Mister Lamont, if he wanted too."

Anne bit her lip. She didn't get one of these offers often. As much as she liked to be seen as a coach or mentor, the kids slotted her into the off limits teacher category.

"It's a celebration," Dirk called out. "Tan got promoted to supervisor."

"Dirk!" The girl's color heightened even more.

"Tanya, good for you." Anne was proud. The job wasn't merely a way for the teenager to make some spare cash, she considered it the start of her restaurant career. "I knew you'd be good at it."

"You did." Brown hair bobbed. "That's why I want you to come, Miss James. And don't worry. It won't cost that much. I get an employee discount and when I asked, the manager said I could use it for the class tonight."

The timid girl had asked her manager. This was a big deal for Tanya. Anne should…

She tilted her head to study Philippe. Yes, she did say that tonight they'd be on her schedule but after two hours with her class, Anne didn't want to push it.

"I haven't had a great hamburger in a while, *vraiment*." Philippe read her mind. "Are the burgers there any good?"

"Man, they're so good, I could eat three." Dirk stretched, rubbing his flat stomach. "Oh, wait, I usually do."

"As a snack," Tanya added knowingly, making Anne laugh. Dirk was a bottomless pit.

"*Ahhh*... a good hamburger and an employee discount, *aussi*, what more could we want? *In-N-Out* it is then. We'll have to put this in the car first." Philippe hoisted the box easily on his shoulder, balancing it with one hand. "Do you want us to meet you there?"

"What're you driving?" car-crazy Dirk asked.

"A Maybach 62," Philippe said that like it meant something.

Anne guessed it did. The boy's eyes went big. "You're shitting me!"

"*Non*, I assure you I'm not," the man's tone was grave.

"Wow, come on Tan, we gotta check it out." Dirk slung his backpack over a slumped shoulder.

Was the car something special? Anne knew nothing about them except that they took her from point A to point B and broke down at the most inconvenient times.

"The Maybach didn't impress *you*, did it?" Philippe's free arm brushed up against hers as they walked.

"Was that the point?"

Philippe nodded. This sexy dynamic man wanted to impress her. Difficult as that was to believe.

"The seats were nice." Anne's comment sounded lame, even to herself.

Dirk snorted, exchanging a disgusted look with Philippe. Philippe then proceeded to give Dirk a run down on his car's, this fancy Maybach, specs, numbers and stats that meant little to Anne, but excited the boy.

"So what are your other cars?" Dirk was deep into his favorite topic as Philippe stuffed Anne's teaching supplies into the trunk.

"No other cars." Philippe's answer surprised Anne. She, too, assumed he had a garage full of Jaguars and Mercedes and other fancy vehicles. "I'm a one car man. One car, one house, one woman."

One woman? *Liar.* But wait, Lamont doesn't lie. He was known for his cutting honesty. So what about Suzanne?

"But you're loaded," Dirk pointed out.

"*Oui*, but I have no need for more." Philippe squeezed Anne's hand. How did her hand get in his? When had that happened? "The power of focus, you know."

"That's what Miss James says all the time," Tanya piped up happily from behind Anne. "Focus on one thing until it's accomplished."

"You should listen to her." Philippe winked at a confused and slightly fuzzy-headed Anne, a lazy smile on his own face. "Your teacher knows a lot."

Knows a lot? He had to be joking. *Anne didn't have a clue. She lost control of this situation hours ago. She didn't know how to regain it. She didn't even know if she wanted to.*

A little over an hour later, that lack of control led to them being jammed into a corner booth, extra tables dragged across the restaurant to accommodate the noisy teenagers. Somehow, Anne ended up sitting on Philippe's lap, her legs dangling off the ground. A couple of the girls were in the same situation with their boyfriends. It seemed natural and she guessed it would be if Philippe was her boyfriend.

Which he wasn't. Sure, most of the kids thought so especially after Philippe held her hand on the short walk to the restaurant. She didn't have the heart to pull it away, not in front of so many curious eyes. That would have been rude, wouldn't it?

Then Philippe bought not only Anne's meal but the meals for the entire class, making a big deal out of using Tanya's employee discount, the girl's fragile confidence blossoming under his praise.

What could Anne do then? There hadn't been room in the booth for all of them and she couldn't tell him to find his own seat elsewhere. So when Anne was pulled into Philippe's lap, she didn't slap his face as she should have. Nope, she let that happen too.

She even let the dinner conversation spin without her usual input, Dirk dominating it with stories about his 1973 Gremlin, the car he had been restoring for months. Finishing off three doubles at the same time involved a lot of talking with his mouth full, grossing out both Tanya and herself.

Philippe paid no attention to the exposed half chewed food, listening intently and asking questions, every once in a while popping a French fry into Anne's mouth and passing her their shared chocolate shake to slurp on. He was being as nice as nice could be and as a result, Anne was in big, big trouble. He was difficult enough to resist when in his cold-hearted bastard mode but this soft Philippe was impossible.

And if she had these feelings while in a room full of kids, what was going to happen when they were finally alone? When they were alone, he would kiss her, Anne knew, he'd kiss her good night and then what? Could she stop there? It didn't look good for that possibility. She wanted him too much to hold back. Anne wiggled nervously, her body heating up from her thoughts.

"Unless you want to give the kids something to talk about," Philippe whispered in her ear, his warm breath upon her neck, "you'd better stop moving."

Oh, geez, Anne stilled immediately. Philippe bit her earlobe and then applied himself to the conversation. His fingers flayed over her stomach, his thumb pressing between her breasts. Yep, Philippe Lamont's hand between her breasts. That made her bottom twitch and she shifted. Wrapping things up quickly.

"Anne and I have to get going. We have things to do."

She could imagine what those things were. "Dirk, here's my e-mail." Philippe flipped the boy a crisp white business card. "Keep me updated on how it goes with the car. I'm not shitting you about that either. Tanya, you were right, it was a great burger, a burger to be proud of. *Merci et félicitations.*"

The girl moved so they could get out, Philippe sliding over until Anne hopped off his lap. There was a chorus of happy good-byes as they wandered out of the restaurant, again hand in hand.

Anne paused outside the door, eyes blinking. It had gotten dark all of a sudden. The stars would be out. But she didn't have time to look up at them. She was pulled toward the car and almost pushed in the front seat. Philippe filled the driver's seat, his face dark and intense, and put the key in the ignition. He didn't turn it. Instead, he slid his seat right back.

"Cherie." The endearment was more a groan, as he reached for her, his hands on both sides of her face, his lips finding hers. Not a soft, innocent first kiss but hard and punishing, making her lips pulse and burn. He forced her mouth open, his tongue filling the space, searching.

They broke with a gasp, chests heaving. They kissed and now? What would happen now? No looking far to find the answer. It was in Philippe's glowing eyes. Everything. They would do everything. He wouldn't stop until he had her completely.

And Anne felt the same. She wanted him; she needed him. Her lips met his this time, expressing this need, giving him permission to do with her what he would. Anne wrapped her hands around his neck and let him drag her back to his seat, shifting her so she straddled him.

He was hard already, straining against his pant fabric towards her heat. *I did that to him,* Anne thought in wonderment, *made this handsome man hard.* She rubbed against him and his eyes rolled back, his mouth pulled into a grimace. Philippe's mouth. This couldn't be happening. It was a dream, it had to be, and in her dreams, she was always fearless. As she was now, Anne moved back and forth, back and forth, riding Philippe fully clothed.

Not that she remained fully clothed for long. Philippe fumbled with the tiny buttons down her sleeveless blouse. Finally frustrated at the slow progress, he pulled the fabric apart, popping them off. The cool air was a blast of unwelcome reality against her skin bringing Anne to her senses. *What am I doing? With Philippe?* She wasn't his type. No amply endowed beauty queen like the women Philippe normally cavorted with. He would find her lacking...

"Cherie, you are so... so..."

Anne's breath caught. *Small? Disappointing?*

"Perfect."

Perfect? Me? Anne braved a peek. His words didn't lie. Philippe's face shone with appreciation and no small amount of desire. While looking his fill, he scooped her silk and lace covered breasts with gentle hands, kneading them until her nipples ached. The front-closed bra was easily discarded, and his mouth found first one breast and then the other, teasing them, his tongue swirling.

At that point, all Anne's thoughts and worries vanished.

Philippe, on the other hand, tried desperately to hold onto rational thought. He had been thinking about this, touching Anne, loving this little brown sparrow, all day and was ready, too blasted ready.

He needed a distraction and fast. Multiplication tables. That worked for him before. It would take his mind off her. *Merde, mais* she felt so good. *One multiplied by one is...*

Anne bucked against him, back arching as he licked her berry-kissed nipples, dark and lovely, her breasts like ripe fruit under his lips. So sweet, so responsive.

Non, don't think about that. Concentrate. Seven multiplied by eight...Mon Dieu, was she undoing his belt? For his sanity, Philippe had to stop that. He had to. He kissed her hard on the lips.

Anne moaned into his mouth, her tongue twisting around his. "Touch me, Philippe."

What could he do? He had been told. He had to obey. If he could hold out for a few more... *What about division? Division was difficult.*

Merde, merde, merde. Was that his pants being unzipped, freeing him, soft yet firm fingers curling around him? And at her touch, Philippe's thin thread of control snapped. He was too hard, too far along. It wasn't right, he tried to capture her hands, those magic hands. "Anne, I can't." He grimaced.

What could he tell her? That he, Philippe Lamont, an experienced and normally disciplined lover, was going to cum instantly like he was one of those hormone raging, teenage boys she taught? But that was going to happen and there was nothing he could do about it, there was no room in his thoughts for anything other than the little brown sparrow astride him.

Her hands kept pumping him relentlessly, the pressure just right. "Anne, oh, Anne." She rode against him, his hands squeezing her cloth covered buttocks. *So round, so...*

Then it was done. *Merde,* he disgraced himself, a hot sticky mess in her hand. Philippe couldn't bear to look at Anne, unable to take the certain disappointment on her face. He was so selfish, thinking only of himself, his great uncontrollable need.

Her bare breasts brushed against his cheek as she reached to get Kleenex from the back seat.

"I'm so sorry, *Cherie,*" and he was. Sorry and confused. That hadn't happened to him in years. Why now? Why with Anne? When making a good impression was so important to him? Why was making a good impression important to him? Pride, that must be it.

"You're sorry? You didn't enjoy it?" She paused, as if uncertain about the answer.

Anne knew blasted well he enjoyed it. The proof was in her hand. "I did, *bien sur*."

"Then why are you sorry?"

Oui, she did sound relieved, her light touch cleaning him up, patting his underwear back in place. She neatly placed the used tissues in the waste basket.

"Why? Because I, *ahh*, I." Philippe didn't know what to say. She knew why. Would she make him say it, make him admit his failing? Would she now use this weakness against him?

"I'm the one who's sorry." His heart dropped at her words. Of course, she'd be sorry. He had fucked up, big time. "You didn't stand a chance, you poor man. I should have warned you."

"Warned me?" What crazy twist was this? Philippe summoned up the courage to glance at Anne. That glance extended into a longer searching stare. Shouldn't Anne be distraught? She wasn't. In fact she looked like she was damn proud of herself.

"Oh, yeah, I should have warned you. You see, it couldn't have ended any other way. You were powerless to resist me," Anne declared smugly. "I have skills." She settled against his body, placing his arms around her, facing the windshield.

"You do, do you?" Philippe didn't know what else to say. What could he say? Anne sounded so confident that he was starting to think her responsible. Could she be? Could she have planned all this?

"Yep, mad skills." Anne nodded, rubbing her silky hair into his dress shirt. He didn't even have it unbuttoned, it all happened so quickly. "And I guess that I should 'fess up completely and warn you that tonight was only a sampling of those skills."

"There's more?" he squeaked. He could have sworn she wasn't that experienced. Could this woman possibly teach him a thing or two? *Non*. Impossible. Or was it?

"You don't mind, do you?" If Philippe wasn't mistaken, there was a bit of laughter in her voice.

She was teasing him, *oui*? *Ou non*? Philippe didn't know. After tonight, Philippe wasn't too sure about anything anymore. "I don't mind, at all." And he should do something for Anne. That would be the right thing, the gentlemanly thing to do. Philippe stroked her breasts. He couldn't say that his heart was in it, his lack of restraint perturbing him, but he'd do it. He wouldn't leave her unsatisfied.

Anne, that mind reading, control sapping seductress, knew. She restrained his hand. "Next time, Philippe. Next time, it'll be all about me."

Next time? There will be a next time? The thought shouldn't have made Philippe smile, his plan was for a one night stand, but it did. Next time, one more time and Anne's mad skills. Despite his suspicions over her motives, he would gladly risk everything for one more time with Anne. One more time to redeem himself.

"*Vraiment*, Cherie?" He looked down at her relaxed happy face, insecure and seeking her confirmation.

"Oh, yes." Anne yawned. "Next time, I'll demand my satisfaction. You know that I always get what I want."

Philippe hugged her close. "You do." And he was determined that in this, she would.

Six

Anne's satisfaction had to wait. The next day, Philippe was called away to Chicago on urgent company business. Some fire-fighting with a big bank, sucking up the entire week.

It wasn't necessarily a bad thing. Things were happening too quickly. Not Anne's style, not at all. She wasn't one for jumping into a relationship, even if that relationship consisted only of business and sex. No, Anne welcomed the slow-down. It gave her time to think. Of course she should be thinking about what Philippe's strategy was, rather than how good his lips felt on hers. That would have been a better plan.

"Wine tasting?" Anne indicated the trays of filled *Dixie* cups circulating the convention center, as she munched on a chocolate covered strawberry.

Nancy wrinkled up her freckled nose. "Nah, none for me today."

"What?" Anne's eyes flew wide open in surprise. Her friend was never one to turn down high quality alcohol, and the vintners certainly didn't sample the cheap stuff. "Nance, are you feeling okay?"

"Yeah, yeah, I'm feeling fine. I'm not that big of a lush, thank you very much." Her friend looked around at the grid of vendor displays, hand holding, dreamy eyed couples filling the spaces like grout between tiles. "When you asked if I wanted to do something different today, Anne, I never guessed you meant this. Not that I'm complaining—any excuse to go to one of these things—but what exactly *is* our excuse? You got a fiancé I don't know about?"

"As if I could, Snoopy Snoop." Anne picked up a pamphlet at a photographer's booth, scanned it quickly and put it back down again. "No, this is strictly work."

"Work?" and then understanding dawned. "*Ahhhh*, for Lamont?" Nancy waved off the over zealous vendor. "That makes more sense. So what business is it? Please tell me it's a florist. I haven't received fresh flowers in a while."

Anne made a mental note to drop the suggestion in Nancy's husband Ted's ear. "Nope, nothing with so many perks, I'm afraid. This one's a guest management website."

"You're not joking. Not exciting at all." Nancy flipped the program open to the exhibitor directory. "What's the name?"

"*Be My Guest.*" Though the name was a little cutesy, Anne liked it. "She's not displaying today, and the owner should be here networking." That much she found out from the woman's voicemail message. The information prompted this spur-of-the-moment field trip, a chance to watch the owner in action.

"Okay, *Einstein.*" The redhead picked up a free pen from a financial planning booth and slid it into her purse. Their office supplies were heavily supplemented with schwag, an attempt to keep costs down. "Do you know where we might find her?"

"Nope."

"Or even what this owner looks like?"

Anne shrugged. That was the problem, she didn't. "I figured we'd ask someone."

"Why ask someone, girlfriend, when you can ask wonderful me?" a boyish voice flounced from behind them.

"Stanley," they both squealed at once. A flurry of hands off hugs and butterfly kisses were exchanged.

"Finally, I get some love." The slightly built platinum blond man pouted. "I saw the two of you sashay right by my marvelous booth and thought, *oh, no you didn't. You didn't just ignore Stanley Harper.*"

Nancy and Anne looked at each other in horror. They hadn't noticed him or his display. They must have been too pre-occupied with chatting. Nancy supplied the excuse. "We knew you were working"

"And didn't want to crowd out your potential customers," Anne joined in, fingers crossed that the booth was busy.

This seemed to satisfy the high-strung makeup artist. "Ladies, I never thought to see you here at a bridal show of all places. Is there something you're not telling me, Annie-kin?"

Annie-kin. Not her favorite nickname. Anyone else and Anne would have made a fuss.

"Just meeting up with someone, Stanley." Her friend had a gift of knowing anyone and everyone; he'd be the one to ask. "Except I don't know what she looks like. You know a Denise Marche?"

"A Denise Marche, you mean *the* Denise Marche," the man confirmed his all-reaching connections with an engaging grin.

"Yes." Anne beamed and Nancy gave her arm a squeeze. "*The* Denise Marche, could you point her out to us?"

Stanley crossed his arms in a perfect *GQ* pose, his expression thoughtful. "Not looking like that, girlfriend. Denise is a style queen, a diamond. She doesn't associate with dross."

Anne rolled her eyes. Any excuse to doll her up. Her lack of makeup made the professional squirm. "Stanley, you can forget about giving me a makeover."

"Then you can forget about the intro, Miss Prissy Missy. I have better things to do." He snapped his fingers and turned in a fluid motion that would have made a supermodel envious.

"Okay, okay." Anne groaned before he could disappear. What harm could agreeing do? It would make Stanley happy and stop her from having to ask complete strangers. "Make-up only and I don't want to look like a five dollar hooker."

"A five dollar hooker?" His elfish smile caught the attention of passing females. Stanley was a good-looking man. "In that boring suit? You're overvaluing yourself, sweetie. You'd be lucky to get spare change. Come, come." His tread was light and excited, almost skipping down the aisle. "I know exactly what I want to do."

"And here I forgot my camera." Nancy was enjoying herself, her eyes laughing. "I can't remember the last time you let Stanley play with your face."

"I can. Your wedding," Anne pointed out as Stanley pushed her into the fold-up directors chair, "and I ended up looking like *Tinkerbell*."

"Posh." Stanley snapped out the plastic bib to protect her clothes. "You looked like moonlight reflecting off a winter forest. Breathtaking."

"I sparkled for a week afterwards," Anne grumbled, closing her eyes as Stanley sponged on the foundation base. "Not professional."

"You and your professional." Stanley dabbed a brush on her eyelids, smoothing it with his thumb. "Professional doesn't mean boring and it certainly doesn't mean make-up free. You don't need much, Annie, but every woman…"

"Or man." Stanley's own good looks were aided with make up.

"Or man," Stanley agreed, "needs a little bit of help. Even a colored gloss would change your look." He pressed a tube into her palm. "Keep that, and don't say I never give you anything."

"You mean besides grief?" She didn't need to open her eyes to see his reaction—an overly dramatic sigh communicated that quite well. "I'm joking, Stanley. Thank you."

"And that's for you to use, not stick in the bottom of your purse."

Drat, Stanley knew her a little too well.

Anne relaxed as her friend fussed over her face, her thoughts immediately wandering to Philippe, wondering what he was doing at the moment. She missed him. Sure, he called every day, he did that with all his direct reports, she supposed, but it wasn't the same as seeing his handsome face.

Direct report or no, not all of their discussions revolved around business. He asked about Dirk and his Gremlin restoration. She told him about Ginny's challenges as a new entrepreneur. He talked about his mom trying to guilt-trip him, as only moms can do, into another trip to France.

And Philippe always asked Anne what she was wearing, wanting to know in graphic detail from shoes to undergarments, especially the undergarments.

"Penny for your naughty thoughts, Annie-pie." Stanley teased as he dusted her flaming cheeks.

"It'll cost you more than that, Stanley." Anne wasn't about to share her secrets, though Stanley would likely find out soon enough. The man had sources.

"Can only be a man. Fancy Nancy, do you know about this?"

"Don't you dare!" Anne held out a finger in what she believed was Nancy's direction.

"That's fine." Stanley wasn't perturbed. "She'll tell me later. Done, and in record time."

Anne opened her eyes to find them surrounded by an audience.

"Got quite a crowd here." She gulped self-consciously. "Exactly what did you do to my face?"

"Don't fret, girlie, you look marvelous. Doesn't she look marvelous, people?" he called out to the group. They cheered, some giving her the okay sign.

Nancy's grin couldn't get any wider. Both of them, awful people that they were, knew Anne didn't like to be the center of attention.

Like it or not, she was. All eyes were on her. "I'm here for business, Stanley."

"No *Tinkerbell* this time, Anne," Nancy assured her, "Stanley went natural."

Natural? He had been working, fingers flying, for about fifteen minutes. How natural could it be?

"Moonlight on a winter forest, not *Tinkerbell,*" Stanley corrected, reaching around for the square mirror. *"Voila."*

Anne stared at her reflection in disbelief. It didn't look like her—her eyes were huge, her lashes Greta Garbo long, her cheekbones high and defined and her lips, they were shiny and full.

"You do magic, Stanley." Anne was in awe of his talent. "Magic."

"Pshaw, I can only work with the materials I have, dearest." Stanley hugged her, and then went to replenish his snapped up business cards and brochures, flitting about the table, making his audience giggle.

Her fingers folded around the lip gloss. Maybe she could do that at least. It couldn't be that difficult.

Anne and Nancy then had to wait patiently until the crowd died down to manageable levels. After the makeover, Stanley's booth was busy with women interested in having their own look updated, too busy for him to leave it untended. Instead, Stanley gave the partners an overly thorough description of the woman they were seeking, outlining everything from the designer of her fresh new outfit to the outrageously-high suggested retail price of her leather shoes.

Anne's heart sunk with each passing detail. *Tall, blonde, beautiful. Exactly Philippe's style.*

She had her suspicions upon receiving this assignment. Philippe hadn't exactly been as forthcoming with details about this entrepreneur, not like he had been with his cousin Henri. Now Anne was sure. This must be the one that he slept with, the past lover, the one even more gorgeous than the fabulous Suzanne. A past lover to be reckoned with. Denise had impressed the difficult to please Stanley with her wit and character.

~ * ~

Less than an hour later, Denise could add Nancy and the even more hard-won Anne to her long list of admirers. Her beauty drew their eyes immediately and then Anne did a second take. This Denise looked familiar, why, Anne couldn't say.

If they had met, Anne doubted she would have forgotten the blonde. More than her classic profile impressed the women. Denise was a born saleswoman with a gift for making connections, crucial for success in small business. Anne and Nancy watched Denise mingle with attendees and exhibitors, picking up contacts quickly and assuredly. When Anne and Nancy chose to introduce themselves, their stealth research complete, they were greeted with a kind smile and a firm grip.

"You work for Philippe?" Big blue eyes lit up, sparkling sapphires in a flawless setting.

"I do." Anne nodded, uncertain of the reaction to this revelation. Denise's romantic relationship with Philippe was over. Were there any harsh feelings left?

It didn't seem so. "He's quite a man, isn't he?" Her plump lips, tinted in the most current shade of pink, turned upwards. "Very charming. No woman alive can resist him for long. I know that I couldn't. So I have to wonder, are you resisting him, Anne?"

"He's my boss, Miss Marche." Her reply weakened by Nancy's not so secret smile.

"Denise, please." The blonde laughed. "And I'll draw my own conclusions from that rather evasive answer, if you don't mind. Are you here evaluating my little request for financing?"

Little request? She was looking for a cool million to start with. Anne wouldn't call that a little request. "Yes, I believe we have a meeting next week."

"We do." Denise smiled. "I'm looking forward to it. The project is at a standstill without financing; can't do anything without more money."

Anne noticed Denise assumed the money would be coming. "I understand your predicament. I hope to do the first evaluation," *stress on first,* "quickly. When I heard you were at the show, I took the opportunity to speed the process along."

Anne's neck started to ache from looking up at Denise. She didn't know how Philippe did it—date such tall women. Maybe they didn't spend much time standing, her evil inner self prompted.

"Denise!" An equally tall brunette approached, arms outstretched. Anne faded back as the two women embraced, talking rapidly. She noted how smoothly Denise folded into the conversation the information about her new venture, careful not to share her competitive advantage but still outlining exactly what the event planner could do to assist her.

"Sorry about that," the entrepreneur apologized, as the visitor left. "She knows everyone in the wedding business. Having her on board will be beneficial."

"Do you have many such alliances built thus far?" Anne enquired. It was all about connections in this business, word of mouth and referrals.

"Fortunately, yes, and many will be future advertisers on the site. I have a list of the interested exhibitors if you wish to see them." Denise handed her a paper from her portable organizer.

The list was long, with some big names on it. Aware that it could be falsified, Anne passed the paper to Nancy. Her partner quickly circled the names in her own directory. They would drift by the booths later and casually confirm.

"You'll talk to them, of course." Denise read Anne's thoughts.

"How did you know?"

"It's something Philippe would do," was her simple answer.

Of course, Denise would know that. Any girlfriend would naturally learn a lot about Philippe's business. That should have been a relief. It would make Anne's job easier, not needing to explain the process or worry about offending the entrepreneur with the standard questions. It wasn't a relief; the feeling Anne experienced was resentment.

"Denise, I should leave you to your business." She checked her watch. Four o'clock, the convention wrapped up at six. She'd have to get moving if she wanted to see all the booths. "I'm sure you have much to do."

"As do you, Anne." The smile seemed genuine. "Meet back up with me before you leave. I'll wait for you by the entrance so I can answer any questions you might have."

"I'll do that." The businesswoman was more than helpful.

"I like her," Nancy offered her opinion once they were out of earshot.

"I do too," Anne agreed. She was secretly hoping that she'd hate this former girlfriend, that she could point at a glaring defect in character to offset her beauty. But no, she was charming and intelligent and gorgeous.

How can I compete with a woman like Denise? Anne's thoughts were glum. Easy Answer—she couldn't.

Denise was not alone when Anne and Nancy met up with her at the end of the day. Immediately recognizing the shorter man beside the blonde, Anne's heart started to race. Not that he was pleased to see her. Philippe looked furious. *At what?* Anne didn't know.

And come to think of it, she wasn't that pleased to see him either. At first, his appearance surprised her, excited her. He was so handsome that her stomach quivered with one look from those brown eyes, but then a hard-to-accept fact sunk in. After a week away, Denise was the first person Philippe wished to see. Denise, not Anne. That hurt. But Anne wouldn't show it. Not to Philippe and certainly not in front of Denise.

"Philippe." Anne tried to treat him casually, her face as smooth as glass. "I'd like you to meet Nancy, my business partner."

"And good friend." Philippe kissed the redhead's hand. Nancy blushed at the unexpected action. He was a slick one, her venture capitalist, always so charming. "But what's this?" Now it was Anne's turn for a greeting. She was uncomfortably conscious of Denise watching them as Philippe traced down a cheekbone and over her bottom lip with one long finger, his brown eyes black as night. "You can't fool me, *Cherie*. I've seen this look before. What have you been up to while I was away?"

He had seen this look before? Not possible. She had never worn makeup in his presence. "Nothing. It's nothing."

"Nothing." Nancy snorted. "Don't let Stanley hear you say that, Annie."

"Stanley?" Philippe stiffened.

What was he so uptight about?

"Our friend Stanley," Nancy hastened to explain. "He was extremely proud of Anne's makeover."

"Makeover." For some reason, Philippe relaxed, the gold specs returning to his eyes, "Anne doesn't need a makeover, she's beautiful enough as she is. Where's this Stanley that thinks she does?"

"Did someone say my name?" The platinum blond make up artist popped his head into the group.

It was turning into a party, yet Anne wasn't paying attention. How could she? Philippe thought her beautiful enough as she was. Beautiful. Her.

"Stanley, how'd you find us?" Nancy shouldn't have had to ask. Stanley could be counted on to arrive when needed and more often when not.

"Were you hiding from me, Dearest?" Stanley fluttered his eyelashes at her. "Not nice, Fancy Nancy. Oh, hello Denise." Stanley's wave would rival a Queen's. "I see that Annie and Nancy finally found you, Beautiful."

"They did, Stanley, thanks for pointing them in my direction." Denise reached over to kiss his cheek.

"And who," Stanley turned to Philippe, his hands on his hips, looking the venture capitalist up and down, "may I ask, is this dashing young man?"

"Stanley." Her wonder slipped into amusement as Anne watched Philippe's unsettled reaction. "This is Philippe. Philippe, Stanley."

"You are Stanley?" Philippe actually smiled at that as he reached out to shake Stanley's hand. Stanley, that pest, wouldn't have any of that. Having witnessed Nancy's greeting, he held out his hand expectantly, palm down, wrist limp.

Disbelieving brown eyes slid to Anne and her lips twitched. They both knew what Stanley wanted. Anne cocked her head, silently daring Philippe.

Her answer was a threatening glower. Philippe, not one to back down from any challenge, raised the offered hand to his lips, kissing the air above it and then releasing as quickly as possible, the back of Stanley's hand not even touched.

The ladies laughed. Stanley, in contrast, was completely charmed, his hands fluttering. "My, my, my, my..." he murmured.

Nancy leaned over and whispered something in Stanley's ear. His dark lined eyes snapped open, darting quickly between Anne and Philippe. "Annie, you lucky girl, you," Stanley sighed. Anne quickly shook her head in warning.

Philippe came to stand beside Anne, his arm snaking around her waist. "You owe me big for that, *Cherie*," his voice was dropped so only she could hear, his lips brushing against her skin.

"Not now," Anne protested, aware of Denise's watchful eyes. Philippe's arm not letting her step away.

The ex-girlfriend smiled at them blandly, pretending not to mind, before turning back to Stanley and Nancy. Denise was a much better woman than Anne. If their roles had been reversed...

"I called you this morning when I got in," Philippe shared, his comment again only meant for Anne. "You didn't answer."

He tried at least, before going to girl two. That made her feel a bit better. "I must have left the condo already."

A silver-haired security guard wandered by, giving the group a grumpy look. The convention center was emptying out, their group being one of the last.

"We should be leaving," Anne pointed out, much as she didn't want to break up the party.

"Annie-kin, you are so right, girlfriend," Stanley spouted, and Anne could feel Philippe's shoulders shake. He had better not be laughing at that inane nickname. "I'm simply starved," Stanley continued. "and I know the most charming little bistro just down the street from here. Delicious food, but more importantly delicious waiters. They wear the tightest little black pants."

"Count me in," Nancy piped up. "The hubby's away for business."

"That's right, Nance Valance," Stanley teased, "free yourself from the ball and chain, you rebel you. Annie-pie, are you in also sweetie?"

Anne was hungry, the chocolate covered strawberries not making up for her lack of breakfast or lunch. Besides, not daring to look up at Philippe, as of yet, she hadn't a better offer. "I'm in."

"And Philippe, you gorgeous hunk of a man, will you be joining us?" It was Annie's turn to suppress laughter. Philippe looked like he wanted to throttle Stanley.

"If you stop calling me that, Stanley," Philippe's deep voice rumbled, "than *d'accord*, I'm in."

"I'll try, Sweet Stuff, but no guarantees," Stanley sighed, "Beautiful?" He turned to Denise.

Her gorgeous face expressed her regrets. "Unfortunately, I have a previous engagement."

"We understand, oh how we understand, Girl, when you look like that." Stanley held both her hands, and then gave her a twirl. "We can expect nothing else."

After they said their goodbyes, Philippe drew Denise apart for a longer, more private conversation. The blonde's blue eyes kept darting back to the group, more specifically Anne.

The way Denise smiled at Philippe, the way they looked at each other—Anne almost slapped her forehead—that was it! Denise was the blonde in the photograph, the one taken a week before LWH went public, the one hanging on his wall, the one he looked at everyday.

"Something tells me they were more than friends, Annie." Stanley noted the casual way Philippe had his arm around the blonde. An embrace Anne tried to ignore.

"They were once an item," Anne confirmed. It was obvious that they had been and, it appeared, still were, very close.

"And what an item. The two of them, so wonderful to look at. Eye candy for the gods. *Hmmm*," Stanley cooed.

Anne's look cut him dead.

"Not that you don't look cute together, Annie-pie. You do, adorable and you're more his height, pocket sized." Her friend quickly tried to recover, "I like him, girl."

"I do too," Nancy jumped in.

"How can we not? Annie-Bananie. No wonder you waited so long if that's who you were waiting for." Stanley blatantly looked Philippe over, making the businessman frown their way. "I'd wait too for a man like that."

"Don't get too excited. It's a passing thing," Anne muttered, embarrassed by the situation. How could it not be temporary? Philippe dated the likes of Denise. For all she knew, he still was dating the fabulous Suzanne. That might not be serious either but it was a lot more serious than what he was doing with her, plain little Anne. *Maybe not so plain.* He said she was beautiful. Beautiful, her, and Philippe didn't lie.

"A passing thing? Annie, you're not that type of girl." Stanley nudged her in the stomach with his bony elbow. "And I'd bet my best eyeliner that you're not his usual type of girl. The *Barbies,* including the beautiful Denise, are his trophy babes, aren't they?" Anne nodded, amazed at Stanley's deduction. "You, you're not like that."

Anne certainly wasn't like that, not even close. "I wish." At least then, she had a shot at holding his attention.

"You might think you wish but you don't really." Stanley shook his blond head. "Those women are a short term fix for a quality man like Philippe. You, girl, you're a life-long addiction, you wait and see."

Anne didn't have a chance to respond, even if she could, Philippe's lingering good-byes with Denise finally over.

"Ready, ladies?" Philippe asked, looking to Anne for the answer.

He got one from an unexpected source.

"Ready? So ready." Stanley flirted, "So very, very ready."

Seven

Philippe found it difficult keeping his eyes off of Anne during dinner. Not that Stanley's make-up job made her look like someone else; that would be easier to accept. *Non*, Philippe had seen that expression on her face before, dark smoldering eyes, flushed cheeks, full pouting lips. His little sparrow looked like she had been kissed senseless, and it made him squirm. All he could think about was putting her in that state naturally. And as soon as possible.

"Are you thinking of getting a dessert?" Anne leaned toward him, her hair slipping over her shoulder, soft as satin, brushing up against him.

"*Mais oui, Cherie.*" He swallowed, staring at her lips. He planned for his dessert to be a true calorie burner but still sinfully sweet. Anne's big brown eyes met his, and Philippe let desire transform his countenance. He felt the trembling in her body. It was so close to his.

"Fancy Nancy and I are going to share the crème caramel," Stanley piped up perkily from across the table.

"Will you share with me, *Cherie*? I wish to save a little appetite for later." Philippe, again, made his plans perfectly clear. He had a favor he was eager to return this evening. He thought about it the entire week and couldn't wait much longer.

"The chocolate mousse looks good." Anne's voice was husky.

"It does," but then, he would agree to anything to please her. Philippe signaled for the waiter that they were ready. He had done all the ordering tonight, Stanley insisting that it be done in French despite Philippe assuring him the waiter spoke perfect English. It now worked to his benefit, Philippe asking for only one spoon for the chocolate mousse. That should get the evening moving in the right direction, his lips curved in satisfaction.

"Annie-kin, do you like pearls or diamonds?" Stanley volleyed across the table.

Where that came from, Philippe had no clue. Such was Stanley's style of conversation, random questions followed by even more irrelevant insights.

"Diamonds," Anne didn't hesitate to answer. A crisp twenty-dollar bill passed from Stanley to Nancy.

Diamonds? That choice surprised Philippe, Anne didn't seem like the bling-bling type, more classic, traditional. He said as much.

Her answer had nothing to do with monetary value or others' perceptions. It was all Anne. "Diamonds sparkle like stars. They make me happy."

Whether "they" pertained to the diamonds or stars, Philippe wasn't too sure. He had the irrational urge to shower her with both, the former significantly easier to obtain than the latter. *How?* He would figure out a way.

"More wine?" Philippe picked up the bottle of white and tilted it toward her empty glass. Anne shook her head.

"Me, please." Stanley waved his glass in front of him for a top-up.

"Nancy? Last chance." Philippe asked. He knew the answer but offered anyway. Anything else would have outed her. "It's good."

"If you do say so yourself." The redhead laughed. He had chosen the wine. "None for me, thanks."

"Nance, you're really on the wagon tonight." Anne commented, "Not a drop of liquor."

Philippe's eyes met Nancy's. For close friends, Anne hadn't yet shared Nancy's secret. No alcohol, a healthy dinner, heavy on the spinach salad, and frequent bathroom breaks made Nancy's condition obvious to Philippe. But then, he knew more than the average man. His two sisters seemed to be constantly pregnant.

The crème caramel was placed in front of her and Nancy hooked her thumbs in her waistband. "Trying to reduce, Anne. Not all of us have your amazing metabolism."

Philippe's clueless sparrow accepted the lie. "It's slowing." Anne then slanted Philippe a look that told him she knew what he was doing with the one spoon. She didn't kick up a further fuss. *A good sign.*

Philippe watched her, guarding his expression, as she bit into the mousse. Her eyes fluttered closed, dark lashes against brown skin. Her quiet moan of pleasure made his palms sweat. *Merde*, she turned him on, simply watching her eat was an erotic experience.

"You'll want to try this." She handed him the warm spoon, their fingers lingering, touching. "It's really good."

"I can see that." Philippe shaved off a tiny piece, leaving more for Anne. There was no way he'd enjoy eating the mousse more than he'd enjoy watching her suck on that spoon.

The friends talked and laughed, Philippe content to listen to the conversation, sipping at his coffee, joining in when needed. Anne was the quietest of the three, completely overshadowed by Stanley's drama and Nancy's bubbly personality, but Philippe found himself nodding his head more at her insights.

Anne's neat and tidy brain was one of the reasons. Philippe enjoyed their daily phone conversations, one of the reasons he looked forward to seeing her again. That and the promise of hot sex, of course. That could not be ignored. But in the past, with his other women, hot sex was all he was interested in. Not so with Anne. Philippe asked for her opinion and wanted to hear the answer. He paid attention. He had to, the woman too damn quick to tune out on.

Anne threw him a grateful look as he picked up the check. He chuckled at her charge for chicken fingers and fries. Not the fancy food type, his girl.

"Stanley, you want a ride home?" Nancy offered as they headed to the exit. "I have to drop Annie off also."

"I'll take care of Anne." Philippe nodded his thanks to Nancy for the opening. *She's a good one, that Nancy.*

"I bet you will." Stanley's saucy comment made his skittish girl stiffen. Philippe cautiously tightened his grip on Anne's waist. She wasn't going anywhere. He had plans for tonight.

Those big brown eyes devoured Philippe as he climbed into the driver's seat. He started the car up and she sighed. *Oh, no, we don't,* he almost chuckled with delight, *this time we'll do this properly. No more hanky panky in the cramped car.*

~ * ~

Anne wanted him, more than she ever wanted anything in her life. She wanted his mouth on hers, his hands on her body, his hard muscle against her soft skin. But, she watched as he concentrated on the road, his determined chin in profile. *That* would have to wait. Until then, small talk. *What to say?*

"Thank you for tonight. Stanley…" Was bringing up her flirty friend conducive to exciting bed play? Likely not.

"It was nothing, *Cherie*." He shrugged her comment off, smoothly parking the Maybach.

It was not *nothing*. Anne knew enough less confident men to dismiss his tolerance as easily. "You're a good man, Philippe Lamont."

"If thinking that helps my cause tonight," he opened her car door and held out his hand, "then I'll be a good man."

She slid her hand along his. It was firm and warm and made her palm tingle. *Yeah, Philippe is a good man, surprisingly so.* "Well, I don't know if it helps your cause," Anne dropped her voice into a whisper, "I wouldn't want to corrupt you."

His eyes burned amber. "You think you can do that, *Cherie?* Corrupt a worldly, jaded man such as myself?"

Worldly, jaded. Oh dear. Philippe is right. What could I possibly offer him? Me, plain little Anne James. She squashed that thought. Philippe was used to confident women. He bedded confident women, and dang it, that's what she'd give him, a confident woman. *Be brave. Be fearless.* "I could try."

"Not tonight, *Cherie*." He tapped a finger against her nose. "Tonight is all about you."

All about her, Anne quaked. Could she do that? Take all the pleasure for herself? Sit back and enjoy? No, it felt too greedy, too selfish. And it gave him complete control. She'd be at his mercy. She didn't like that.

Since their encounter in the car, Anne thought about the next steps. A lot. So much so that in this week apart, she plotted out a brazen action plan. It took courage, guts, to implement. She didn't know if she had it in her. But worldly, jaded—was it really such a risk? The usual could bore him. What she planned... well, if it went wrong, at least she tried. If anything, she could laugh about it later. Alone.

Anne weighed the risks as she led Philippe into her living room. What now? "Would you like a drink?" she offered, nervously watching him prowl around the room, his sharp eyes not missing anything, picking up photos and putting them back down again. Her place wasn't that large. They already passed the microscopic kitchen. The only other room was, *gulp*, the bedroom. And she wasn't ready for the bedroom yet.

"No, a drink isn't what I'd like." He returned to her side. "You are." Before Anne said another word, Philippe kissed her. His kisses were hard like his body, urgent, hungry. They drove all air from her lungs until she was left gasping, hanging onto him.

Philippe unbuttoned her blazer, pushing it over her shoulders, letting it fall to the ground, his hand running over her ivory camisole. She was backed up until her calves hit the edge of the sofa. Then he tilted her down to lie on the cushions so he was over top her, braced against one arm. "*Tres douce*, very soft," Philippe murmured against her neck, his free hand cupping her breast, bringing her nipple to hard peaks underneath the silk. "I know what you like too, *Cherie*."

This was it, her sign, her chance, and she took it. "I don't think that you do," slipped out before she debated it further.

The impact was immediate. Philippe pulled away, his face one of stunned disbelief. "*Comment?* You don't think I know how to please you?"

"I don't think that you do." Anne looked as sultry as she could manage, trying to diffuse his anger, bring the passion back. Had she made a mistake? She didn't know. It was too late to back out now. "I think I'll have to show you."

Anne rose to her feet, leaving him confused and angry on the sofa. *Be brave, be fearless, concentrate on the task at hand.* First step, secure the man's attention. Anne reached around behind her to unzip her slim skirt, all the while watching him. *Accomplished.* Philippe waited expectantly, his brown eyes flashing gold. *Next step, get naked.*

Wishing she had the foresight to put on music, Anne hummed as she edged the skirt down teasingly over her hips, slowly revealing first her midriff then the top of matching ivory panties, lower, lower. Wiggling a little more gave him a peek of the top of her tan stockings, and then the skirt fell to the floor in a swish of fabric.

His mouth dropped with it. *Good, good, very good.* That gave Anne enough courage to rest one high heel on the cushion by his thigh, and bend over slightly to smooth her stocking from ankle to thigh, drawing his eyes upward, well aware that her camisole gaped open while she did so.

Now what? Talk, that's it. Not small talk, no mention of Stanley; sexy talk. "Do you want me to show you, Philippe?" Anne stepped back, running a hand over that camisole, down to her panties. "Show you how to please me?"

"*Mon Dieu*, woman, this was supposed to be about you," he groaned. From the tightness in his voice, she guessed his control was stretched.

Anne had no bloody idea how stretched his control was. Philippe told himself that it couldn't happen again. He thought he ensured this morning that it wouldn't. But *non*, this blasted sparrow was turning him into a sex maniac. *Oui*, her actions were unpracticed, a little nervous, a little awkward, the humming adorably off key. Philippe would bet big dollars this was her first time doing something like this. That made it all the more erotic. Like he was peeking into a private moment. *The little brown sparrow flying free.*

"This is all about me," and Anne's words were right on the money. It was about her. There was no room in his mind for anything else.

Philippe tried to look away. He couldn't. Those long fingers of hers trailed over her thin body. Did he ever think it was too thin? He had been a fool. It was lean with subtle curves in all the right places.

Her camisole slipped off those dainty brown shoulders, slowly, slowly, until dark nipples were freed.

Merde, did she just lick her finger before she circled the darkness, leaving a glisten of moisture in its wake?

"Anne, I can't." He shifted, so hard that he was uncomfortable. He wouldn't get through this without grabbing her. Or something.

"You can touch yourself too, Philippe," her voice was sultry as she read his mind. "I don't mind."

He couldn't do that. She wasn't some stripper. To be used for purely visual entertainment. This was Anne. This was the woman he asked advice from, the killer businesswoman with the keen brain.

But then she licked her finger again and moved it under the band of those silk and lace panties and all thoughts of not touching himself fled.

~ * ~

Hours later, spent and satisfied, Anne lay cradled in Philippe's arms, back fully on the sofa though in partial denial over her actions. *Had she done that?* Pleased herself in front of Philippe Lamont? Worldly, jaded Philippe Lamont? No sense thinking about it now. *What is done, is done.*

"What am I going to do with you, *Cherie*," he murmured

against her forehead, hugging her close.

Anne ran her fingers through his short curly chest hair, finding comfort in the strength of his heartbeat. *"Hmmm*...I thought you were tired."

Philippe put his hand over hers, stopping her movements. "That wasn't what I meant and you know it. Though, hold onto that thought for later." He kissed her fingertips one by one.

So what had he meant? What was he going to do with her? In what capacity? Not sex. Had to do with business then. Business, business. Always business. Could business still be done between the two of them? With Philippe going out of town after the last encounter, they hadn't discussed it. Now it happened again.

"Do you want me to continue working for you?" Anne framed her question for the affirmative she wanted.

"Maintenant, Cherie? Now?" Did she want to talk about business now? Of course not, but it had to be talked about sometime.

"Yes, now."

"Then of course, I do," Philippe's voice held no doubt.
"This changes nothing. You don't need my approval to turn down the plans. It's like you're working solo."

"And if it's a thumbs up?" Anne's experience with Denise today told her the woman could have a viable business.

"You have no emotional or financial attachment to my decision, so what will you care? They aren't your clients."

And later, when they were her clients? When she did care? Had she screwed her company literally by masturbating in front of their largest financier? Anne knew the answer but was not brave enough to ask the question. Instead, Anne tackled the other touchy question she wanted to know about. "What's the story with Denise, anyway?"

"Cherie, you might want to work on your pillow talk."

"Advice from the expert. Thank you." Anne's triteness earned her a playful pinch. "Seriously, Philippe, I'd like to know."

"Then I'll tell you." Anne rode the wave of his chest as Philippe sighed. "We were once an item."

That was what he was worried about telling her? "Tell me something I didn't know."

"Did Denise...?"

"No, it wasn't Denise. I have eyes. I can see it. She's your type and you act, well, lets say you act closer than just friends." Anne was careful to keep all hurt out of her voice. "So why'd you leave her?" *How would it end?* Anne and Phillipe's relationship. If she knew then maybe she could prepare. Forewarned is forearmed, and all that.

"I didn't leave her."

What? Had she heard that correctly? Anne sat up straight, moving away from his comforting warmth.

"Denise left me."

"Really?" *Why would any woman leave Philippe?* Denise looked and acted sane.

"*Vraiment.* You may find it hard to believe." His tone was dry. Anne doubted he was proud of Denise's actions. "But we were friends more than lovers."

"Oh, yes. A platonic relationship." The sarcasm slid out. *Who is he trying to fool?* Philippe had a very healthy sex drive.

"Don't be bad, *Cherie*, not that friend-like, *evidemment*. We had no future and she fell in love with someone much more compatible. We remain friends. I'm happy for her."

Sure, he is because everyone knows Philippe Lamont likes losing. Tell that story to someone who doesn't know him. Intimately. And friends more than lovers—didn't that sound familiar? Wasn't that what Anne and Philippe were? Business buddies who slept together or got darn close to, Anne amended, they not yet doing the deed. Not yet doing the deed. A technicality. It was a matter of time.

Especially since there wasn't anything left stopping them from reaching that logical conclusion. After tonight, their business relationship was messed up, ruined beyond redemption, Philippe telling her in not so many words that Anne's clients wouldn't be able to pitch to him.

And she had done this, for what? A fleeting relationship? Some hot sex? Was that a big enough payoff? Was that fair to her business? It's not that she didn't know what she was doing; she did. Even Nancy warned her. *Nancy.* Blast it, but her partner wouldn't be too happy with Anne's lack of willpower. The thought of explaining the situation to Nancy made Anne's black mood even darker, shredding the last remnants of romance. Anne didn't bother to try to put the pieces back together again.

She rose, ignoring Philippe's raised eyebrow, and searched for her clothes, flung around the living room during her first and last striptease attempt. Anne couldn't see Philippe to the door in her stocking and heels. No, she wasn't yet that brazen. Anne slipped on her suit, not bothering with the undergarments.

"*Cherie?*"

She didn't answer, tossing Philippe his clothes as she ran across them. He wisely didn't ask again, dressing quietly.

Finally fully clothed, Philippe stood at the door with his arms crossed, watching Anne warily. He looked confused. Indulging her terrible mood, she didn't enlighten him.

"Guess I'm done here," he had the nerve to say. *What had wrapped up? A business meeting?*

"Guess so." Anne opened the door.

Eight

Anne could have finessed the confession, spinning it into a positive rather than a negative. It was doable. She was a skilled salesperson and Nancy was an easy prospect, one she knew well. Anne didn't bother.

"Nance, we can't pitch plans to Lamont in the future."

"Really." Her friend sipped her very healthy glass of milk. "And why's that?"

Anne fiddled with the remains of her garden salad, chasing a piece of lettuce around her plate. "It's gotten personal."

"No, Annie!" Nancy's eyes grew big. "Tell me you didn't."

Oh, yes, she did and it couldn't be any less professional. Philippe was a crucial part of their business. Now, Anne's actions had cost the company money, cost her good friend money. "I'm so sorry Nancy, I couldn't resist him."

"Well, let's be honest," the redhead clucked. "Who could? Even Stanley with his crazy high standards was halfway in love with Philippe by the end of dinner. You've lusted after the man much longer."

"I haven't lusted after him," Anne started to protest. Nancy's reprimanding look forced her to admit, "Okay, maybe a little, but Nancy, be serious, we won't be able to target him any more."

"That isn't because you did the nasty with him. Think Annie. You're the strategy woman. Did you believe Lamont would allow us to sell to him? You'll have spent three months as an insider."

"Well." A tiny part of Anne did. A part of her hoped it would go back to business as usual.

"He's not an idiot, Annie. He's what you call a bastard, remember? Cutthroat and business savvy. Too savvy to allow your entrepreneur an unfair advantage."

Anne's shoulders slumped. She secretly wished that Nancy disagreed with her conclusion. "He's a big part of our business, Nance."

"Because you focused on him. If you focused on some other V.C, they'll become as big a part of our business, maybe even bigger."

"I suppose." The thought of doing all that groundwork on someone else, someone other than Philippe didn't appeal to Anne. There was no one quite like him.

"Well, what's done is done, as you always say. Our little Annie with

Philippe Lamont, imagine that! So spill it girl. How was it?" Nancy grinned. "Is it true that he can go for hours, making women howl for mercy?" Some of Philippe's ex-girlfriends were quite loose lipped about his sexual prowess, contributing heavily to the Lamont legend.

"Nancy!" Anne protested, her face flaming at her friend's crudeness. And then she thought about it a little more. *Hours? Not hours.* He was skilled, there was no doubt about that, but he didn't last that long.

"Okay, okay. I'll be kind and not dig for details," her friend relented. "But Annie, sweetie, play safe. Promise me you won't get in too deep." She grasped Anne's hand. "You know what Lamont is like."

"I know." Yeah, Anne knew only too well what he was like, never long with any woman, no matter how glamorous, no matter how sophisticated.

"As long as you know." Her friend's voice was gruff. Anne didn't think she fooled Nancy one bit but her friend mercifully changed the subject. "Remember that I'm off to San Diego with Ted next week."

That's right. She mentioned something about that the other day. It struck Anne as peculiar, Nancy not often accompanying her husband on business trips. "Ted's been in San Diego a lot lately, hasn't he?" Too much for Anne's liking.

"He adores the city, as I do." Her friend smiled. "It's livable with the zoo, and tight communities and great schools."

Great schools? Since when did Nancy care about great schools? Anne didn't have a chance to ask as Nancy moved on to her next subject. "I have a temp coming in this week, training to take over in my absence. She's been doing a great job, a very fast learner. I'm impressed."

"She can't fill your shoes," Anne piped up loyally.

"I don't know." Nancy's words were quiet. "I think she might be able to. And she's interested in full time too."

Full time? Healthy lunches, no alcohol, long trips to a remote city with good schools, now a qualified temp for a one-week absence. They should address the situation.

"Do you want to talk about it, Nance?"

Her friend's look at her watch, confirming today's date, all but announced her pregnant state. "Not yet, Anne. Too early."

"I only have one and a half months left with Lamont." That would be one miserable day. Anne tried not to think about it, plopping down her credit card on top of the bill. A business lunch with her partner, maybe one of their last.

"I know." Blue eyes met brown in understanding. It was settled. They would talk about it then.

To add to her increasingly bad day, as soon as Anne sat down behind her desk, a sour faced Mrs. Depeche entered her office. Was this what Anne looked forward to working with in the future? A woman like Mrs. Depeche? The thought was depressing.

With a disapproving sniff likely at her long lunch, the stiff backed executive assistant placed a thick file on her desk. "Remember, Miss James, that you have the one-thirty with Denise Marche." Anne was aware of the meeting. It was a quarter after one.

"Do you know Denise well, Missus Depeche?" Anne wasn't yet worthy of calling the woman by her first name.

"Philippe and Denise…" Philippe's executive assistant paused, as if uncertain of what to say next.

"They had a thing, I already know." Anne tried to put her at ease.

Mrs. Depeche slid into the guest chair, sitting at the edge of the seat, like she wanted to flee as soon as she could. The executive assistant opened up a little. "They've remained friends, spending time together, so yes, I would say that I know her well."

And Mrs. Depeche liked Denise while she didn't like Anne. Anne tried not to be so sensitive but it hurt. "I value your opinion, Missus Depeche. What do you think of Denise?"

"I think she's kind, intelligent, very adept at making people comfortable…" She drifted off, her eyes not meeting Anne's.

"You like her," Anne stated baldly. Mrs. Depeche's gray head nodded. "I do too."

Mrs. Depeche's jaw dropped.

"That surprises you?" Anne didn't wait for the answer. "It shouldn't. Denise is a nice person."

"I thought because…"

Anne wouldn't make Mrs. Depeche finish the thought. "You thought because Philippe dated her I wouldn't like her? This is business, Missus Depeche. I'm a professional."

"Professionalism is important." The comment held more scold than observation.

So that's it. Anne should have realized. That was when her uptight behavior started, after that first discovered embrace. "You don't approve of my relationship with your boss."

"It's not my place to approve or disapprove." But Mrs. Depeche's face said it all, she disapproved with every ounce of her body.

"That's okay." Anne waved her hand. "I don't approve of it either."

Brown eyes behind glass widened. "You don't?"

"Who could? You're right. It's unprofessional and if known, would make other employees uncomfortable."

"It's known, Anne."

What? It's known? They had been so careful. Mrs. Depeche took pity on her and explained, "Philippe doesn't meet with all his executives daily and he certainly doesn't look at them the way he looks at you."

Anne groaned, holding her head in her hands. She was getting a headache, a big pounding headache. Not one for medication, she now knew why some people popped pain relievers like candy. "I'm sorry," she had been apologizing a lot today, "I didn't want that to happen."

"Then why risk it?" came the question she dreaded.

Why? Why? Anne didn't have a good answer. "I couldn't say no." And she couldn't. She couldn't deny him anything.

"You like him." It was the older lady's turn for blunt speaking.

"Yes, well, that's my challenge to overcome, isn't it?" Anne said briskly, shuffling the papers, trying not to think of how her problems were rapidly compounding. "I'm sorry if it makes your position awkward. I never intended that, Missus Depeche."

There was a pause. When she spoke, Mrs. Depeche's voice held a softer undertone to it. "I'll handle it, Anne, but please call me Sylvie."

Anne hadn't time to think of her new batch of problems before Denise arrived, breathtakingly beautiful in a blush pink designer suit, her polished nails a perfect match. Her beauty further enhanced by the genuine smile on her porcelain face.

"Anne, so glad you could see me." The woman forewent the handshake for a brief buss on the cheek, her light flower scent reaching out to surround Anne.

"Denise, welcome. Please have a seat." Anne noted how she drifted into the chair with perfect grace, her generous proportions filling out the suit in ways Anne's slight form never could.

She felt like a flat-chested little girl seated across from Denise, a bit intimidated. But, as her confidence threatened to evaporate, Anne reminded herself that she was the one with all the power, the control. And she was the expert. She couldn't forget that. Anne pulled out the business plan. Its strength lay in the proposition rather than the format. The gems had to be searched for, hidden within layers of unnecessary text.

"Not one for small talk, I see." The blonde nodded down at the paper spread on the desk. "So like Philippe that way. He is always cuttingly to the point."

Anne cocked her head, considering the woman with cool brown eyes. Had she done that deliberately? Drawn attention to her relationship with Philippe? "We are alike in another way. Business is business." Anne liked Denise but she wouldn't let her personal feelings affect her judgment.

"Oh, yes, you're a bastard also." This made Anne start and Denise explained, "He mentioned that you called him that."

"Numerous times," Anne mumbled, unnerved that he shared their personal conversations with Denise. *What else had he told her? Surely not...* her cheeks pinkened. "Denise, I reviewed your business plan and I have a few questions."

"I'd find it peculiar if you didn't." Denise smiled a tad less easily.

"Where did you get the idea of a integrated guest list system?" Anne needed to assure herself that this was Denise's original idea. She didn't want any lawsuits.

"I was helping with my sister's wedding and I noticed that she had many guest lists. One for the invitations, one for the replies, one for seating arrangements, the gifts received, the hotels needed and so on. Basically it was the same names on all the lists and I thought to myself, this is absurd, why not work off one master listing? I was in data management at one time, if you didn't know."

Anne didn't. *Blast it, the tall blonde has a brilliant brain in that pretty head of hers. So far, her logic makes perfect sense.*

Denise's monologue continued on a tangent. "Funny how many of Philippe's girlfriends had an information technology background. You must be one of the only exceptions. Even Suze has a—"

"About *Be My Guest*, Denise," Anne redirected her client. She didn't want to hear about all of Philippe's ex-girlfriends. With his history, that could take days.

"Oh, yes, where was I?" Big blue eyes blinked rapidly. Anne got the impression that the beauty wasn't used to being interrupted.

"One master listing," Anne prompted helpfully.

"That's right, one master listing, then I took it a step further. What if there was a site that handled all this? Automatically fed to thank you cards, table cards, gift registries, hotel and rental car reservations? The possibilities are endless. The advertising and affiliate deals alone would make the site profitable!"

Anne was stirred by Denise's passion. Passion was good, essential, and the business excited the entrepreneur. That was clear. "How long would it take to get up and running?" First-to-market would be key, especially for the gift registry portion. The on-line and bricks-and-mortar retailers would want to team with one company only. They had to be the first to approach them.

"Less than a month after receiving financing." There was confidence in even Denise's shrug. "Most of the programming is done, only fine-tuning the graphics left."

Most of the programming is done? Anne flipped through the business plan. If Denise felt the site was ready to go live, that wasn't how the plan read. It was very brief and top level. No screen snaps of actual web pages, no commentary on back end support. "Do you have some documentation with actual content?"

"It should all be in the latest plan." Denise's forehead wrinkled.

It wasn't there. Anne memorized the business plan; she looked at it so often. "Could you show me?" Anne slid the papers over to her.

Denise scanned it quickly and shook her head. "Anne, this is the old plan. Didn't you get the latest version? I sent it to Philippe last week."

"Philippe has been out of town. He likely hasn't had time to go through his mail yet." Anne supplied a reasonable excuse. She had to talk to Philippe. It didn't reflect well on Lamont Ventures to be so disorganized.

"I didn't mail it. It was hand delivered." Denise bent over to search through her briefcase, pulling out a thick binder. "Doesn't matter, I have another copy."

Anne silently scanned through the pages. There was much more detail here. *Looks good.*

Meanwhile, Denise filled in the gap in conversation with her running commentary. She talked a lot, too much for Anne to concentrate fully on the technical pieces. *Likely it's nerves.* Anne heard about entrepreneurs breaking down completely at a business plan pitch.

"Can I keep this?" With Denise's affirmation, Anne continued, "I'll peruse this in full later. So the financing would be...?"

"To complete the programming but mainly for marketing and securing affiliate exclusivity. Advertising in the bridal magazines alone is outside of my budget. I used up all my personal financing with the programming."

"Understandable," and impressive that she got this far without outside financing. To hire a good programmer was expensive. "Anything else I should know?"

"That I'm determined to make this work and I wouldn't have approached Philippe if I didn't think he'd get a good return on his money."

Well said. "Then I'm pleased to say that I'll be promoting your business to the next level."

"Thank you so much, Anne." Denise clapped her hands in excitement, her blue eyes glowing. "I knew you were a nice person from the second I met you."

Anne gave her best scowl. "This has nothing to do with nice. Your business plan is solid, and if successful, should give our company a healthy return. Don't spend the money yet though. *Be My Guest* has to pass a few more levels, each more stringent than the one before."

"Sounds like a long process." A shadow fell before Denise's face.

She had been waiting a while for financing. No doubt any delay was nerve-racking. "We'll try to speed it up as much as possible. There are also the usual concerns. Share of ownership, monthly audits, and of course, if we agree to the financing, we'll bind you personally to the company for a minimum of three years. I assume you have no issue with this." Much of the company's early success hinged on Denise's extensive personal contacts.

The blonde drummed her perfectly polished nails on the desktop. "I don't think binding me for three years is necessary, do you?"

Now that is peculiar. An entrepreneur wishing to jump ship so quickly? Normally entrepreneurs were wedded and bedded to their companies. "It's a standard requirement."

"I'll have to talk about it." Denise bit her lip.

With whom? Denise was the sole owner. *Relax, Anne. Don't be so suspicious. Give the girl a break.* Denise probably wanted to discuss it with her legal counsel or accountant. Most successful entrepreneurs had an informal board of directors.

"You'll have time, Denise. As mentioned, we have due diligence to complete before the contract is drawn up."

"How long will it take?" Denise's voice wavered.

Again, with the time concern. Sounded like Denise was a little overextended at the moment. Mortgaging to the hilt to feed a hungry little start up wasn't unusual. Anne didn't bother asking for confirmation. It would embarrass Denise and Anne would find out soon enough, a credit check being standard for all applicants.

"We'll have your answer in less than a month," Anne promised. She'd put a rush on it and pull the team together immediately after this meeting.

There was a knock on the door. Before Anne could answer, Philippe poked his dark head in. "Did I hear a familiar voice?"

"Philippe," Denise squealed, dashing out of her chair to give him an enthusiastic hug and kiss.

Anne watched the interaction from her seat at the desk. Philippe's handsome face glowed with happiness as the blonde wrapped herself around him. Although he only came up to her shoulders, they were an eye-catching couple.

"What no kiss for me?" Gregory also appeared at the doorway, and Denise hurried to do the honors.

Great, the whole gang is here. A regular good times reunion. Anne, feeling very much like an outsider as they chatted, opened back up the latest business plan and buried herself in it. She sensed him approach before he spoke.

"So I take it from Denise's happiness, *Cherie,* that you didn't kick her to the curb like you did poor Henri." Philippe's husky voice dropped in volume so only Anne could hear.

Her heart skipped a beat, with him sitting casually on the edge of her desk. Philippe wore another dark navy suit, a rich blue tie, blue lined white cotton shirt, even his shoes were buffed and polished. But it wasn't about the power suit, more how he wore it. Confident. Cocky.

Her intense attraction to Philippe made Anne overly blunt. "You saw the plan."

Philippe furrowed his brow, his long dark eyelashes flickering. "Months ago. I barely remember it."

He must be thinking of the old plan. "No, no, the new plan. Denise sent you a copy last week."

"Not to me." Philippe shrugged like confidential documents disappeared all the time at his company. "Does it look half decent?"

"Better than half decent." Anne pushed her concerns away. It wasn't her place to comment on how he ran his own business. "It's solid, deserving of further investigation."

"Did you hear that Dee? Anne thinks your plan's solid," Philippe repeated louder so his ex-girlfriend could hear. "That's a real compliment coming from my hired gun."

Blackmailed gun more accurately.

"Isn't Anne nice, Philippe?" Denise laughed, drifting closer, her arm around the blond lawyer.

"Once again, I'm not nice," Anne muttered, completely disgruntled. *How many times do I have to say it?*

"She's right, Denise." Philippe's grin grew. "I don't think Anne knows how to be nice. She's a little too honest for that."

"Sure, she's a real bastard," Denise informed the group.

"Denise!" Gregory granted Anne an apologetic look.

"It's okay. She told me she's a bastard," Denise explained. Not that Anne had, but then she hadn't refuted Denise's proclamation either.

"That explains everything. Like attracts like, right, *Cherie?*" Philippe purred.

Gregory stepped in to defend her, "I don't think Anne's a bastard. Just the opposite, she's always very nice to me."

Defending her or not, Anne didn't like the spin Gregory put on the last comment. Sounded like she gave him more than friendly hellos and smiles in the morning.

"She's nice to me also," Denise confirmed more innocently, "And Stanley says that, what does he call you, Anne?" Her face scrunched up and Anne groaned. *Here it comes.* "Annie-kin, that's it. He says Annie-kin is all bluster, no punch, a cream puff dressed up as a sledgehammer."

"Annie-kin" Gregory repeated, his eyes lingering on Anne's face a little too long. His glances, she didn't know why, they made her feel uncomfortable.

And that nickname was spreading like the blasted flu. *Great.* Add that to her growing list of problems. "Remind me to kill Stanley." Anne frowned up at Philippe's laughing face.

He was no help. "*Ahh, Cherie.*" Philippe rubbed her shoulder, his body so near she felt it shaking.

His amusement didn't last long, Denise not done with her

storytelling. "Did you know that Philippe kissed Stanley?" she confided to the lawyer.

"No! Really? Philippe?" Gregory's attention switched to his friend.

"Need any help hiding the body?" Philippe asked Anne.

Nine

Philippe smothered a smile as Anne impaled a few leaves of lettuce with the tines of her fork, a look of complete determination on her face. She struggled to finish her food, not willing to waste any of it. It was her second lunch of the day. Anne used that reasoning to try to wiggle out of this impromptu celebration but Philippe wouldn't allow her. For some not to be explored reason, it was important to him that she be there.

Since her situation was fully his fault, it was only fair that he help her out. Philippe, without bothering to ask, picked up her plate and moved some salad to his own. *Rabbit food*, not his favorite, but his sacrifice made her happy. She darted a silent look of thanks his way.

Denise and Gregory chatted up a storm across from them, allowing Philippe to devote full attention to his little sparrow. Anne didn't need to be the center of attention, content to sit back and listen, letting others carry the conversation.

And Denise was more than happy to. The woman could talk, one of the many reasons that she was not compatible with Philippe. It was difficult to think clearly with so much verbal clutter. No, he was more than content with the silences he shared with Anne, each exploring their own thoughts before opening their mouths. Philippe could be assured that Anne wouldn't unload half-cocked ideas onto his already full mental lap.

"Didn't know you to be a salad eater, Philippe," Denise piped up, indicating his plate. It formerly held a perfectly grilled steak and mashed potatoes. As far from salad as possible.

"I'm trying to eat healthy to make up for dessert." Philippe put the dessert menu between Anne and himself. "What say you, Anne, to sharing some decadence with me?" His face was a picture of innocence though he fully intended the double meaning. He looked over the listing. *Something with a spoon for her to suck on would be preferable.*

"I'd love to but I don't think I have any room left." Anne tugged at the waistband of her pants. Philippe caught a tantalizing glimpse of white lace and then almost growled out loud as he realized Gregory leaned towards Anne also.

Trouble. Big Trouble. Gregory had been sneaking looks at Anne all through the meal, acting the gentleman, oh so considerate. It wasn't the way that Gregory would treat a girlfriend of a friend. Philippe didn't like it, he didn't like it one bit. He draped his arm along the booth behind Anne, making his possession of her attentions clear to the lawyer. "No room?"

"None at all." She sighed regretfully, unaware of the sudden tension at the table.

"Not even for such sensual pleasures?" Anne wouldn't appreciate this heavy-handed approach but the demon in him demanded he drive the point home with all the finesse of a demolition derby.

He was right. She didn't appreciate it and frowned. "Especially not for those."

"Philippe, you can share the apple pie with Gregory and me," Denise threw out as a peace offering.

"I'd even let you have a little taste before I do," Gregory had the nerve to tell him.

Little taste? Philippe had the burning urge to give his friend's handsome face a little taste of his fist. "Aren't you afraid I'll want the whole thing?"

Gregory's lips turned upwards but his eyes didn't share the smile. "I doubt that would happen, dear friend. There are too many desserts out there for you to sample."

"*Alrighty* then." Denise was not amused as she put in the order. "One piece of apple pie it is, and three forks."

Philippe dared to look at Anne. She watched him with those big brown eyes, sweetly concerned. That was his girl, oblivious of her effect on two seemingly grown men.

"Gregory, do you have some spare time this afternoon?" Anne used the gap in conversation to ask. "Sylvie's trying to pull the team together so I can meet with you all briefly."

Mon Dieu. The team. Philippe remembered the long nights of hashing out contract details. They'd be spending a lot of time together, Anne and Gregory.

Gregory's blue eyes flashed in triumph. "My entire afternoon is yours if you wish, Anne."

She bit her full bottom lip, drawing Philippe's gaze to her mouth. *No doubt that was where Gregory looked too, that dog.* "Well, I don't think I need that long."

"Good, because I'd like to talk with you, Gregory, when we return to the office." Philippe had to clear the air before Gregory and Anne started spending time alone. He would go insane otherwise.

"You boys will behave, won't you?" Denise pleaded.

~ * ~

An hour later, they were behaving, being perfectly civil. But then they hadn't started talking yet. Gregory slouched in the guest chair, like a child about to get a scolding, and Philippe rustled some paper, trying to think of a way to broach the topic without sounding like a raging Neanderthal.

"I think Anne's a great girl," Gregory finally offered, "She's very intelligent. She has a good heart. She's good looking in a quiet sort of way, the way that I usually like. You may go for the *va-va-va-voom* blondes but me, I like my women like Anne, classy and dignified."

Except there are no other women quite like Anne. There is only Anne and..."She's mine, Gregory." So much for delicate positioning.

"I know that." He picked a piece of lint off his suit jacket. "I would never impinge on your turf."

"Then what exactly are you doing?" Philippe reminded himself that Gregory was his best friend.

"I'm ensuring that I'm next in line."

"What?" Philippe sprang from his chair, the thought of the good-looking lawyer touching his sparrow making Philippe see red. He paced to the window, his fists clenched at his side. *I will not hit Gregory, I will not hit Gregory, I will not hit Gregory.*

"You know, like Derek did with Denise," Gregory explained.

"That was different." Philippe scowled. *Oui,* Derek was Philippe's friend also, *et oui,* Denise was Philippe's girlfriend at the time, *et oui aussi,* Philippe noticed Derek moving in before they broke up but that was different.

"How?"

How? What to tell him? There was no logical explanation except for "That was Denise, this is Anne."

"If it were Suzanne...?"

Gregory and Suzanne. Now, that would be a good solution. Philippe wouldn't have to worry about Gregory with Anne, and Suzanne would stop bothering him. "You have my blessing with Suzanne."

"No thanks. She's not my type. Comes across as fake. A little too desperate too." Gregory walked to stand beside him, the fool. If he knew how Philippe felt, he wouldn't be within beating range. "But if Anne and Suzanne's positions were switched..."

"If I ended it," Philippe supplied, trying to think this through rationally. He had to see this from his friend's point of view. Normally Philippe scrambled for the exits as soon as he became involved with a woman. Gregory couldn't know that the thought of Philippe not being with Anne again, not talking to her, was unimaginable.

"Then yes, I'd be interested. Anne's a rare find, a one in a million woman, I'd be a fool not to."

"And I'd be a fool to walk away from her." Philippe knew in his soul that was true. "And if I never ended it? What would you do then?"

Gregory stepped back, his face frozen with shock. "I, you... what?

My friend, I had no idea."

"I trust her," was all Philippe said in explanation. He didn't have to say more. The people he truly trusted he could count on his fingers. Gregory knew that.

"You trust her?" Gregory sounded like he found that hard to believe. "That was fast."

It was, very fast. "When I see a bargain, I move. That's what has made me so successful in life. No hesitation." And Anne was the true deal in every sense of the word.

"You do, Philippe." Gregory didn't appear that heart broken. He stretched out his hand to grasp his, pounding Philippe's shoulder with the other. "That is great news. Wow, I never thought to see the day."

"It's early yet," Philippe cautioned but his grin grew. This was when he should be flipping out over commitment. Instead it felt good. It felt right.

~ * ~

Anne, in contrast, felt terrible. The two lunches were not setting well with her, her poor little tummy uncomfortably stretched. Then there was the tension between Gregory and Philippe over that second lunch. What that was about, she didn't know. Could be due to Gregory flirting so outrageously with Denise. Philippe would still have some feelings for the gorgeous blonde.

Who wouldn't? She was beautiful, intelligent and nice. Philippe was no dummy; he must have noticed Denise's sterling qualities. To top it all off, should they have a celebration luncheon at this early point in the analysis? What if it fell through on some minor point tomorrow? Philippe would be so disappointed in her. It was a lot of pressure. She wanted to help Denise out, and she wanted success for her own ego—and she definitely didn't want to let Philippe down. Anne had worked hard to impress him.

Mrs. Depeche, Sylvie she could call her now, knocked on the office door and entered. "Here are the copies I made of the *Be My Guest* business plan for your meeting."

Anne was grateful for the interruption. "Sylvie, thank you so much, but you didn't have to put a rush on them. You had enough on your plate for this afternoon."

"It's important you make a good first impression, Anne." Philippe's executive assistant wouldn't meet her eyes, like she knew something but didn't feel comfortable sharing it.

"I could have talked to the points and distributed the plans later." Anne thumbed through the pages. "The team would have understood."

"Not all of the team," was muttered under the older woman's breath. *She did know something.* Anne suppressed the urge to ask. Whatever it was, Anne would handle it. No sense pressing their new found truce for a trivial matter.

Trivial or not, it added to her already strained nerves around this first meeting. Anne, on her way to the boardroom, glanced at Philippe's closed door. Gregory was still in there. Sylvie would direct him to the meeting as he exited. Anne hoped he wouldn't be long. With the lawyer in the room, at least one person would be on her side.

She arrived to find the group huddled together. At her entrance they scattered, breaking into smaller groups. A meeting before the meeting—no doubt about the new project manager. That was normal, Anne supposed. She couldn't hold that against them.

She went around the room, talking with each member of the cross-functional project team. Although this was her first Lamont Ventures business analysis, the rest of the team had worked closely together before. Anne, prior to this meeting, made a point of getting to know each team member, sitting down to better understand what each person did. She felt that she had made some pretty good connections with everyone.

With everyone except Kevin Maple. Their relationship had started rough and gone downhill. The executive resented her for some reason. And just her luck, Kevin was in the room already, talking with the finance rep. Anne dreaded making small chat with him but she couldn't avoid it. Not as the project lead and not without making it obvious.

"Kevin, I'm glad you could make it on such short notice." She extended her hand.

His grip was a bone crusher, Anne managing to hide her pain with a smile. "Yes, the short notice was unfortunate. Proper planning is essential to smooth project management."

His point being that if she planned better, she wouldn't call rush meetings. "But when an exciting opportunity presents itself, as it did this afternoon, a good manager should move as quickly as possible to capitalize upon it."

Kevin wasn't letting this go without a fight. "And as quickly as possible requires taking two long lunches in the same day?"

So he *was* watching her. "If the lunch is with a prospective business partner, then yes, it does." Anne noticed with relief that Gregory entered the room. "And on that note, we will get started."

Anne handed out copies of the business plan, going over the broad points, sharing the issues that they should look out for. She also handed out the timeline, based on previous successful projects, with dates and people responsible.

At first the team was disenfranchised, staring at her with blank, dead eyes. They responded to her questions with the shortest of answers and didn't volunteer information. Anne caught them sneaking looks at Kevin before speaking. That didn't faze Anne. She had years of experience getting apathetic teenagers excited about business opportunities. In contrast, a highly driven, educated team was a breeze.

So fifteen minutes into the meeting, most of the team ranged between acceptance and enthusiasm. They had a few solid concerns that Anne addressed quickly. Most of the team. Not all.

Kevin, the source of Anne's problems, asked question after question after question, many unreasonable for such an early point in the analysis. Anne gritted her teeth, plowing away at answering as best she could, her game-face on, unwilling to show her dissatisfaction in front of the group.

"Has anyone else, besides yourself, met with the business owner?" Kevin stood as he asked each question, his superior height making Anne uncomfortable.

"At this point, no. As the project manager, I didn't feel it necessary," Anne responded, her chin tilted up in defiance.

"You didn't feel it necessary," Kevin mocked, implying that the opposite was true, "so we're to rely only on your opinion? Someone who has been with the company a little over a month?"

Anne could hear the gasp from the rest of the group, Kevin going too far this time. Her eyes did not waver from the VP's face. "I'm heading this project, so yes, yes you are."

"I don't know about the rest of you," Kevin looked around the room for support. "but I have a concern with that."

"Really." So this was the goal of the pre-meeting. Kevin was staging a coup. *Well, he could try.* If he'd listen, Anne would tell him not to waste his time. She wasn't going anywhere.

She slowly and deliberately went around the table, staring down each team member. The goal was to ensure that the group knew she was a force to be reckoned with, to gauge support, and to put a human face on the leader they were trying to oust. What she saw was a bunch of fence sitters, no one holding her gaze for more than a couple seconds, content to stay neutral, to let Kevin and her duel it out, prepared to follow the victor. When Anne finally got to Gregory, seated closest to her, he nodded in full support. He would be the only one to defend her.

"Kevin does not speak for the entire group." Gregory stood up, addressing the team. "I, for one, have no concerns with Miss James' leadership, but more importantly, Philippe Lamont, our CEO, has no concerns." He paused dramatically. "He confided today that he trusts Anne James completely."

A buzz of unease rippled through the group as that last bit about trust was absorbed. Whether it was the truth or not, Anne appreciated the words.

"We all know that our CEO isn't thinking clearly at the moment." The way Kevin's eyes roamed up and down her communicated what he thought Philippe was thinking of.

Anne felt a rush of noise in her ears as her temper raised. How dare the man treat her like some executive-chasing bimbo. She was so overcome with rage that she didn't hear the click of the door behind her.

"Mister Maple, are you daring to question our CEO's leadership?" Anne demanded, thumping her fist so hard upon the table that the pens rattled.

The room went deathly quiet, silent except for the whirl of the ac unit. Kevin's already pale face whitened a couple more shades and his mouth moved compulsively.

"Answer the question, Kevin," Philippe's demand made Anne jump. How long had he been standing behind her? Anne didn't dare look at him. She continued staring straight ahead.

"I'm not," Kevin mumbled as he sat down, deflated and defeated.

Philippe hadn't been there for anything but Anne's last passionate declaration over his leadership. However, a quick look around the room made the situation vividly clear to him. Participants were visibly uncomfortable. Kevin glared at Anne. Anne glared right back. Philippe now appreciated Gregory's warning about Kevin and this meeting. That he planned to ensure Anne wouldn't make a run for Kevin's own position.

Not that she would ever consider taking that position. And not that she couldn't handle the confrontation. Kevin might be bigger and louder but Anne... Anne was a true leader. She would win by sheer force of will. And VP or no VP, Philippe was certain that Anne had been one step away from telling Kevin to leave the boardroom.

She shouldn't have to. Her temporary appointment was Philippe's decision. His staff should accept any rearrangement of hierarchy, at least publicly. And that Kevin badmouthed Philippe, his own CEO, in his attempt to bring Anne down didn't please Philippe either. Philippe had zero tolerance for betrayal.

"I'm disappointed that Miss James had to ask that question. *Non,* more than disappointed, embarrassed." Philippe propped his fist knuckles down on the table and leaned forward, glaring at Kevin. The tall man visibly shrunk in front of him. "My first duty is and has always been to this company. If you doubt that, then I, frankly, doubt *your* judgment." Philippe paused, looking around the room, ensuring that everyone was on board. There were wide-eyed nods and some deep throat swallowing, his staff not having seen him this angry in a while.

"As for the question of Miss James' leadership, as a personal favor to me, this businesswoman rearranged duties at her own very successful company, loaning us her skills. Finely honed skills acquired by years of experience." Philippe played up Anne's background. "Miss James, how many business plans have you evaluated?"

"Thousands," the word was rock steady, her eyes trained on Kevin.

My little brown sparrow has her feathers up. Philippe would have chuckled at the sight but he was too damn angry. "Thousands, far more than I've looked at. Certainly far more than Kevin has had even cross his desk." Philippe made it clear that he hadn't forgotten about the backstabbing executive. "And we will be using Miss James' skills to benefit Lamont Ventures, albeit for too short a duration. I'm honored and grateful for this gift. I know that she will treat any project member at Lamont with as much respect as her own employees. It's only right that we return that respect."

Anne didn't turn her head but Philippe thought her clenched jaw relaxed a little. *She is a warrior, this one. Quiet normally, but well able to smite her enemies down.*

"But that isn't why I joined you this afternoon." Philippe forced a smile to his face. He wouldn't leave the meeting on a down note. "This is a happy time. I understand that Lamont Ventures has an opportunity to add yet another member to our family. I'm counting on this team, under the guidance of Miss James, to carefully evaluate and prepare recommendations. I will, as usual, base my final decision on your analysis. Remember, you're driving the direction of the company and for that, I thank you."

Ending there and without another word to Anne, Philippe left the room, stalking back to his office to fully vent his fury. By the subdued atmosphere in the office, the feeble smile on Sylvie's face, the news of his reprimand had already spread.

Good. Then there shouldn't be any surprises when the restructuring news is posted.

Kevin would have to go. That this happened wasn't a shock to Philippe. He never trusted the Vice-president. *Oui,* he had a great resume. *Oui,* he came to the company with impeccable references. *Oui,* he was well educated, a Harvard man. But Philippe never felt comfortable with him. He felt obliged to look over the executive's shoulder.

Now Philippe knew why. Once again, his gut proved correct, as it had with the little brown sparrow. The memory of Anne thumping her tiny fist on the boardroom table made his mood lighten. She was such a fighter. *Oui,* his dear Anne was the bright spot in the meeting. Not only had she not tolerated disloyalty to herself but she hadn't tolerated it to Philippe. There was no question, she was a strong woman, a good alliance. An alliance he planned to strengthen.

Ten

"If you stare at her with any more heat, Philippe, she'll burst into flames." Angela McKenzie studied Philippe's prey, with discerning blue eyes.

"You're not supposed to notice, *mon ange*. This is a business function, *se comprendre*." Philippe watched as Anne laughed at something the taller blonde woman said. The blonde was pretty and she arrived with Anne so they must be friends. She didn't interest him though.

Anne had his full attention. She was dressed all in black, as were most of the attendees at this IPO celebration, but even with her lack of color, she drew his eye.

"And how," Angela took a sip of her champagne. "does she know your entrepreneur, I wonder?" Anne kissed and hugged the man enthusiastically, communicating to all that they were well acquainted. Understandable. She worked on his business plan.

"It's her job," Philippe quipped with an elusive smile.

"Then I see I have been remiss in mine. I should have solved this mystery sooner," and off the determined Angela went to join the group.

Philippe stayed put, watching the commotion from a safe distance. The blonde mystery woman broke from the group, making a run for the bar. He took the opportunity to find out her connection, to learn more about his Anne.

He was granted a sunny smile, touchingly familiar, as he approached the woman. That was all he needed to make his intro. "You're a friend of Anne's, aren't you?"

"Actually, I'm her younger sister." The voice was perky with remnants of Anne woven into it. "Ginette James, Ginny to friends."

This was the sister she always talked about? They were so very different, barely a resemblance. A shame, but proving his point, Anne was truly one of a kind. Philippe took Ginny's offered hand and kissed it, winking teasingly. "Anne's sister? Then I hope to be a *bon ami*, a good friend. Philippe Lamont."

"Oh, I've heard of you. You're Anne's boss," the blonde beauty proclaimed.

"Amongst other things." Philippe made his position clear, glancing across the room. Anne watched them, an unreadable expression on her face. As soon as he made eye contact, she turned away.

He frowned. That was out of character.

"Really." Ginny curled her arm around his. "I didn't know. Anne doesn't talk about that with me."

No wondering why. Her overflowing bosom pressed against his body and Philippe tactfully stepped away. "I'm her nasty little secret."

"Not so nasty." Blue eyes devoured him. He felt dirty from the experience, like it was one of his own sisters ogling him. "And I would never keep you a secret."

"You and your sister are different," Philippe attempted to clarify. *Very different.*

"Some would say that the newest version is an improvement." She ran a red tipped nail down his arm.

Merde. Rudeness was the only solution to this problem. "Some would say that the quality drops."

Full lips curled in a childish pout and Philippe glanced away. How anyone found that attractive, he had no idea. Ginny laughed and slapped his shoulder lightly. "You'll do, Mister Lamont, you'll do."

"Excusez-moi?" What is going on now?

"Do you find me attractive?" Ginny batted heavily darkened eyelashes at him.

Two months ago, maybe. Now... "Non, I don't," was his blunt reply.

"And you like my sister?" At Philippe's tentative nod, she continued, "Thank goodness. I thought Anne would never find a man worthy of her."

"You were testing me." His mouth dropped at the notion. Did Anne know her little sister did this? From his sparrow's flushed cheeks, he would say no.

"Don't get upset, Mister Lamont." Ginny's blue eyes danced merrily. "You passed with flying colors. Most men would have caved at the full frontal press."

He wasn't most men. "It was impressive." Philippe laughed at her audacity. Maybe there was a bit of Anne in her. "You must really love your sister."

"Oh, I do, not that you're unattractive." Seeing his chagrin, she hastened to add. "But I'd never date someone who dropped my sister like that. I learned that lesson years ago."

Dropped Anne? That sweet sexy girl? Men could be such fools.

"So?" Her blonde head tilted, an Anne mannerism.

"So?" he repeated. What did Ginny want now?

She wrapped her arm around his again. "So what do you need to know to impress my overly discerning, older sister?"

~ * ~

If looks could kill, there would be two less people in the world. Anne glared vehemently at the couple. She didn't expect Ginny to act any differently; she always hit on the one man in the room Anne was interested in. But Philippe, well, Philippe disappointed her. She thought that he was different. Clearly he wasn't. Just like the rest, *that bastard.*

"They make a cute couple." Ms. McKenzie drew nearer.

Anne played ignorant. "Who?"

"Philippe and that pretty blonde girl." The angel investor waved in their vicinity.

"That pretty blonde girl is my sister." Anne sniffed. "And I didn't notice."

"Of course you didn't, child." Her shoulder was given a squeeze.

"I'm not a child." The protest was weak. Anne felt more childish by the minute, one of her childish impulses to pull Ginny's long blonde hair.

"No, you're not, Anne James," the gray haired sophisticate agreed. "You're Philippe's ace in the hole, the mysterious business plan coach feeding him all those delicious opportunities."

And you too, but Ms. McKenzie hadn't figured that out and Anne wouldn't enlighten her.

"I'm correct, aren't I?"

"I might have tossed a couple his way." Anne took a gulp of her screwdriver cocktail. She didn't normally drink at business events. Tonight was proving to be an exception.

"And now you're working for him full time."

Anne's eyes flitted over to the couple by the bar. Why was Ginny standing so close to Philippe and why was he letting her?

"Working for him temporarily," Anne murmured. If she had known…

"Really?" Ms. McKenzie's face lit up.

Ginny touched Philippe's arm again and Anne couldn't stand it anymore. "If you'll excuse me, Ms. McKenzie, there is someone I need to talk to."

"About time," she heard the businesswoman say, as Anne set down her drink and crossed the room.

Anne ignored the welcoming smile on Philippe's face as she approached, ignored the way his brown eyes glowed, ignored the way he made her feel. She would deal with him later. Right now, Ginny was her focus. Her sister foolishly beamed at her, her perfect complexion glowing, unaware of the pain she was causing.

"Sister dear, may I speak to you a moment?" Anne's voice was dead steady.

"Of course, Annie. Philippe, it's been a pleasure." Ginny then had the nerve to kiss Philippe's cheek, Philippe's, her man's cheek. He was her man. Didn't Ginny know that? Or hadn't Philippe told her?

"The pleasure was all mine, Ginny." Philippe flipped a business card in his hand. "I have your number. I'll give you a call and let you know how things are going."

Great, he had her number already.

"I'd like that." A furious Anne didn't stick around to hear the rest of Ginny's reply. She turned on her heel and strode so quickly, it was almost a run, out the door.

Anne kept walking until she was well outside, stalking around the brightly lit gardens of the convention site, gulping deep breaths of the cool night air. The room had been so suffocating, she thought she would pass out.

"Anne?" Ginny's voice trembled a bit. She should be worried. Anne had never been so angry before. "What's wrong?"

"What's wrong? What's wrong?" Anne chopped the air with her hands. "What's wrong with you, Ginny? Don't you have enough men? Do you have to flirt with every man I like too? Do you?" Her eyes filled with tears and Anne blinked them away.

Ginny's mouth opened and closed and then opened again. "I'm doing you a favor, Annie. If they cared for you…"

"Cared for me? They don't have time to care for me." Anne felt like screaming. "You start off where it takes me weeks to get to, freely handing everything to them, like a gift, all pretty bows and wrapping paper. How can they resist?"

"Philippe…"

"I care for Philippe, a lot." Anne was overwhelmed, so very overwhelmed. "But we've only known each other two months. He hasn't had time to build up feelings for me. If I knew…"

"If you knew, what?" Ginny threw her shoulders back. "Would you keep him a secret, from your own sister? Well, congrats, you did! How's that supposed to make me feel? When I go to a party and find out my sister has a boyfriend?"

"Figures. Me, me, me. That's all you think about. Well, I was thinking of you too. I didn't bring you here to pick up men, Ginny," Anne yelled back, "I brought you here so you could build contacts, build your business."

"You shouldn't have bothered," Ginny spat out, "I can build my own business, thank you very much."

"Right." Anne snorted. Everyone knew start-ups need help.

"Right." Her sister's eyes sparkled. "Just because I'm not the smart one." She acted out *smart one* having finger quotes around the words. "Or let's be honest, shall we? Just because I'm the dumb one."

"You're not the dumb one," Anne corrected her. Anne was labeled the smart one because, well, she certainly wasn't the pretty one but that didn't mean Ginny was dumb, not by any stretch of the imagination.

"Don't patronize me, Anne. I know I'm not as smart as you." Ginny sniffed. "But that's okay. I don't need your charity, Miss Successful Business Hot Shot. You can keep your hoity-toity big-money friends. I'm going home."

"Ginny." Anne held up a hand to stop her but then dropped it again. She knew from experience that it was better to let her go. Ginny's snit would blow over soon enough.

"Oh and by the way, smartie pants, two months is long enough to build up feelings. Philippe turned me down flat." Her sister flung the words over her shoulder as she stomped away.

Anne rubbed her temples. What was happening to her? Blowing things out of proportion, so unlike her. Ginny loved her in her own crazy way. And what had she said about Philippe? About turning her beautiful sister down flat? That would be a first. If that was possible, could it also be possible that he had deeper feelings than simple lust for Anne? She would ask him, clear the air.

Anne re-entered the room, determined to pull Philippe away for a private talk. She arrived in time to see the fabulous Suzanne embrace the venture capitalist in the middle of the crowded party.

~ * ~

Angela McKenzie wasted no time hustling over to Philippe's side after the two sisters' stormy exit. Philippe watched her approach him with amusement. "Causing trouble, *mon ange?*"

"Truly, Philippe, I don't know what game you're running, flirting with one sister in front of the other," the older woman puffed, her breath a little wheezy from her smoking habit.

"Is that what it looked like?" He thought he made it clear that he was not.

"You bad boy, you flirt so naturally that you don't even notice when you are doing it."

"I suppose." That troubled him. Philippe didn't want to cause Anne any hurt. He definitely didn't want to cause friction between siblings. He shrugged the concern off. Anne would sort it all out. She was very good at getting misunderstandings out in the open.

"How long will you need Anne?" Angela lowered her voice so no one else could overhear.

How long will he need Anne? Years, maybe even decades. It had been two months and that time hadn't even taken the edge off.

"For business, Philippe. Stay focused," Angela clarified.

Oh, that was her angle. She wanted to steal Anne away from him. "I'll let you know when I'm done with her." He patted her hand.

Philippe was then treated to Angela's pitch for why she needed Anne's help and what she could offer Philippe in exchange. He suspected

Anne would not be pleased with being haggled over like a piece of office equipment.

Though how she was dressed tonight, *hmmm*, definitely worth negotiating for. A loose skirt often meant a garter belt, black to match her hose. Black hose, black panties, lace or silk, maybe both.

"I thought you broke up with that Suzanne woman?" his friend's question breached his very pleasant reverie.

"I did. Two months ago." The same night he truly met Anne, Philippe lost all desire for Suzanne.

"Then what's she doing here?"

"Pardon?" Philippe's head snapped up, his eyes scanning the room. He didn't have to search far, the woman headed in a beeline toward him. Suzanne was alone, no friends in tow. Especially concerning as there was no one to witness a scene.

"Life is never dull with you, is it, Philippe?" was Angela's parting shot as she disappeared into the crowd.

Deserter. Not that he blamed her. He'd disappear too if he could.

"Philippe, darling." Suzanne reached out her arms. "I knew you'd be here."

Merde, does she always wear so much perfume? Had he a cold all the time he was dating her? Philippe hugged his ex close, his mouth near her bejeweled ear. "But you should not be here. I want you to leave, Suzanne. Immediately."

"Surely, you don't mean that, Philippe?" She stroked his jawbone, making his top lip curl in distaste.

"With all my heart." Philippe gritted his teeth. What God-awful timing he had. Anne resurfaced, sisterless, to witness the full embrace.

Her face was expressionless, classic Anne, but she changed direction abruptly, going with Gregory to the bar, her arm around his waist. Gregory was surprised at first, looking nervously in Philippe's direction over Anne's shorter brunette head. Seeing Suzanne attached to Philippe's, he looked like he won a jackpot without even entering.

Oui, mais. His friend had better enjoy the feeling while it lasted. Philippe was about to reclaim the winnings. First he had to get rid of Suzanne. That damn viper, undeterred by his blunt comments, brushed her breasts against his side.

"I've missed you Philippe. Surely you've missed me."

"I haven't." He had some difficulty removing her arms from his body, his eyes on Anne.

"Liar, I'm sure you have. Are you reconsidering our split?"

"Never, Suzanne." Philippe watched Anne toss back another drink. "We're done."

When Philippe stepped towards Anne, Suzanne grabbed his arm. "It's that plain brown thing, isn't it? I was told that you were with her, but I couldn't believe it. I thought that you had better taste."

"I do." *Enough is enough.* Philippe's cold tone reflected his lack of patience. "And I've chosen to indulge it." He looked her up and down and then dismissed her, leaving her gasping angrily after him.

One dark look from Philippe and Gregory backed away from Anne. *Smart move.* He wouldn't want to have to damage his friend's boyish good looks.

"We need to talk, *Cherie*."

Anne stared up at Philippe, her eyes black as tar, her chin jutted out defiantly, and then, without a word, turned away, showing him her shoulder.

"We need to talk *now*, Anne." Philippe circled her wrist with one hand, spinning her around, her drink spilling on the bar top. *Mon Dieu*, he was about to explode. *Not here*, he looked around them. *Somewhere private. Outside.* Without waiting for any confirmation, Philippe dragged her out of the room. He headed to the gardens, Anne stumbling after him.

There, that was far enough from everyone. They would talk but Philippe had to vent some of the emotion first. He couldn't think, otherwise. He folded Anne in his arms, his mouth hot and hungry on hers, grabbing her rear, driving her against him. *Merde*, she made him crazy. He could never get her close enough.

When they parted minutes later, Anne caught him unawares, throwing the remaining drink in her glass at him, dousing him with a sticky concoction of orange juice and vodka. But she wasn't done. Anne flew at him, pummeling his chest with her small fists, her arms moving like windmills, her long brown hair flying.

"Why, you little vixen." Philippe laughed, easily catching her hands, a flea having more strength than Anne. "You like to play rough, don't you?"

"*Rrrough?*" she spat, slurring her words, "you *ssslllleep* with everything that walks and you *ttttalk* to me about *rrrough?*" Anne staggered into the garden, gait unsteady, heels sinking into the soft grass. She stopped briefly to lean against a tree, kicking off her shoes, before continuing into the night.

What was up with her? He'd never seen Anne this way before. And he didn't know where she was going. There wasn't anything out there except more gardens. And fountains, there were fountains. She might fall into the water, the way she was behaving. Hit her head. Drown. *Hell no.* Not while he lived and breathed. Philippe followed her.

~ * ~

She hadn't fallen into a fountain. Philippe found Anne sitting relatively calmly on an old swing, legs dangling, the seat slab looking wide enough for both of them. "Scoot over," he instructed. She did so, silently, head turning in the opposite direction but not fast enough for him to miss the glittering of tears in those big brown eyes.

Had he hurt her so much? Enough to make Anne cry? Philippe tugged on the rope and tested the stability of the board, ensuring that it could hold his weight, before sitting down.

"I'm not sleeping with Suzanne, *Cherie*."

"At this exact second, I guess you're not." Her words sounded muffled.

Trust Anne to take him literally. "I broke up with her two months ago. Around the time, I met this little brown sparrow." Philippe had never gotten around to telling her that. He assumed she knew.

Anne's answer was a very wet sniff.

Did he have a handkerchief? Philippe patted his pockets. *Non*, he didn't. "I didn't sleep with your sister either. For a number of reasons. I just met her today." Philippe knew enough to keep humor out of his voice. "The bigger one being that I'm not attracted to her. My only interest in her is that she happens to be the sister of this woman I truly care about." He waited for her response. Minutes ticked away.

"She said something like that," Anne admitted.

So he *had* caused trouble between the sisters. That didn't make him happy at all.

"Ginny loves you." Philippe hoped this would soothe things.

"I know." The words were quiet, yet certain. Philippe wished he had so much confidence in Anne's feelings for him.

"What about you and Gregory?" Philippe had to know. *Were there any feelings there?*

"He's a friend of a guy I like."

Philippe let out a breath that he didn't even know he was holding. *Bonne, bonne, tres bonne.* He pushed the swing out with one foot.

At that point and without any warning, Anne promptly fell over.

"Anne?" Philippe looked down, horrified that she had fell and disgusted with himself that he hadn't caught her.

She didn't seem any the worse for wear. Anne was peering up at the stars, feet propped up on the swing, an expression of complete happiness on her face. "Lets not fight anymore, Philippe, lets lay here and look at the stars." Her brown hair was spread around her like a halo, her shoeless feet balanced on the swing, exposing a lot of stocking and a bit of garter belt. She looked wild and free. Relaxed like they had just made love.

Mon Dieu, she was adorable. And acting damn peculiar. Philippe bent down, feeling under her head for a bump. There was none thankfully, she had fallen on the soft grass. Then why the quick change in emotion? Why the strange behavior?

A very fragrant yet ladylike burp revealed the culprit.

"You're drunk," he stated flatly.

"You, sir," Anne reached up both soft hands to cup his concerned face, "are right." And then she smiled a smile that would soften the hardest of hearts.

Eleven

The way Philippe looked at it, he had a couple of options. Only one interested him. He laid down on the grass beside Anne, shifting so she was resting in the hollow of his shoulder, and propped his own feet up on the swing seat beside hers. His reward was Anne snuggled close to him and a satisfied sigh. Philippe didn't have to see her face to know she was smiling.

"The stars are moving, *je pense.*" He pointed to the dot of light in the sky.

"That's a plane, goofy." Anne laughed. When was the last time Philippe Lamont, venture capitalist, had been called goofy? When was the last time he star-gazed? He didn't know but he considered both worth it to hear her laugh. "I see I'll have to eradicate your ignorance concerning the solar system."

She sounded so prim and proper that he squeezed her tight. "Yes, teacher."

"Pay attention, if you get lost…" Anne warned.

"And don't have my GPS." The Maybach, hell, even his watch had one.

"And don't have your GPS…"

"And it's night," Philippe pointed out yet another restriction in her plan.

"And it's night," Anne amended. "This could come in handy. See that formation…"

"I like to call it a constellation," Philippe couldn't help teasing.

She glared at him, her bottom lip quivering suspiciously. "Do you want to hear this, Mister Know-it-All, or am I wasting my time?"

"*D'accord, d'accord,* I'll try to be quiet."

"I won't ask the impossible." This sauciness earned her a roll in his arms, the freshly mowed grass rustling under his back.

After a moment needed to recollect her inebriated thoughts, Anne continued with her lecture. "See that big cup with a handle?"

"The big dipper?"

"Yep, and see the little cup?"

"The little dipper?"

"You know this already," she was getting exasperated.

"That's all I know, I promise. Please continue," Philippe lied badly, counting on Anne being too drunk to notice.

She was. "The little dipper or *Ursa minor* is the most important of the two."

"The smaller anything usually is."

"Why thank you." Anne took that as the compliment he intended it to be. "See those two stars at the end of the cup?" She pointed up at the sky. "Those are called the 'Pointer Stars.'"

"I see them." Truthfully he was busy breathing in the fruity scent of her hair. *Why did she smell so good?*

"They point to the North Star," Anne's voice washed over him, "If you get lost..."

"At night with no GPS," he murmured, nuzzling her cheek.

"You can use that star to let you know which way is North," Anne concluded happily.

"Have you ever used that piece of trivia?"

"It's not trivia. It's useful information, and yes, I have, once or twice. Well maybe just the once," Anne amended tritely, nodding, her hair rubbing against his jacket, "when Ginny and I were teenagers."

Vraiment? Philippe found that hard to believe. "In the wilds of California?"

"Yep, in the wilds of California. Malibu Creek, to be exact. We went camping and Ginny and I were having so much fun swimming that we didn't head back to the campsite soon enough. If not for the North Star, we'd be wandering lost today." The happiness of the memory lent a touching warmth to Anne's voice.

"You love your sister, don't you?"

"Of course, we have our differences but I love her and she loves me," Anne declared.

"You sound confident about that," Philippe teased.

"What can I say? I'm completely lovable." Anne laughed. And what could Philippe say? She was.

Philippe was content, lying there in the grass, Anne in his arms, both lost in their thoughts. The experience ended all too soon for his liking, the lights in the garden flicking off and on in warning.

"That's our sign to leave." He could have stayed there all night.

"Wh... what?" From the sounds of it, Anne had almost been asleep.

"Come, *Cherie*." He rose to his feet and then bent down to scoop her up. She cradled in his arms nicely.

"My shoes." Anne stretched out her stocking clad legs to show him her toes.

Left, by the tree. Philippe knew where the shoes were. He was feeling too lazy to retrieve them. "I'll buy you a new pair."

"You will, will you? You might want to reconsider that. I like expensive shoes. Only the best for me, and oh, that reminds me, I need a ride home, Ginny…"

Must have driven. "You're coming with me."

"Are you okay to drive?" she asked, like the thought had just occurred to her.

Better shape than she was. "I have a driver tonight." Philippe hired a driver so he could drink at these events.

"You let him drive the Maybach?" Anne may be drunk. She may be tired. That didn't stop her from asking a thousand questions.

"I bought the Maybach especially so a chauffeur could drive it," and tonight Philippe thanked his foresight. There was nowhere he would rather be than holding her in the backseat during the long trip back.

It was a long trip. They started deep in the suburbs, miles away from downtown. All was going well until a little over midway. Anne started groaning, holding her stomach, her beige skin turning a greenish hue. "Philippe, I don't feel very well."

Merde, she is going to be sick. Philippe frantically looked around him for something to contain the mess. He grabbed the plastic bag out of the wastebasket to prepare.

Anne fumbled at the car door. *Good thinking.* Fresh air. That might help. Philippe found the controls and rolled down the window, allowing Anne to stick her face out, the wind pushing her hair over her shoulder.

"Hold on a little longer, *Cherie*, you're almost home." He rubbed her back in a calming circular motion, hoping all this would buy them some time. It did. No mess in the Maybach. *Now, to get her to the condo.*

Philippe brought the plastic bag with them as he carried her into the elevator. Luckily the elevator was vacant, an express trip stopping only on Anne's floor. Philippe felt her stomach jerking, trying desperately to empty, Anne keeping her mouth stubbornly shut.

Merde, where is that key? Philippe searched through Anne's tiny clutch purse. There it was. Finally opening the door, he kicked it closed behind them, carrying Anne directly to the bathroom. Made it with only a second or two to spare, Anne sticking her head in the toilet bowl, heaving.

"There, there, you'll feel better now." Philippe coaxed, holding her hair out of the way. *How could such a small person have so much in her stomach?* He didn't know but he wasn't going to drink orange juice anytime soon. As Philippe ran a wet face cloth over her face, Anne avoided his eyes. All this must be embarrassing for his dignified sparrow.

"Philippe, I'm fine now, you don't have to stay." Predictably, Anne wanted to get rid of him as soon as possible.

"I'm staying." Someone had to take care of his damned independent woman and that someone was himself. Philippe doled out a dab of toothpaste on her brush and handed it to Anne. "Here, *Cherie*, you need this."

"Rat." Her smile was wobbly. She took the toothbrush.

Philippe then picked up her monster sized bottle of mouthwash, scanning the ingredient listing, and shook his head. "You need something stronger than this, *Cherie*. Do you have any industrial strength?" Philippe made a big show of opening and shutting the bathroom cabinets. He chuckled at the organized stockpile of hygiene products, the severe sparseness of her medicine cabinet. She was a neat freak, his Anne.

She spat and rinsed. "Don't tease, I feel bad as it is." Anne portioned out a thimbleful of mouthwash, gurgled, and spat again.

Philippe smoothed her hair back. "There, feeling better?" Hugging her close, he moved them into the bedroom. She had to be exhausted.

"Philippe, I don't think I'm up to…" her big, brown eyes pleaded.

"Don't worry. I don't make it a habit of coercing inebriated women," Philippe assured Anne, dryly. Not that he didn't find her sweetly attractive but he would rather she be sober for any lovemaking. That, and not having to worry about her vomiting up anything left in her stomach. From college days, he knew nothing ruined the mood faster. "I'll help you undress."

Anne sat with a thump on the bed. "I can do it…" Even as she said the words, she laid back, her eyes already fluttering close.

"Sure you can." She wasn't in any condition to do anything. Philippe reached around her to unzip her black dress, sliding the fabric up her body. She was as loose as *Jello* in his hands. And this *Jello* turned him on, even passed out and sleeping. He tried to ignore the way her black bustier pushed her small chest up and together, creating the illusion of more. Tried, but couldn't. That wouldn't be comfortable, no matter how soft it was. Philippe undid the tiny hooks. Yes, definitely uncomfortable. He traced the ridges dug into that supple brown skin of hers.

No shoes to remove, those didn't survive the night. Philippe looked down at her shapely legs. The stockings had to go. He picked one foot up, resting it over his shoulder and then carefully rolled down the filmy material. Soft, but not as soft as the inside of her thigh. He moved to the other leg, repeating the process, hesitating only a minute before pushing the stockings into his pocket. Not one for lover mementos, why he wanted them, he didn't know. *Peut-etre*, a reward for tonight's restraint.

Philippe stared down at Anne, now naked except for the briefest of panties, tied with flimsy ribbons at her hips. He sucked in his breath. *Merde, she is beautiful.* It was almost a shame to cover her up.

"Where would your nightgown be?" Philippe asked out loud, not expecting an answer.

He got one. "No nightgown. Too hot," muttered from the bed.

Hot? She brings new meaning to the word. Philippe drew the sheet over that sexy body and then bent down, kissing her cheek. "I have to go, *Cherie.* Sleep well."

"Don't go." Anne frowned, her eyes closed. "Stay." She patted the space on the king sized bed. A big bed for a little woman.

Philippe should refuse. The driver waited downstairs. Anne was intoxicated. His control was weak. But he couldn't. There was nothing he wanted more than to sleep, even if it was only to sleep, beside her. To wake up with her in his arms. Besides, she might need him. What if she was ill again? She'd be alone. A corner of his brain said that it was unlikely but even the slightest of possibilities was rationale enough for Philippe. "*D'accord.*"

After a quiet call to his driver, Philippe shrugged out of his tie and jacket. He couldn't sleep in his pants so he took those off also. Should he leave his shirt on? Philippe sniffed an armpit and decided *non.* The fabric was quite ripe, the vodka and orange juice soaking through. The underwear, they had to stay on. *Oui*, if he had any hope at all of getting through this night.

Should he take a shower? He would smell fresher, *mais* the water would wake him up. Was being awake conducive to sleeping, only sleeping, next to his near naked sparrow? *Non.* So the shower had to wait. *Maybe tomorrow morning? Together?* On that happy thought, Philippe lifted the sheet and crawled in behind Anne, wrapping his arms around her.

Anne murmured his name contentedly, backing up until their skin touched and was breathing heavily again almost immediately. It took Philippe many more minutes to join her.

~ * ~

Anne woke first in the early morning light, turning in Philippe's arms to stare into his sleeping face. *He is here!* She touched his bristle covered cheek in wonder. Philippe was in her bed. She was almost naked. He was almost naked. How they got that way, Anne didn't know.

The bits and pieces she did remember of the evening weren't exactly her shining glory. Despite all that, Philippe hadn't run for the hills, he stayed. She didn't know why. There was no reason for him to stay, to be so very kind to her. *It's almost as though…he cares. That's a foolish thought, isn't it?* No, it had to be revenge. And if it was revenge then there was nothing to protect her from it now. He'd seen every possible ugly side of her personality. Nope, no going back, might as well enjoy the forward for as long as it lasted.

Be brave, be fearless. Anne kissed his bare shoulder, sucking on his skin, and when she glanced up again, his eyes were open. Warm brown eyes with dashes of gold dancing in them.

"How are you feeling?"

No guts, no glory. "I don't know you tell me." She brazenly stroked him with her entire body, brushing her breasts against his chest, his body reacting immediately.

"Are you sober now?" His rumble made her skin tremble.

"Unhuh." She traced the vein on his neck with her tongue. Salty.

"How many fingers?" He held out three.

She took one finger into her mouth and sucked on it. When she was done to her satisfaction, Anne smiled at him. "Are you going to make me walk a straight line?"

"Never." Philippe tenderly stroked her side, resting his hand on her hip, fingertips hesitating on the tiny black ribbons. "Are you sure, *Cherie?*"

Anne pulled her hips back, undoing the ties. "Oh, I'm sure."

"*Dieu merci,*" he managed before his mouth came down on hers, soft and lazy.

Philippe continued with that speed. Could Anne tempt him into picking up the pace, even by clasping him tightly to her? Nope. He refused to be rushed, kissing her long, and deep and thoroughly. When he was done with her mouth, his lips moved to her neck. Anne was left, hanging onto his shoulders, swiveling her hips against his body.

"Philippe," she gasped as he captured one dark tipped nipple between his lip-covered teeth, tweaking it to painfully tight attention. His tongue circled first one breast than the other.

"I need." Anne pushed her hips up. The sensation was too much.

"I know what you need, *Cherie.*" His hand slid down between her breasts, over her belly to her neatly shaved strip of hair. "You showed me, remember?"

Not this, she didn't show him this. He positioned a finger at her entrance and waited. She couldn't stand it, raising her hips again, legs spread to push that finger in. "Oh." It felt so good, she pulsed. She let her hips fall and the finger withdrew.

"Again, *Cherie,*" he prompted, his mouth against her breast.

This time it was two fingers, stretching her, his thumb against her tender nub, caressing it. She thrust twice then twice again. It felt wonderful but not enough.

"I need…" She couldn't find the words to express her need.

She didn't have to. Philippe knew. He rolled her in his arms until she was astride him, his hardness before her. Philippe grasped her wrists, licking the tender palms of her hands before Anne began to pump him.

"Impatient little sparrow, I know what you need. I'll give you it."

And he did. Hands on her hips, Philippe raised her. Anne positioned him properly and sank down with a satisfied moan. He filled her, fitting her perfectly. That was what she wanted, what she needed. She moved, slowly at first, Philippe remaining motionless so she controlled the speed. Up and down, up and down, Anne felt the passion building. Then Philippe began to thrust, hard and sharp upwards, reaching the deepest corners of her body. Anne grasped on to his shoulders, her fingers digging into his skin, trying to hold on.

"Let go, *Cherie*, let go," he panted.

Anne was confused. *Let go? No way.* She'd fall off.

"Let go, *Cherie*," another grunt.

Pushing her fears aside, she did as she was told. Anne released his shoulders, flinging her arms back, arching her back.

Oh, lord, it felt, it felt.

"That's it, fly little sparrow." And she did, she truly did.

~ * ~

In an ideal world, they would have spent the next day in bed, loving each other, exploring bodies, experiencing pleasures unimagined. This wasn't the ideal world. Both Philippe and Anne had obligations, things to get done. The best they could manage was spending the time together accomplishing them.

"How much of the business is engagement rings?" Anne kept one eye on the steady stream of shoppers moving into the high-end jewelry retailer's new store. Potential *Be My Guest* customers.

"Over twenty percent." Philippe slipped a large diamond on the ring finger of Anne's right hand. "What about this one?"

"Too large. It'd shred my hose," she absentmindedly dismissed, her mind on her own issues. Something wasn't quite right with the *Be My Guest* project. Denise remained anxious, too anxious about timing. Her credit report, as Anne suspected, revealed that she was stretched to the breaking point.

"Would the store see the happy couple after the proposal?" Anne tapped on the glass display case with her left hand.

Philippe placed the ring back and pulled out another. "To size the ring, *je pense*."

A chance to sell to the bride-to-be. And yeah, Denise had to realize that her tenuous financial situation wasn't going to change soon. Anne glanced down and wrinkled up her nose. Pink. She wasn't a fan of colored diamonds.

Philippe put that ring back without a word, asking for another tray.

She explained that, although they could provide funds for future costs, there wouldn't be enough money to cover past costs. Financiers didn't like it when entrepreneurs pulled their own contribution out of the company. That hadn't gone over well with the blonde. After that, Denise was harder to get a hold of. Almost as though she changed her mind about needing financing. Though when asked, Denise denied it.

"Would they sell their customer list?" Anne asked Philippe.

"Only with customer approval. Sounds like we have a live one." The half-carat ring fit snugly, like it was meant for her.

Anne tilted the ring, blinking at the dazzling reflection. She wasn't a big jewelry fan but, "It is nice."

"An estate piece. Older cut." Philippe smiled. "I thought you'd like it. *Mais.* By live one, I meant Denise's company. If the project's a live one, I'll have you for a while longer, *Cherie.*"

Longer? Anne returned to the present with a thump. "What do you mean?"

"You can't dessert the project in the middle," Philippe dismissed that idea as absurd, pulling the ring back off her finger. "It would be disruptive."

"Well…" Anne hadn't really thought about it. She committed to three months. After that, it was up to Philippe to manage.

"If it's a green light, might be additional weeks, months, maybe even years," he continued, "*Oui*, could take a while to get things settled, *Cherie.* These things don't run smoothly."

"Months? Years?" Anne straightened. Her own company was currently on life support, running off previously accepted business. She had no time to evaluate new projects. "Not an option. I can't go much longer than the three months we agreed upon, Philippe. I won't have a business to go back to."

Philippe shrugged, not concerned, that self centered man. If it were his business…

"No, I'm serious." Anne faced him, hands on her hips. "Running long on this contract isn't a possibility."

Philippe's eyes glowed black, back to being the bastard businessman. "It's a very real possibility."

"We agreed…" The contract was only for three months. *Had Philippe suspected?*

He hadn't. "We did, but agreements change, extensions happen. I honestly didn't think any of the plans had legs."

Anne believed Philippe but she couldn't humor him. "No, agreements can't change and I won't allow an extension."

"You don't have a choice," Philippe sounded certain.

Anne was as certain. "I do have a choice. I can't do it. I won't do it." To do so, combined with losing him as a financier and Nancy, well, Nancy's situation, would destroy all she had worked for.

"Then you'd better hope that this project falls apart," was Philippe's advice as he stomped back to the beckoning entrepreneur, "because you're on it until it's concluded."

What the… Anne was ticked. How had she gotten herself into this no win situation? No matter what she did, she was screwed. She could walk away at three months; the contract binding only to that point, Philippe would have no legal recourse. But then there'd be no hope of either a personal or professional relationship with Philippe.

This project had already lost him a VP; Kevin having been walked out of the building a few days ago. Was that her fault? Not really. Kevin was disloyal and that personality trait would have come out eventually.

Unfortunately, it was now, in the eyes of Philippe's employees, paired with Anne's project management competence. They were watching her closely to see if she disproved Kevin's negative opinion, to see if she lived up to Philippe's glowing evaluation.

So it would cause Philippe loss of face if she left in the middle. It would also be unprofessional. She would have let her hard working team down, a team she rushed for results, any other project leader needing time to ramp up. But by helping Philippe, she would hurt her own business. Maybe not merely hurt her business, maybe kill it. Dead. All that she had worked for. Gone. Entrepreneurs were already going elsewhere for coaching. They were losing referrals from those clients. They wouldn't make their goals for the year.

Anne would have to hustle to reclaim her presence at the top of clients' minds.

Anne sighed, she knew what her decision was. She wasn't happy about it, how could she be? But she knew what it was.

Twelve

"Nance, we have to talk." Anne was sitting down, legs crossed at the ankles, in her partner's messy office. It was early evening and they both worked, putting the final touches on a business plan designed for the Angel. It was a good solid plan, one Anne was proud of, with the entrepreneur coming in tomorrow evening to be coached.

A tired Nancy summed up the problem immediately, "I thought you wanted to do this next month, when you wrapped up with Lamont?"

"That was the original plan. Things have changed. If the *Be My Guest* business is a go, Philippe wants me on board until completion." Anne eyed the redhead. Nancy didn't seem overly concerned, so she clarified, "Could be months or even more."

"Not willing to let you go just yet, is he?" Nancy's double meaning clear.

"Not yet." The unspoken assumption being that he would eventually.

"It does complicate things." Nancy slanted the papers Anne straightened, a long running contest they had, the goal to see how long Anne could go without tidying them. "We'd have to drum up business."

"Yeah." Anne's fingers itched to straighten the mess. How Nancy could work that way, she didn't know.

"So you'd have the Lamont full time gig, our business plans to do, and the new client evaluations, not to mention your *Young C.E.O.s* volunteering." Nancy counted off the tasks. "Can you manage all that?"

Anne broke down, again lining up the papers flush with the edge of the desk. "Frankly, no, and that's why we have to talk."

Nancy studied the very masculine calendar posted on her wall. Schwag from a rental car company, it featured vividly colored muscle cars and half naked women. "It's a couple weeks too early, Annie."

"I know, but it can't wait. It'll be between only the two of us, Nance, I promise. I won't tell anyone." Anne needed to settle this. Nancy's plans played a key role in her decision.

"You won't tell Stanley?"

Sharing secrets with their good friend Stanley was like taking up a front-page ad in the *Los Angeles Times*. It was possibly the fastest way on earth to spread information. "Certainly not Stanley, Nance."

"If you do, I'll hear about it," the warning was unneeded.

"If I do, everyone will hear about it. Stanley isn't exactly the cone of silence." *Far from it.*

"More like the bugle horn of broadcast. Oh, and speaking of Stanley, he wants to know if you prefer roses or orchids."

Roses or orchids? A couple days ago, he wanted to know if she preferred a D-J or a live band. Where were these random questions coming from?

"What the...?" Anne sent a perplexed glance Nancy's way.

"Don't look at me, Annie-kin." Her friends shrugged. "You know how Stanley is."

He was always one for crazy questions and seemingly superficial polls. Most had a purpose, at least in Stanley's unique mind. It was up to the answerer to figure it out. Anne hadn't the time right now.

"Regular ol' roses, I guess, like in my mom's garden. Orchids are too exotic for me, I don't see their appeal."

"That's what I told him, roses for you. I like orchids myself but you're different and we have to..."

"Nance." Anne stopped her. Nancy could talk around in circles all night if allowed. "Are we going to discuss your secret or not?"

"Okay, okay," Nancy agreed, "I suppose I can tell you. You wouldn't be the first so it can't be bad luck, can it? Ted knows, of course and I think my mom suspects already too and maybe Ted's mom and..."

Again Anne broke in, "Nance, are congratulations in order?"

"How did you know?" Nancy's mouth dropped open.

"Well..." *Where to start?* Anne would have to be totally self-absorbed not to notice the clues.

"I'm not showing, am I?" The redhead rubbed her hands over her flat belly.

"Not at all, but you're not drinking either, at least not alcohol. Milk, yes. Alcohol, no."

"I hate, hate, hate milk." Nancy's bottom lip curled.

"I know." Nance was a long time hater of liquid dairy. Anne couldn't remember her ever drinking it before now. "That was one of the giveaways, that and all that spinach."

"I'm getting sick of spinach too. The doctor said I should eat it," Nancy grumbled.

"Then you have to eat it, *Popeye.* So it's a yes. Girl, I'm so happy for you and Ted." Anne hugged her good friend across the desk.

"Thank you, Annie." Nancy glowed. "I'm getting used to the idea. Wow. Imagine that. Me—a mom. Scary."

"Not scary. You'll be a great mom." *Nance will be. She takes care of*

everyone. "How far along are…?"

"Three months in two weeks. That's why I didn't want to say anything. They say it's bad luck and…" Nancy worried; she was a tad bit superstitious.

"But you didn't tell me, I guessed." Anne skated around the issue, not wanting to cause her friend any additional stress. This seemed to relieve her. Nancy's face cleared. "And your other news?" They might as well talk about everything. "How's real estate in sunny San Diego?"

"Annie James, have I no secrets?" Nancy gasped.

"Not from your best friend, no." Again, Nancy's not-so-stealthy house hunting activities weren't that difficult to detect.

"Ted was offered a good job there. So good we couldn't turn it down," Nancy admitted, "We love the city and the company really wants him. They're generously paying the difference in real estate values. That, combined with his increase, means we can live on his salary alone. It'd be tight but we can do it."

So there it was. Nancy's plan. Anne wanted to ensure she knew what her friend was saying. "Are you planning to?"

They sat down and stared at each other, each knowing the answer. Neither wanting to say it. "Well." Nancy's eyes darted away.

"Are you interested in working remotely?" It was a long shot, she knew, but Anne had to try. This was her best friend and long time partner they were talking about.

Nancy slowly shook her short curls. "We've done so well over the years, you and I. I think about all that we've accomplished."

"We've built this business from the ground up." Anne's face softened as she thought of the hard times, the good times, the wins, the losses. "It's like our child."

"I know," Nancy paused, "but, Annie, I think I have to focus on my new child now."

So that was that. The sense of loss weighed heavy on Anne. "Understandable."

"You could get a new partner," Nancy offered, "I'd be okay with that."

"But I wouldn't. To add that to my list of things to do…" Anne wouldn't be able to handle it. "No thanks."

What to do? What to do? Anne looked up at the ceiling, like another answer would appear there. It didn't. "I'm thinking we wrap this up, Nance. Take the next month, finish the existing cases and then close it down." *There, the words were out. No taking them back now.* Anne didn't know what solution Nancy was thinking of. This wasn't the one.

"Close the business? Annie, what will you do?"

"Work one job for a change. Finish my time at Lamont Ventures and not have to worry about burning out." Anne hid her emotions behind flippancy. It wasn't all bad. It would be nice to have a personal life again, some time to do things for herself. Spend some more time with Philippe without having to multi-task. "Then take a breather, go on a trip."

"A vacation? You?" Anne hadn't taken a true vacation since opening the business. "That's a unique concept, isn't it?"

It had been a random thought but it felt good. "Yep, a vacation. Maybe France. I've heard it's nice. Take some quiet time to think about what to do."

"You deserve it, Anne. You've been working way too hard."

"I have been, especially lately with the double job."

Nancy, in full mother training mode, was concerned. "Will you be okay?"

Anne shrugged. "I've saved my pennies." A single gal, she didn't have many financial concerns.

"You always were a good little investor." Anne never hid that from Nancy. "So are you finally going to do it?"

"What?" She never discussed any of her post business plan prep plans.

It turned out Anne didn't have to. "Teach, of course." Best friends knew these things. "You know you love it."

"I do." It would be a big decrease in salary but she could do some consulting on the side to supplement. Anne had her investments also, not that she wanted to dip into them yet, not if she didn't have to. "You think I should?"

"It's what you were meant to do. Your gift."

It was. Anne studied her friend's earnest face. All this could be for the best except for... "I'm going to miss you, Nance." Anne's eyes teared up and she had to look away. She didn't want to cry. She should be happy for her friend.

"I'm only a phone call or an e-mail or a long drive away." Nancy's voice sounded suspiciously muffled also. "You're on vacation. You could visit."

"Nah, you crazy kids need to enjoy your last months with only the two of you." Anne smiled half-heartedly. "Besides, once the baby comes, Auntie Annie will visit so often, you'll be sick of me."

"Never." Nancy clasped her hand and they held onto each other. "And we'll visit you... and Philippe?"

"I hope," but Anne had only hope riding on that relationship.

Nance's laugh was shaky. "How's that going, anyway? Do you still think he's a bastard?"

"Nah, he just plays one on T-V." Anne glowed as she thought of his softer side. "It's a bad-ass act for business, scares people in submission."

"I'm not surprised. After he kissed Stanley's hand, I had my doubts. And his wandering eye?" A truly concerned friend, Nancy didn't hold anything back.

"He told me from the start that he was a one car, one house, one woman kind of man."

"He didn't?" Nancy laughed in wonder.

"The power of focus, you know." Anne swirled her hands in magic circles.

"Okay, *Anthony Robbins*." Nancy shook her head. "As long as Philippe's focusing on you."

"As far as I know, I'm his girl of the moment."

"A brunette lacking his required double *D's*." A red eyebrow raised. "You are good at sales."

"No guts, no glory." Anne grinned. "Though some of my techniques need a little polish." She shared her adventures praying to the porcelain gods.

Nancy's eyes grew wider. "And you're still seeing each other? Ted can't even stand to hear about my morning sickness and he certainly doesn't wipe my face afterwards. He'd hose me down from a distance first."

Morning sickness, Philippe would be good at that, the morning sickness bit. Anne got a funny feeling when she thought about him and her and pregnancy. *Stop it, girl, you're running way too far ahead. First concentrate on seeing him tonight, leave tending to babies to later... although two would be nice. A little boy and a little girl. Brunettes obviously, not too tall either—*

Stop it!

"So Nance, could you start on dissolving the partnership?" Anne asked, trying to drag her mind away from the thought of kids. "There won't be that much to do, since it's just you and me."

Nancy sighed. "I suppose. It seems like the end of an era."

"Or a beginning of a new, more exciting one," Anne presented brightly, in spite of the stomach twisting fear.

This fear she knew. It was the fear Anne felt when she left home for college, knowing no one else on campus. It was the fear she felt when she moved to the very expensive Los Angeles to open her own business, not having a single source of income lined up.

Yep, it was nothing to be worried about. Fear and Anne were old friends.

~ * ~

Two passion-filled weeks later, fear and Anne had a falling out. Anne wandered in from a long, enjoyable lunch with her sister, Ginny, to find Sylvie hovering like an unpaid bill collector near her office. "Anne, Philippe..."

"Anne James, get your ass in here," Philippe bellowed through his open door.

Anne's head snapped up. She had never heard him use that tone before. It was rude, insulting and the entire floor heard him.

It also didn't surprise Sylvie, meaning he had been that way for a while. The executive assistant squeezed Anne's arm in support as she passed.

Anne glowered at Philippe after the door shut behind her. His look far outshone hers, his face dark with a fury she had never seen before.

Philippe was ticked.

"Sit the hell down!" His deep voice shook the windows.

Anne didn't sit. "What the hell is your problem?" she threw back at him. His hair looked like he had raked his hands through it a half dozen times. A bad day? Yep. A reason to curse at her? Nope.

He felt he had reason. "You. That's what my problem is." Philippe stood, his whole body shaking. "I knew you were trouble from the first minute I met you. I should have stuck to my original plan."

"Which was?" She was curious to hear this. Anne had always wanted to know what his master plan was.

"To squish you like a bug under my foot," he snarled, "to destroy you, your company, and all you stood for."

Revenge—that was what he had been after. Ironically, without even trying, Philippe succeeded. Her company was gone, closed, finis, and now it sounded like she was next. Anne sat down and calmly folded her hands. Ignoring Philippe's temper was the best way to drive him crazy. "And what, may I ask, stopped you?"

Philippe opened his mouth and then closed it again. Whatever it was, he thought better about sharing it. "*N'importe*, I didn't and that was a mistake, one that I might now rectify."

"You could try," Anne dared him. She didn't know what he was so angry about. That didn't stop her from fighting back.

"Don't tempt me, *petite ensorceleuse!*" He sat back down with a thump. "I have half a mind to sue your ass off."

Dang, but that would be ironic. Anne did him a favor by dropping the lawsuit with Bruce, not necessary now that the business was wrapping up, and Philippe turned around to sue them to kingdom come. "On what grounds?"

"Corporate espionage, intellectual theft, being lower than slime," Philippe tossed a package into her lap.

The package, obviously a clue to his temper tantrum. Anne opened it and shuffled through the pages, snaps of web pages from *Wedding Pings*, a competitor to Denise's company.

"What am I looking at?" She, no tech genius, was frustrated to not see the cause.

"You know full well. Look at the third page," he barked

like it would explain everything.

It did. "Oh, my Lord." Anne felt faint. She closed her eyes to stop the room from spinning. "Oh, my Lord."

"Oh, my Lord," Philippe mimicked, "Don't bother selling little miss innocent to me." His voice was hard. "I'm not buying."

He thinks… oh, my Lord. He thinks I'm responsible. Anne was sick to her stomach. He thought she sold out Denise to the competition, letting them scoop her concept. That he could think that of her. It was too much. She pressed a palm to her throbbing forehead.

Philippe stared at her with those cold eyes of his.

Say something, he wanted to scream at her. *Tell me that you had nothing to do with it. Give me some proof, something, anything to convince me that you weren't the one to leak the information, information that destroyed a good friend's business.*

Philippe felt the hurt on Denise's face when she approached him. She didn't accuse anyone, not him, not Anne, not his company but he knew that when she gave him the file, she also handed over the responsibility. It wasn't until they touched the business plan that the information was transferred.

Correction, it wasn't until Anne touched it, until he made it clear that she was on the project until it was settled, that the information got shared. She had been angry. It would destroy her own business. What had she said that first meeting? Holding all the cards left her nothing to bluff with, *To win, she'd be forced to cheat.* This was cheating. If it wasn't then it was a big coincidence. Smart businessmen didn't believe in coincidences. Philippe didn't believe in coincidences. As much as he wanted to.

"Explain." Philippe would give her one more chance. He hadn't told Denise about his suspicions, a part of him refusing to believe it, couldn't believe it, and he wanted Anne to give him a reason, something, anything he could grab onto.

"You think I did this?" she spat.

Anne appeared hurt, angry but then, she was a good actress, his little sparrow, she held her emotions close. It made her the best.

"And why shouldn't I?" *Give me a reason, any reason,* he begged her with his eyes.

She wasn't looking at him. There was silence in the room, just the sound of her breath and his breath rushing in and out. And then Philippe realized. *She doesn't have a reason.* The thought slammed into his stomach, almost doubling him up. This woman, this darling woman whom he trusted so much, that he cared for more than he cared for himself. She had betrayed him. All this time and when it came down to it, she put her own interests first. He should hate her. He should reach out and destroy her like only he could. But it was Anne, and Philippe couldn't. He, for all her awful actions, all her deceit, couldn't bring himself to hurt her.

"You had better leave." His voice was now quiet, defeated, hollow.

"Philippe," she looked about to argue. *A little too little, a little too late.* He couldn't listen to her lies. Philippe turned away so his back was facing her.

"Don't bother packing your things. Sylvie will do that. Just leave. Immediately. I never want to see you again." *Liar.* How his foolish heart could be holding on, he didn't know.

"Okay." She sounded as wiped-out as he felt. Philippe waited until the door clicked shut before collapsing in his chair, folding up, laying his forehead on the cool wood of the desk.

~ * ~

This isn't happening. It can't be happening, Anne told herself, standing at the door. *This is all a big mistake.* It would be corrected. Philippe… no he couldn't. He couldn't believe that of her.

Sylvie watched her with a concerned expression on her face.

Anne straightened, her body held rigidly upright. *Breathe in, breathe out.* Cool, calm, controlled. She was a professional. She could do this.

"Sylvie." Anne went up to the executive assistant, reaching out her hand, unsure of her reception. *Take it, please take it,* she begged silently. There was only a slight hesitation before it was grasped firmly. "Thank you for all you've done. It's been a pleasure working with you."

"With you too, Anne." The woman's sympathy almost undid her. She would not listen to it, no she would not. Only later, when…

No, worry about later, be in the now. "There shouldn't be too much for you to pack up. I travel light." Anne made a half-hearted joke. Sylvie didn't laugh. "If you could send it to my home, I'd appreciate it." Less for Anne to move at her office. An office that wasn't her office anymore. She had no office.

"I will. Come. I'll walk you down, Anne." Sylvie smiled gently like Anne was a child to be comforted.

"You don't have to do that," Anne protested. She needed to be alone. Away from sad eyes.

"Actually, I do."

It took her a full minute before Anne realized what Sylvie was saying. *That bastard.* Not only did Philippe think she sabotaged Denise's business but he thought Anne was a risk to his own company. That hurt. No matter, she would get through it. She was strong.

Anne walked, head held high through the office, smiling and saying goodbye to the few brave souls that did the same. The entire office knew. What they knew, Anne didn't know. She did know that it was these types of situations that defined people. The weak hid. The strong shook her hand. Philippe was lucky to work with some very strong employees.

Then they were alone, Sylvie and Anne, standing in the elevator.

Anne stared ahead, watching the bright red digital numbers change.

"I know you didn't do it," Sylvie said quietly, breaking the silence.

Anne blinked. Of all people, Mrs. Depeche, with her unflinching loyalty, should have sided with her boss. "How?"

"I saw the way you worked on this project, twisting and stretching the rules to make it happen. The late hours, the constant revisions. Not even Philippe would have tried so hard."

"It was a good idea. Obviously." Anne tasted the bitterness in her words. Bad ideas weren't often stolen. In all her years, nothing like this had ever happened. And now on her last plan...

"And you don't have it in you. I trust you."

"I appreciate that Sylvie, more than you'll ever know."

At least someone trusted her. How could Philippe not? How could he think that of her? Philippe, the man she trusted. The man she cared for. The man, oh Lord, the man she might even love. Philippe thought she was a thief, and a liar and a backstabber. Anne couldn't contemplate the thought, it made her so sick.

"Philippe will realize this too. After he has calmed down," the executive assistant assured her.

"It doesn't matter." Not a single corner of her heart believed her own words.

"I think it does." The elevator stopped at the parking garage. Sylvie shook Anne's hand one more time, took Anne's pass, and then let the door close.

Anne was alone. Alone with no job, no company but most of all, no Philippe. Anne walked through the parking garage, heels clicking on the ugly gray cement, tears falling down her face.

Thirteen

Anne sat cross-legged in the middle of her office with a filing cabinet drawer open, sorting the files into three different boxes, one for shredding, one for storage, one for transfer to the client's site. It was almost surreal, how many companies she had touched over the years. Some never got off the ground, Anne turning down the opportunity to complete their plans. Some now enjoyed multi-million dollar revenues and were publicly traded. There was a lot left to do before they closed the office completely. The business plans were completed but the packing had to be done, the rest of the office furniture had to be sold, and all by the end of the month.

Anne didn't mind the hard work. She trudged home at the end of the day, physically exhausted. It helped her not think about Lamont. *Has it really been two weeks since Philippe fired me?* Two weeks and nothing, not even a call. He should have figured out by now that she hadn't been responsible. *If he cared enough to investigate.*

"You didn't eat the salad," Nancy accused, standing in the doorway, hands on her hips, the lunch she brought to Anne untouched on the desk. Anne wasn't a big eater to start with but lately, she had been hard pressed to force any food past her lips. "Ya gotta eat, Annie. You're going to make yourself sick."

What does it matter? She could afford the sick day. She could take a sick day, a sick month, hell, even a sick year and no one would care. Anne shrugged glumly, not looking up from her files.

"And were you meeting with Ms. McKenzie today?" her friend asked.

The angel of the angels? Where had that question come from? "Nope."

"'Cause she's sitting in our reception area. Alone." Truly alone. The receptionist's last day was the previous Friday. "Says she wants to speak to you."

"Then I guess I'll listen to her." Anne dusted off her khakis and moved the box off the guest chair. She didn't have much choice. The woman was waiting.

"What do you think she wants?" Nancy ran a hand over her belly as they walked.

"Don't know. I imagine she'll tell me." Ms. McKenzie must have heard by now. Heard her, judged her.

"You'll be fine." Nancy squeezed her arm. She was a good friend, Nancy. With everything else going on in her own life, she put up with Anne's denial, rage and then extreme sadness.

It was like a death really, a death of everything she knew and loved. *Loved. Philippe. No. No time to think about him now.*

"Ms. McKenzie." Anne stretched out a hand to the well-dressed woman, Nancy disappearing back into the hallway.

"Anne." The financier looked around her. "You run a tight ship here."

Her return smile was weak. "We're dissolving the business. Please excuse the mess." Anne led her through the eerily quiet hallway to her own office.

"Dissolving the business?" Ms. McKenzie lowered herself gingerly onto the rather dusty chair. "Does Philippe know?"

"I don't know what Philippe knows." *Nor do I care*, Anne silently added. "I no longer work for him."

"So I heard." The older woman wiped her hands on a tissue.

"And did you hear why?" Anne decided to lay all the cards on the table.

A heavily powdered nose wrinkled. "Some nonsense about leaking confidential information to the competition, or what not."

Ms. McKenzie knew. This didn't surprise Anne but it still hurt. Years building a reputation and now she saw it destroyed in minutes with lies and innuendos. "Did Philippe tell you that?"

"Child, Philippe told me nothing. He didn't volunteer the information nor would he answer any of my questions. He has been unusually tight-lipped."

Honorable, that was the Lamont she knew...and loved. "Then how?"

"A couple sources. First that Suzanne person." Ms. McKenzie scrunched up her face. "Let it drop at a cocktail party."

At a cocktail party. With Philippe. Suzanne and Philippe, back together again. He didn't waste any time, did he?

"Then Philippe's former executive came pawing at my door, looking for a job." No respect from Ms. McKenzie there either. "Thought the information about you would help his case. It didn't."

There was only one former executive that Anne knew. "Kevin Maple?"

"That's the one. Stupid man, as if I would hire him."

Maple had heard too. Must have made his day.

"But that's the past. Let's talk about the future."

The future? What future? Anne didn't have a future. At least, not with Ms. McKenzie.

"I assume you're done with Philippe." A valid assumption. "And you're done here. What are you doing next?"

Anne didn't know. The colleges had their full complement of professors for the fall semester, leaving her unemployed. Not that Philippe would ever know that, Anne pressed her lips together mulishly.

"I see." Ms. McKenzie tapped her own painted lips with a fingertip. "I want you to work for me."

What? Had the Angel not fully understood the situation? "Philippe fired me."

"Yes, unusual for him to be so impulsive. He's seldom so irrational. His loss…" was Ms. McKenzie's gain, the unspoken implication.

"He felt he had just cause." Why Anne defended him, she didn't know. "He believes I sold information to the competition, destroying his client and damaging his own company's reputation."

"He listened to the facts," *facts* being said sarcastically, "and we all know how the facts can lie. Philippe made a mistake."

Ms. McKenzie sounded so confident, Anne asked, "How can you be so sure?"

"Look, child, Philippe might not trust his gut but I do. He trusted you. I believe he still trusts you. He simply let that horrid temper of his get in the way of good business."

"He made a mistake with Kevin," Anne pointed out.

"He never trusted Kevin, not since day one," Ms. McKenzie confided. "Why do you think Philippe was so hands-on with him? Did Philippe micro-manage you?"

"Nope." He had let her run with the ball, make her own decisions.

"He felt a need to hold Kevin's hand. Why? Simple. He didn't trust him. Turns out that Philippe was right."

"And you feel he's wrong about my involvement?" Anne didn't make an effort to defend herself.

"Not feel, I know he's wrong." Ms. McKenzie spread out some files on the desk. "Are these yours?"

Anne's eyes skimmed over the names. *Good companies, great business plans.* For the first time in two weeks, Anne felt her old confidence returning. "Yes."

"I thought so. All I had to do was take a sample of the very best plans presented to me. With a couple exceptions, it was clear that one person drafted all of them, someone especially skilled, the best. Philippe works only with the best. He hired you so you must be the best. Stands to reason that they're yours." Ms. McKenzie looked quite pleased with herself.

"So?" *Where was the financier going with this?*

"So, Philippe's gut aside, no one putting this level of work, of art, of love into a complete stranger's business would ever sell out their integrity for a handful of dollars or a couple months less work. Am I right or am I right?" Ms. McKenzie gathered the files back up into a tidy stack.

"I suppose you're right." The two women studied each other, Anne waiting for the Angel's next move.

"Child, what did you say when Philippe accused you?"

What did she say? *Nothing, absolutely nothing.* Anne continued the trend now.

Ms. McKenzie's sigh was deep and heartfelt, like she was too weary for all this. "You didn't defend yourself, did you?"

Anne shook her head. Why should she have to? He automatically should trust her. Wasn't that what a relationship was? Mutual trust?

"Did you, at very least, tell him that you didn't do it?"

"Nope."

Ms. McKenzie looked to the right, off into space. Anne watched different emotions flicker across her face. Finally she seemed to come to a decision.

"I can't believe I'm saying this. I must be getting soft in my old age," the financier muttered to herself. "Child, I'll walk through this with you slowly. You clearly aren't thinking rationally."

Great. Now she was getting insulted, in her own office. Anne straightened. She didn't have to take this.

"I'm telling you this because I like you." The Angel stopped her protests before they started. "So when you coach entrepreneurs to pitch to Philippe, what do you tell them to do?"

And the point of this is? "Be confident; be certain; be strong."

"Right." The Angel nodded. "And what do you tell them to expect?"

"Push back," Philippe always pushed back, to see how far he could.

"And what is your entrepreneur to do when that happens?"

"Push right back." This was a difficult concept to sell to capital-starved business owners. They had to risk losing financing in order to obtain it.

"Why?"

"Because Philippe's a bastard and bastards respect only other bastards." Anne could see where this was heading and she didn't like it.

"So when Philippe pushed back, when he accused you, what did you do?"

"Nothing." Anne sagged. "I know, I know. I should have pushed back but he should have…"

"Forget," Ms. McKenzie slammed her hand down on the desk, startling Anne, "what he should have done. That is irrelevant and out of your control. Accept the responsibility for your own failure, Anne. You, better than anyone, should have known what Philippe's reaction would be. His actions were no surprise. He did what he always does— push. You got emotional and failed to respond properly."

Anne had. She had failed, failed him, failed herself, failed their relationship. What could she do about that now? Nothing. "What's done is done."

"Hell no!" Ms. McKenzie snorted. "The first failure is not the end. Your entrepreneurs fail time and time again and still they try. They have to. Just like you have to talk to Philippe, tell him that you didn't do this, that he was right to trust you."

Put myself out there to get hurt again? No way. "Why would he believe me?" Anne questioned aloud instead. She had no proof, nothing but her word.

"Because he wants to," Ms. McKenzie stated, "and because you're going to figure out who did this. Who put this black mark on your reputation. With or without his help, you're going to do whatever it takes to clear your name."

"Why should I?" Her destroyed reputation would never recover.

"You have to. Until you do, a part of your brain always will be fretting about it. You won't be able to do this level of work." Ms. McKenzie slapped the files on the desk. "And I don't want any less from you. So settle it. Then come to me. I'll make you an offer worth your while."

Ms. McKenzie rose, like it had been all decided. *Has it?* Anne debated as she accompanied the Angel out. Ms. McKenzie was right; the accusation ate at her. The unfairness of it. An accusation that should have been leveled at the real culprit, the thief, the coward.

She could bring him to justice. "I just might follow your advice," Anne told Ms. McKenzie.

"Do it," the money woman urged, "Whatever it takes. Get it done."

Whatever it takes including meeting with Philippe?

Could she do that? Again, she had no choice. She had to. Anne needed access to Lamont resources to prove her innocence. And when she did and Lamont found out he was wrong, so very wrong… Anne's lips curled into a mirthless smile.

~ * ~

Anne wasn't as confident the next day, sitting in the Lamont Ventures reception area. She arrived first thing in the morning and put her request to meet with Philippe in with the front desk. Philippe was there, she was told, and he would see her. Anne didn't know when. By noon, she was having second thoughts. Still no meeting and no sign of Philippe. Former co-workers came in and out of the doors, looking at her curiously, a few brave enough to say "Hi," but no one lingered. No one wanted to get caught talking to the exile.

Anne didn't dare move, even to go out for lunch in case she missed the appointment. When her stomach started rumbling, her appetite coming back with a vengeance, the receptionist, out of pity, brought her a sandwich and a bottle of water from the downstairs deli.

At least Anne had the foresight to bring reading material. She was halfway through Sun Tzu's *The Art Of War*. Appropriate for the battle she planned against Philippe yet familiar enough that her mind could wander.

Five o'clock came and the receptionist packed up. Yes, Philippe would meet with her. No, she didn't know when.

Six o'clock, Sylvie wandered out, her briefcase in hand. Seeing Anne, Philippe's executive assistant walked towards her.

"Will he...?" Anne asked as the older woman kissed her cheek. Sylvie would know better than anyone.

"I shouldn't say." Her kind eyes sparkled. "But this is the only exit."

So Anne was to wait and hope. "His mood?"

"The same as the past two weeks." In other words, not good. If Philippe was in a good mood, Sylvie would have said so.

"I hope this isn't a mistake." What could this solve with him in a lousy mood and not wanting to see her?

"It's not." Sylvie squeezed her hand in support. "I'm going, Philippe won't see you with me here, but don't give up Anne. Some things are worth fighting for."

And then Anne was alone again. Alone with her thoughts and fears and misgivings.

By nine o'clock, Anne was asleep in her chair. She finished her book, finished counting the ceiling tiles, finished studying the dust on her shoes. The boredom numbed her mind, quieting the worries and, exhausted, she finally drifted off, her body needing the rest. Anne hadn't slept at all the night before, being too anxious about today.

~ * ~

Philippe checked his watch. Ten o'clock. He sighed. *It's time.* He waited long enough and if Anne was out there stubbornly waiting for him, he'd see her. He didn't know what she wanted. Philippe had expected, had hoped, that Anne would return shortly after he fired her. Return to give him a reason why. Something to justify why he continued to think about her. Despite disgust over her actions, he cared for Anne, trusted her. It didn't make any sense.

But a week passed and then two, and Philippe came to terms with her not returning. He moved on with his life. What was left of it. Which wasn't much. Work, that kept his mind busy. Sex? Suzanne attempted to seduce him. He wasn't interested. Not in Suzanne, not in any woman. That part of him was dead. Anne killed it. Or so he had thought. When Philippe opened the main doors to look at the source of his thoughts, all the desire he thought long gone was rekindled.

She slept, looking as innocent as he wished her to be, small enough to curl up comfortably in the chair, her feet tucked underneath her body. Was she even thinner than before? He thought so. And there were dark circles under her eyes. Philippe wanted to take her in his arms, forget about the past, love her. He couldn't do that.

"Anne James," he barked, feeling a tinge of guilt as she jumped, her brown eyes blurry.

"Philippe." She stood, smoothing down her skirt.

Oui, she had lost weight. The skirt hung around her hips. A straight skirt, no garter belt today. Those, what did she call them? *Stay ups?* Something like that.

"*Maintenant.*" Philippe couldn't look at her any more. Not without his traitorous body responding. Not that he had to look to see if she was following him. He could hear the click, click, click of her heels on the hardwood. He could smell the fruity scent of her, light on the air. He could hear her taking deep breath after deep breath, her normally indestructible composure pierced. Philippe strode to his desk, standing behind it, using it as a barrier between them, but not bothering to sit down. He forced her to tilt her head up to hold his gaze. "*Qu'est-ce que c'est?*" He was too upset for English.

"I didn't do it." Anne looked at him rock steady, not even blinking once. Not that she blinked when she lied.

No, Philippe watched for the guilt indicating slight pursing of her lips. That's what her tell was, the clear sign she was lying. There wasn't any, her mouth remained partially open, that full bottom lip begging for a good long kiss. Or had he deliberately missed it? Because some part of him didn't want to see it? Had his attraction for Anne colored his judgment? Philippe couldn't even trust himself anymore.

"What proof do you have?" That would put this to rest for good. Proof he could hang onto, proof he could verify with cold, hard facts.

"I have none. Yet." Anne rested her fingers on the desk top, leaning forward determinedly. "But I intend to uncover who did this and why. I'll do whatever it takes."

She sounded so sincere and Philippe desperately wanted to believe her. "So do it." *What's stopping her? Why is she here?*

"I need your help to investigate."

That's it. She can't do it on her own.

"You need my help." Philippe laughed harshly. "You have some nerve."

Anne's smile was sad. "Nerve is all I have left. Without your cooperation, I won't have access to all the information. I need that information to clear my name."

Philippe could feel the hurt as acutely as if it were his own. He didn't know why he cared. She was the source of her own unhappiness.

"Why should I help you?"

"I don't know."

"Come on, Mademoiselle James, you know the rules of negotiating." He couldn't help the sarcasm. "You ask me for something. You must have expected to give me something in return."

She was silent, that brain he loved most likely working at full throttle, running through various scenarios.

For her to come up with a plausible lie. He didn't have the time for that.

"So Mademoiselle James, what do you have to offer me?"

"I'll do whatever it takes," said in a whisper but Philippe heard her.

Anne's brown eyes met his and his breath caught. He knew before she reached up to undo that first suit jacket button what Anne was going to offer him. Was he interested? Damn straight. She still turned him on. His body heated up at the thought of touching her. It defied all that he thought he stood for but she had that control over him.

"Any interaction with my company goes through me," Philippe clarified, trying to keep his expression disinterested even as he watched her intently.

Anne nodded, continuing to unbutton, the jacket gaped open, showing the blood red camisole underneath. A slutty, primal color.

"I don't want you talking to anyone at my company or Denise's company directly." The jacket slipped to the ground.

She reached back to undo her skirt.

"*Non.*" He walked around the desk, clearing the top as he moved, stopping her. He turned her so she was facing away from him, and pushed her against the desk. "I'll take what I want the same way as you'll get what you want. Fast, expedient, purely a business transaction." He yanked up her skirt, pressing her shoulders down to the wooden surface with his other hand. She gasped as her skimpy red satin panties ripped.

His fingers tracked the angry indents the straps had made on her hips and then he moved lower, her skin soft like the satin under his palms. *Mon Dieu*, she was wet for him already. Despite his intentions to simply take Anne, Philippe couldn't help stroking her, giving her a bit of pleasure.

She didn't protest. The exact opposite. Her back arched, that full mouth of hers opened, her eyelids fluttered closed.

Her responsiveness. The red panties. The camisole. Whatever it takes.

Did she want this? Had she known? Is this her plan? *His own pants puddled around his ankles as he kicked her feet apart. The tip of him ready teased her opening. Philippe paused. He had to be sure. He wouldn't take a woman by force. He couldn't hurt Anne.*

"Do we have a deal?"

She didn't say anything, only arching even more, giving him easier access. Philippe felt her heat, smelled her, this woman who enflamed all his senses. She made him insane, violent. Although all her actions said yes, Philippe needed to hear the words. He had to be absolutely certain.

"Do we have a deal, *Mademoiselle* James?" Philippe repeated, placing his hands on her hips, shaking her a bit.

Anne looked back, brown eyes glowing and then she smiled, a tight little taunting smile. "You know we do, *M'sieur* Lamont. So seal the deal, damn it."

And Philippe did, slamming into her with a force that surprised even himself.

Fourteen

Whatever it takes. This was her new mantra, Anne reminded herself, as she tagged along after Kate Winslow, the PR manager for *Wedding Pings*, main competitor to *Be My Guest*. Good thing too, as there was no turning back now. Anne was well behind enemy lines, her *Birkenstocks* flopping through the corridors in time to *Muzak* from hell. Stanley dressed her in a snug ribbed knit tank top and long multi-colored broom skirt, assuring here that this was what all the artsy university journalists were wearing.

Stanley might have been right. Ms. Winslow hadn't even blinked.

"Your audience is exactly the demographic *Wedding Pings* is targeting," she told Anne. "Young, educated, tech-savvy, starting to think about marriage. We were thrilled when your editor approached us."

Her "editor," a long time friend at a nearby university paper, approached the company upon Anne's request. Sure, she would actually write an article up, that wasn't a lie, but the real purpose was to snoop around.

"We were thrilled that you could slot some time in for us." Of course, the company jumped all over the opportunity, this was free advertising. "I was surfing, doing some dreaming, and came across the clever way you manage guest lists. I haven't seen any other site do this."

The woman beamed. "And you won't. No one else has it. It's an innovation, exclusive to *Wedding Pings*."

Right. Exclusive after her company stole it from Denise, putting the blonde out of business before she even started. "Did he mention I'd like to make that technology the focus of the article, follow the project from conception to implementation?" *At least that was what she had told her buddy to say.*

Heavily mascara laden eyelashes fluttered.

Drat...that sounded too nailed down. The woman was suspicious. Nothing would be leaked if Anne went at it too hard-nosed.

"I mean...it always amazes me how people think of these things," Anne hastened to add, "so creative, so freeing to the brides. Doing your part to make the world a better place." *Complete crap but was it enough peace and love?*

Must have been because the P-R woman relaxed and smiled, a little condescendingly. "That's who we are thinking of. Busy brides who already have enough on their plates. They shouldn't have to worry about seating arrangements and thank-you cards, don't you think, Marie?"

Marie? Oh, yeah, that was her. For an extra layer of invisibility, Anne gave her second name as her first, her surname being common enough to keep.

"Thank you cards? As in snail mail? That's so prehistoric," Anne bubbled, sickening herself in the process, "I mean send an e-mail, already."

"Unfortunately, weddings remain very traditional with mailed cards being the norm." The door to a boardroom was opened and Anne was offered a pink cushioned seat. Did the place actually smell like flowers too? Too, too much. "I've set up interviews with a number of my associates so you can have different viewpoints."

And different quotes with enough information to dominate an entire article. Very clever. It worked out to Anne's benefit also. A polished P-R person was unlikely to let something slip while a programmer or an admin person might be more forthcoming. Anne scanned down the list she was handed. Peter Flun, developer, Heidi Jibbs, marketing, and then her mouth almost dropped open. Kevin Maples, Innovation. *Holy crap, when had he jumped to the competition?*

Anne's voice was perfectly neutral. "Awesome. So have all these employees been involved in this project since the beginning?"

Ms. Winslow looked at the paper and frowned. "Yes all, oh, except for the Innovation contact. He joined the organization two short weeks ago."

"Would it add value for me to talk to him then? If he recently started?" Anne certainly didn't want to talk to Maple. He would have her thrown out of the building immediately. *Geez, that would cause a scene.*

"Yes, you definitely should meet with him."

Figures. The woman wants her extra quotes.

"He has experience with the competition. He can tell you what it is about *Wedding Pings* that switched his allegiance."

Let me take a wild guess. Hmmm, he got fired perhaps? And then sold company secrets to land this new job?

Should Anne immediately make an excuse to leave? She had her answer. It would be easy enough for Philippe to confirm. One thing didn't add up though. Why had Maple asked Ms. McKenzie for a job if he already secured this gig? Was that request made before or after? Anne had to confirm the timing with the Angel. So she might as well stick it out, asking the questions, probing for more answers, and then beat a hasty exit before Maple's interview came up, his conveniently her last slot of the day.

The first slot, the interview with the developer was uneventful. The pale nervous man was purely an implementation vehicle, having been given everything from design to the programs to use. Of course he had. It was all there, outlined in the business plan.

The minute she walked in, or half walked in as it were, Anne knew that Miss Jibbs, the marketing lead, would be another story entirely.

"And I told Sally, what am I supposed to do with the rest of my marketing campaign? It's impossible. I can't advertise anything without money." The woman braced the meeting room door open as she had this honest conversation with a coworker. "I know, I know. They should have told us. Oh, I've got a meeting. I almost forgot. I'll talk to you later."

"Hi, there." The perky brunette wriggled her fingers in Anne's direction and sat down with a flounce, her short skirt floating up even higher. "So Marie, you're from the university. How exciting. My ol' alma mater. Do you belong to a sorority there?"

Anne's mind went blank. *Would a journalist belong to a sorority?*

"Oh, of course you don't," Heidi Jibbs answered her own question. "You gotta be neutral, don'tcha? Free speech and all that. Has much changed?"

"We got a new food court." Anne knew that much. Her editor friend mentioned that any coverage outside of the new food court would be welcome. He had that more than dealt with already. Some controversy with nutrition and big company commercialism.

"Really." Heidi's tone stated that she didn't much care. "I guess that's a 'No.'"

"Well, not like here." Anne tried to transition into the interview as gently as possible, maintaining the chattiness of the opening. "I mean, wow."

"I know. One day I have over a million dollars to play with and the next, nothing." The woman remained on that subject.

"Man, oh, man, a million dollars is a lot of money." Anne remembered it was, when she was a starving student. "Where did all that cash go?"

"How the sugar snaps would I know? Some mystery development costs that I can't get a straight answer on." The rest of the organization must have realized Miss Jibbs had a serious case of verbal diarrhea, not telling her anything.

"A million smackeroo's for development?"

"That new guest management system." Heidi rolled her eyes. "The savior of our company. As if. Marketing drives business, everyone knows that."

A million dollars for developing the guest management system. Since the guest management system was stolen fully developed, that sounded like a payoff and if so, why would they pay Kevin off in a lump sum? Why wouldn't they gradually flow it through an inflated salary or a one time signing bonus?

"I'm confused. If marketing drives business then what does

innovation do? This Kevin Maples person I'm meeting with?" Anne prompted, hoping that her query was enough to send the pony tailed woman into another run on tirade. It was.

"Well, that's a new position so I don't even know what he's supposed to do. We never had it before and I don't think it is needed. It must have been created to hire..." but then she was interrupted by a knock on the glass door.

Anne blinked a couple times and then tried to frantically hide her face behind her temporarily burgundy curls before she was noticed. She wasn't fast enough, meeting the widened blue eyes of Gregory Myers.

Don't blow my cover, don't blow my cover, don't blow my cover, were her first thoughts. Her second was what was *he* doing here?

"Oh, goodie, goodie. I was hoping he'd drop by. Don't go anywhere." The pretty young marketer told Anne like she actually had an option. "I'll be back in a jiffy."

Anne peeked out, Gregory was looking at her. She shook her head and he transferred his attention to the bubbly marketer. Anne's attention drifted back to them. They appeared pretty chummy, with Gregory's hand resting intimately on Heidi's hip. Philippe's friend gave Anne a couple more stealthy glances, but from the woman's relaxed, happy face, it appeared that he hadn't said anything.

When Heidi returned to the meeting room, Anne blinked her brown eyes and forced a girlish giggle. "Who's that hottie and is he on my list of people to interview?"

Heidi laughed, blushing sweetly. "That's a guy I'm sort of seeing and no, he's not. He is a hottie though, isn't he?"

A guy she's sort of seeing? Gregory was going out with an employee? That was a huge conflict of interest he hadn't bothered declaring. "He is. Does he work here?" *Please say no*, Anne prayed. She didn't want to have to tell Philippe that too. The girlfriend bit was bad enough.

"No," Heidi shook her head, much to Anne's relief. "He dropped by to tell me something. He does that, when he's in the neighborhood, very sweet."

"Very, but wow, I can't get over what you said before, a million dollars. Wow." Anne leaned forward, her palms facing upwards, inviting the woman to share. "The project manager must have really known what she was doing. Where is she anyway?"

"Penelope, oh, she's taking some time off." The marketer's eyes darted to the closed door before continuing. "Just between you and me, I doubt if she'll be back. Big, big scandal."

The woman hung back expectantly and Anne knew she only needed a little push. "Big?"

"Oh, yeah." A brunette tendril was twisted around a finger. "Pen had a big fight with the boss. Said she was unethical or something like that, right to her face. Missus Dumont didn't like that much and next we knew, Pen was taking time off. Oh." Her rather free mouth shaped into a circle.

Anne knew what she was thinking. "Don't worry, Miss Jibbs, All this is off the record. I would never betray an alumni." That was the truth. Nothing would go into the paper, might be used to clear her name sure but not in the paper.

"I appreciate that, I knew you wouldn't be that way, and don't worry, the company will make back its money," Heidi shared, "only that it digs into my marketing money. I need recruitment money, what with us being short-staffed and all."

"What do you mean short-staffed?" Anne smelled opportunity.

"Why didn't I think of this before?" Heidi grabbed Anne's hands. She hoped that the marketing woman wouldn't notice that they were older than her youthfully made up face. "I need some short term staff members, floaters more like it, to help out with marketing activities. Fun things, like going to conventions and bridal shows."

Ginny. She was the perfect solution. Her sister could build up her own connections, make a bit of extra cash and continue to snoop around for Anne. As a staff member, she might have access to the files. If Ginny could figure out who received the million dollars, it would tie everything up neatly.

"I know someone who would be perfect," Anne volunteered, "Could I send you her resume?" A resume specially created for the marketer.

"Better yet, tell her to give me a call and I'll set up an interview." Heidi's genuine appreciation causing Anne discomfort. *Whatever it takes.* "That would help me out a lot."

The rest of the conversation plumped up the school article, but didn't add to Anne's investigation. It did call into question Gregory's involvement with Miss Jibbs. Sure, the woman was nice and likely good at what she did but she was also lacking in depth. Somehow, Anne couldn't imagine her piquing Gregory's interest.

So what was Gregory doing with Heidi Jibbs then? Was it a sex only arrangement? Nothing more than that? Was it merely a coincidence that the woman worked at *Wedding Pings*? Was Anne creating connections that weren't there?

After Heidi bounced out of the room, Anne wiggled in her chair. Maple's interview was next. How would she get out of that? As was the trend thus far, Ms. Winslow would pop into the meeting room in between appointments to see if she had any questions. Yet another lie to be told. None was thankfully necessary. Ms. Winslow regretfully informed Anne that Kevin was pulled into a last minute meeting and would be unable to meet with her. More like, he thought her a lowly student reporter and couldn't be bothered with her. Good. Her last name hadn't raised any suspicions.

Ms. Winslow walked her to the elevator, an insipid version of "My Heart Will Go On" blaring in the background, and again offered that if she had any questions, to give her a call.

It would have to be a call. Lying was difficult. They were nice people, with maybe the exception of their CEO, she sounded like a piece of work, and, of course, Kevin Maple. He was an ass. The rest, they couldn't be blamed for using information provided to them. It would be almost impossible to turn down.

No, the fault rested on the person providing the information. It would take someone without any sense of loyalty or honor. Someone who badmouthed his own CEO? Probably. Or a lawyer who didn't declare a conflict of interest? Anne thought that less likely.

She was ninety-nine-point-nine percent positive that the info thief was Maple, and once Ginny secured that last point-one percent, Anne would plop the irrefutable proof in Philippe's lap. She smiled as she walked to her car. *Cocky, self-righteous bastard*, he was intent on dishing out punishment for her imagined crime against him. Or at least trying to dish out punishment.

Philippe tried, oh how he tried, to give no pleasure with his lovemaking. Fortunately for Anne, he couldn't help but please a woman. He did it without thought, without effort. Caresses transpired, words of endearment spilled out without consciousness. He didn't want to please her and he certainly didn't want to want her. That he could resist neither erased any lingering doubts she had about Philippe Lamont not truly wanting plain old Anne James.

She had control over him, as he had over her.

~ * ~

Philippe thought along the same lines as he sat in Anne's sparsely furnished living room, waiting for her to return home. Why he was there, he didn't rightly know. Gregory had given him a call, saying that he saw her at Denise's main competitor, the competitor that scooped Denise's guest list idea. Gregory told him some airy-fairy story about Anne posing as a university student. Like she'd be able to pull that off, give him a break. *Oui*, she might have been a student once but Philippe couldn't picture it. Anne was too uptight, too conservative in dress and speech.

Not in bed though. There anything and everything went. That thought alone made his body harden. Philippe told himself coming over here that he only wanted to know why Anne had been there. He planned to ask her straight out if she was working with the competitor. But then, sitting here, Philippe faced facts. Forget the investigation. He waited for a chance, any chance to see her, to touch her, to taste her.

The key turned and the door opened. At first, Anne didn't notice him sitting in the dark. She wandered into the condo, hips gently swaying, arms full of groceries.

At least Philippe thought it was Anne. *What the hell did she do to her hair?* That gorgeous honey brown silk he loved was frizzy and a harsh reddish pink color. He hoped that wasn't permanent. And the outfit? Philippe had never seen her wear anything like it. It was funky and flowing like she was some sort of gypsy. The sandals slipped off at the door, her feet now bare, one slim ankle having a hemp strap around it.

She could very well be a university student, all sweet rebellion, rainbows and daisies. Was that what his little brown sparrow had been like? And could Gregory's crazy version of the story be correct? Was she doing some investigating of her own? *Was she truly innocent?*

Philippe watched Anne place the bags on the kitchen counter and then start to put the groceries away, singing to herself softly off key. *What was the tune? Ahhh, oui, that horrible Titanic song.* Even with the vile disguise, the bad song choice, the appalling selection of instant meals... *was that condensed soup? Do people still eat that stuff?* It was Anne, and Philippe wanted her.

Would he want someone that couldn't be trusted? Was his heart all the proof he needed? Too many questions. Not enough answers. Time to resolve that disparity.

"Welcome home, *Cherie*." Philippe flicked on the lamp behind him.

Anne jumped, startled at his voice but didn't turn around. "How did you get in?"

"Your landlord. He let me in." There was no point hiding his methods. "Cost a few dollars but it was worth it not to wait in the hallway."

"Why would you wait in the hallway? I'm not aware of any meeting with you this evening." Meetings were what they had now. Not dates, not intimate moments, but meetings.

"I took a chance on you being free." Philippe strode towards her, grabbing the can she struggled to place on a top shelf. The cheery face of *Chef Boyardee* smiled back at him. The woman might be able to find the North Star but she sure couldn't cook. *One more thing to teach her.*

He slid the can onto the shelf and turned. The kitchen was small. She was so close, he could smell her. Philippe leaned against the counter top, and reached out to grab a curl. "This is new."

"Do you like it?" Eyelashes batted against her cheek like butterfly wings. Damn woman was flirting with him. What it would take for her to fear him, Philippe didn't know. He tried to come across as dangerous as possible and she laughed at him.

"*Non.*" Philippe was honest. He liked her the way she was. His little brown sparrow.

"Well, that's too bad." Slight shoulders shrugged.

She didn't care what he thought and that bothered him. "Where were you today?"

"None of your business." Anne put the dishwashing liquid away in the cabinet under the sink. *She must be expecting some heavy duty washing for those instant meals she was serving.* There were already two unopened bottles neatly lined up, ready to go. "I don't work for you any more, remember?"

How could he forget? He asked himself everyday whether he made a mistake. That decision hadn't felt right from the start.

She wasn't done. "I'm my own woman. I work for myself, me, numero uno, or *moi*, if you need it in French."

Mon Dieu, she is adorable. "Merci pour la traduction."

"Not a problem." Anne opened the fridge door and bent over to put a lonely tomato away in the crisper. At least she knew what a fresh vegetable looked like.

Should he tell her about Gregory seeing her? If he did, she'd ask why Gregory was there. And then Philippe would have to admit that he sent his friend in to do some investigating. She'd ask why again, she always asked why, damn pain in the ass woman. He'd have to admit that he had doubts. And that his doubts were compounding with every passing day. Gregory had informed him in the same phone call that Kevin Maples, his former executive, was working for Denise's competition.

So Anne might be investigating, trying to prove herself to him. And if she was doing that, then she couldn't herself be guilty, a small annoying voice inside him said. Philippe humored the voice. "How's your investigation going?"

"I don't have proof yet, if that's what you're asking," her words were gruff. He could hear the hurt in them.

Philippe wanted to reach out and hold her in his arms.

Non. He couldn't. Not yet. Not until he was sure. "Any leads?" *Say yes, Anne.*

"Only the same ones I always had." She turned to look him straight in the eye, "Philippe, why are you here?"

He didn't have a good answer for that. Why was he there? What did he want? He wanted to spend time with her. To go back in time. To believe in her again. Was that too much to ask? It was, so instead, "There's a charity event tomorrow." A date, that was it. "I'd like you to go with me."

Suspicion was written over her made up face. She didn't trust him and that stung. "Why?"

Why? Why? Why? Always why.

Good thing he hadn't told her about Gregory. "Since you're serious about this investigation, you should be more proactive, take some risks. If we spent time together, it would make the real guilty party nervous." *Oui,* that sounded like a good solid excuse. "Nervous people make mistakes."

Anne tilted her head and Philippe watched those harshly colored curls rearrange themselves. She was cute even with a bad dye job, he decided, very kissable, even with purple stained lips. Her legs were bare. *Do hippies wear underwear?* He didn't think so.

"I guess that makes sense." She smiled at him, buying his weak excuse, and his heart lightened. He was seeing her now and he would see Anne again tomorrow. Philippe missed seeing her everyday.

"I'll pick you up around seven." He cupped her chin, raising it so he could look into her eyes. "And since we want it obvious that you are attending, you might want to look more…like you." Philippe curled one tendril around his finger. Still soft, smelling like a fruit salad.

She chuckled at this, the sound husky in her throat. "I'll try my best."

"You do that." Philippe couldn't resist. He swooped down to graze her full lips lightly with his and then, before he could get swept up in Anne, he walked away.

Fifteen

What in the world am I doing? Anne wondered that for the hundredth time as she sat parked outside of the Cyber Café. It was hot in the beat up old station wagon, Anne's wig with skull cap itched under the baseball cap and the binding around her chest was uncomfortable. No use turning on the car; Anne didn't think the A-C had worked for the last decade. It was an unpleasant way to spend a Friday morning and not one of her better ideas. Last night, she thought it brilliant. Of course last night she had also been a bit tipsy.

~ * ~

Stanley popped into the condo after Philippe left, all aflutter to hear how his university student makeover went. He arrived later than planned because Denise had dropped by the studio to get a freebie spruce up. Stanley didn't make Anne feel any better, telling her how Denise looked wiped out, not her normal beautiful self. Anne might not have been directly responsible but she couldn't forego all the blame. Someone on her team leaked the information.

And then Stanley said something strange. He mentioned that Denise was taking some time off, to regroup and recoup.

Regroup and recoup, that's what he said. All well and good except that Anne's credit check on Denise told her that any time off by the blonde would end with her in bankruptcy court. Denise was so overextended that her first action should have been hustling for income.

So why didn't Denise feel a need to rush out and get a job? Where was she getting the money? And what was she doing with her time? A couple glasses of white wine later and Anne pondered those questions. What was that girl up to? The question nagged at her. Well, heck, Anne didn't have anything to do, she already had painted the condo three times, why didn't she follow Denise around and see?

Stanley, jumping into detective work, advised that she go in disguise. Better, he said, to avoid detection. Anne was made over into a teenage boy. He even got a friend to lend her his car.

Should have been exciting, right? *Nope*. What Anne hadn't counted on was how unbelievably boring surveillance work was.

~ * ~

The morning was uneventful. Anne was there waiting when Denise, dressed semi-casually for Denise, in a cute little sundress, left her apartment around eight a.m. and headed to the Cyber Café. Anne knew the neighborhood, the café located a block from Lamont Ventures.

Then Denise stayed there all bloody morning. What she was doing, Anne hadn't a clue. Denise could be working there, playing video games, or running a booming on-line company, for all Anne knew. She couldn't go in, the place too small to enter without being noticed. Her disguise, though good from afar, wasn't the best up close.

No, she had to wait. Anne sat in the rust-bucket, windows rolled down to get some sort of air circulation. Luckily she thought to bring some of her *Young C.E.O.s* business building projects with her so she wasn't completely bored, last week's assignment to draft a simple contract between two individuals. Not that contract law was exciting. It was an important part of business but about as dry as the first and last roast Anne ever cooked.

Around noon, there was some action. Though not much. Denise exited the building, walking a couple blocks down the street to a funky little bistro. It was far enough away that Anne had to move the car and she lucked into a parking spot right out front. *Now*, Anne rubbed her hands together, excited, she'd get to do some real detective work. The bistro was busy, she could wander in for a drink at the bar, situate herself so she could overhear the conversation. *Yeah, finally some fun.* But no, it being a great fall day, Denise chose to sit on the sidewalk-facing patio. *Drat*, Anne had a good view and the patio was too small to get closer. No excuse to get out of the car.

Bored, Anne dug out a peanut butter sandwich and nibbled on it. *Hmmm...*warm, and gooey from the hot car. Surveillance was hungry work. A wave of dark suits passed by the car and Anne slumped down, trying not to draw their attention. Good thing too because those familiar suits headed to the table where Denise was sitting.

Philippe kissed Denise on both cheeks. Anne's fingertips, without any thought, pressed against her own face in the same spot. Her eyes stayed on Philippe even as Denise was passed along to Gregory.

Dang. Of all people, it would have to be him. Her blasted bad luck. This lunch wouldn't add a thing to her investigation. Anne set her sandwich down on the passenger seat to devote her full attention to Philippe. *Geez*, he was good looking. He smiled, his face animated as he related some story. If only she could hear what he was saying.

But watching him was enough. She loved the way he gulped down his not so healthy lunch like he hadn't eaten in days. The way his face changed with his commentary, his lips moving quickly, drawing in the audience eyes, the way he made the server laugh.

A half hour passed. Anne got out of her car to stretch and put more money in the meter. She acted as natural as she could to not draw attention but in her nervousness, her fingers fumbled so badly she dropped a quarter. Anne scrambled to grab it before it rolled away. There. Finally the meter was topped up. Good for another thirty minutes. Anne settled back into the car and resumed her viewing. *Funny. Is Philippe looking right at me? No.* Probably gazing into space. From this distance, her costume would hold; he'd think her to be some boy.

~ * ~

Philippe not only knew that was no boy feeding the meter, he knew exactly to whom that perky little derriere belonged.

That reminded him—"Anne will be attending the charity event this evening," Philippe blurted out to the table, interrupting whatever Denise was discussing. He couldn't spring her presence on them, not after all that had happened. He had to give them some forewarning, had to gauge their reaction. Philippe told himself that it was for their benefit but, in all honesty, if their responses were too negative, he'd spare Anne the humiliation.

"Good, we didn't really get a chance to chat before. Business is business and all that," Denise's dead on imitation of professional Anne lightened Philippe's mood.

Only the disquieting thought of Denise confronting Anne kept him from smiling. "Denise, you'll be nice to her, won't you?"

"To Anne?" Blue eyes rapidly blinked. "But of course, Philippe. Why wouldn't I be?"

Because she destroyed your start up company, peut-etre? Sold you out to the competition? Was he the only person present thinking logically? "Denise, you aren't upset over the *Be My Guest* fiasco?"

"Oh, God, Philippe. You're not still on that, are you?" Gregory asked in disbelief, "Thinking that Anne leaked the information?"

"I don't have any proof that she didn't."

"Proof? Who cares about proof? What happened to trust?" Denise glared at him. "There's no proof that I didn't leak the information. Yet for some reason, you trust me. So why don't you trust Anne?"

Why didn't Philippe trust Anne? He wanted to. But he couldn't evaluate Anne's involvement rationally like he could with Denise. His feelings kept getting mixed up in it, coloring his judgment. *Oui*, that was the whole damn problem. He couldn't go on his gut alone, not with his heart involved.

"I told her she had to work for me as long as your business was viable. Anne was upset. It was cutting into her own company's billings, and then suddenly your business plan was leaked. Come on, Denise, what else could it be?"

"You're serious?"

Like he would joke about something like that and why exactly were the two of them looking at him like he was the bad guy? "I don't believe in coincidences."

"You don't know, do you?" The quiet note in Gregory's voice got Philippe worried. His friend did that, lowering his volume, right before springing an indisputable fact on an opposing legal team.

"Know what?" *What was it?* What vital piece of information was he missing?

Gregory was about to tell him. "Remember when I told you that Anne dropped the lawsuit against Bruce?"

Vaguely. Philippe nodded. He had other things on his mind then, like a pair of shapely legs in sheer black hose but he did remember.

"That was a couple weeks before the transfer of information. Anne was suing an entrepreneur Lamont Ventures picked up," Gregory quickly brought a confused Denise up to speed before continuing, "My friend, did you ever wonder why the lawsuit was dropped? What her motive for doing so was?"

Philippe thought it had to do with their personal relationship getting stronger but he wasn't willing to offer that reasoning, not now. "Not really."

"I did, so I looked into it. Wanted to make certain everything was okay."

Mais oui, more like Gregory wanted to make certain that Anne was okay, Philippe thought wryly.

"You can imagine my surprise when I found out Anne was wrapping up her business."

What the... "Wrapping up her business? Anne's quitting?" Denise gasped out the words Philippe couldn't yet say. "But she's so good at what she does. She loves it."

She's good at what she does but she couldn't do both, that was what she told him. She had to choose. Only his damn Anne would put another company before her own. Only his damn Anne. His? She wasn't his Anne anymore. *Mon Dieu, what have I done?*

"I didn't know," Philippe's voice was hushed. Amongst friends, he didn't try to hide his torment. He was past pride.

"I'm sorry, my friend. I thought you did. I thought you knew and you were deliberately holding that information back from me," Gregory admitted, revealing some of the hurt he felt.

Denise was silent for once, looked at them thoughtfully. Finally she said, "I really ought to get to know Anne better."

So should I. Philippe thought he knew her. He didn't. She was far stronger than he would have ever imagined. There was still monetary gain as a motive. Philippe already knew the answer but he had to wrap up any lingering doubts. "How much was she suing us for?"

"More than *Wedding Pings* paid for the information," was Gregory's confirmation.

Denise finally put two and two together. "That isn't why Anne is no longer working for you, is it? Tell me it isn't. Tell me it was because my start up went under."

"It was." Philippe might as well own up to all his bad moves. "I thought she sold you out and I fired her."

"You—" Denise was again struck speechless.

Denise trusted Anne. Gregory trusted Anne. *L'Ange* had told Philippe he was an emotional idiot. Even Sylvie, his executive assistant, supported Anne. Everyone could see that Anne couldn't, wouldn't do such a thing. Everyone except for himself. Even now, Philippe's head turned toward that dreadful station wagon. His brave, strong Anne was out there, trying to gather up enough evidence to prove her innocence. To prove to him, the only person who thought her guilty. He was an ass, and said so out loud.

"You certainly are," Denise wholeheartedly agreed.

Even Gregory had to nod his head, a sad smile tugging at his lips. "You've dug yourself into a big hole, my friend. What do you tell me when that happens?"

"You can wallow in that hole or climb your way out," the two of them recited in unison.

Philippe, despite his despair, had to smile. It was a frequent piece of advice, as they'd been in a lot of holes over the years. This one, however, was his biggest yet, a crater, a global killer.

"So what will it be?" Gregory asked, "Will you wallow?"

Gregory would like that, Philippe suspected, if he wallowed. He might have a chance with Anne if Philippe left the field, if he walked away.

Walk away from Anne? The woman who wouldn't walk away from him, even after all he had done? Not a possibility. "This time I don't have a choice."

"Then how can we help?" Denise grinned.

~ * ~

With the sun beating down on her little tin can, Anne sweltered, perspiration dripping down her backbone. Next time, if she was foolish enough to do this a next time, she'd wear a cooler disguise. *Dang, but that's a long lunch.* What did they have to talk about? Don't they see each other all the time? Gregory and Philippe even worked together. They couldn't have anything left to say.

They were standing up. *About friggin' time.* Luck would have it that they stopped to talk right in front of her vehicle. Anne kept her head down, studying the newspaper laid out on the steering wheel. Words drifted to her through the open window.

"I need to get back to the café," Denise chirped, "Derek will be in a tissy if I'm too late. We've got a lot to do."

Who was Derek and why was she meeting with him? Anne didn't know.

"We'll see you at the charity thing tonight," Gregory replied.

Was that the same charity do that Philippe was taking her to? Likely.

Anne felt a little—no, a lot—nervous about seeing Denise again. Philippe was Denise's friend. He would have told his ex-girlfriend his suspicions by now. And Denise must hate her. It was going to be a hellish evening.

"Looking forward to it. It was a lot of fun last year."

Sounded like Denise didn't know she was coming yet. Philippe must be waiting to spring it on her. *Nice. More stress.*

"It'll be more interesting this year, isn't that right, Philippe?" Gregory laughed.

"I don't know about fun," Philippe groaned.

Was that a bit about her attending? Anne frowned. Did he not want to spend time with her? Was it a chore for him?

"Oh, it'll be fun for us," Denise threw at him.

"Glad to increase your entertainment, Dee. We'll see you tonight." Anne heard what sounded like lips smacking and then the voices drifted off.

Anne waited for a few more minutes. Denise was going back to the Cyber Café. That meant turning the car around. Anne didn't want to draw attention as she did the U-turn. She tugged at the overly moist binding. The get-up was getting exceedingly uncomfortable. She didn't think she could stand it much longer. *So is it even worth anything going back to the Cyber Cafe?* She couldn't go inside. Anne knew the first name of the man Denise was meeting with. She could ask Stanley about this Derek person.

Yes, asking her gossip queen friend was an easier way to figure out what Denise was up to. Cooler also. So forget it. She did enough PI work for today. She was going home. Anne placed her hand on the key to turn the ignition when the passenger door opened and the seat was filled.

"*Salut, Cherie.*" Philippe grinned at her cheerfully. "What are you up to?"

Busted again. Yesterday by Gregory. Today by Philippe. She was terrible at this undercover work.

"You're sitting on my sandwich," Anne grumbled.

Philippe pulled the flattened bread out from under him, smelling it. "Plain peanut butter on white processed bread. You really are a cheap date, aren't you?"

Anne took the uneatable sandwich from him and tossed it in a plastic bag. So much for her lunch. "This isn't a date, Philippe. I'm busy."

Philippe ran a hand over the ripped up dash, wrinkling up his nose at the dirt on his fingertips. "Nice car. Did you trade in the Volvo?"

"Ha." Anne rolled her eyes at his sarcasm. "I borrowed it from a friend."

"Oh, I wouldn't exactly call her a friend." Philippe opened the glove compartment only to shut it again quickly as things starting falling out. "You got a death wish?"

"It runs okay." Anne didn't know why she was defending the junker. It was a piece of garbage. "Can I take you somewhere, Philippe?" Like back to his office or anywhere else as long as it was out of her car?

"I guess you can take me home, *Cherie*." Philippe, after a couple tugs, managed to put on his seatbelt. "I have to change my clothes. Can't go around with peanut butter stuck to my *derriere*."

But oh, what a fine derriere he had. He probably knew it too, conceited, bossy man.

Anne started up the engine. It backfired, turning heads. Embarrassing. Next time, if there were a next time, she'd do the undercover work in her own reliable and clean car. A Volvo wasn't a look-at-me type of car anyway. Very common. And it was quiet.

"I can fix that," Philippe told her, unperturbed by the loud bang. "Dirk and I finally fixed the problem with the Gremlin."

My, aren't you being helpful and so very chatty. "Thank you. I'll tell my friend. Who knows? Car repair could be a second career for you."

"It could. I'll keep that in mind." Then his face grew serious. "So whom are you tracking, *Cherie*? Me, Gregory, or Denise?"

"Couldn't be you," Anne blocked, "I had you chipped once while you were sleeping."

"Guess you didn't think I could find the North Star." Philippe nodded, his arm out the window, tapping on the roof, annoying Anne. "So that leaves Gregory or Denise. You're wasting your time, Anne. Neither, I think, is your guilty party."

"Since you think I'm the guilty party, please forgive me if I don't take your opinion into account." Anne let the car coast to the stoplight, not wanting it to stall. The station wagon was a little touchy with stopping and starting. The brakes squeaked as they were applied, almost masking his words.

"I don't think you're the guilty party, *Cherie*."

What? He doesn't? Well, that's news to me. Anne thought herself tried, convicted, and on death row. "No? Why the sudden change of heart?"

"No sudden change of heart," Philippe sounded so earnest she almost believed him. "More like an alignment of head with heart."

Alignment of head with heart, huh? Although Anne wanted to believe him, his story didn't quite hold together. If he truly didn't think her guilty, why'd he fire her? Why weren't they investigating this together? Why make her believe that she was on her own? Anne thought all this but didn't ask. She kept quiet, not ready to talk about it yet. It hurt too badly.

He sighed, not pursuing it further. "What are you doing?" Philippe ran a finger along the bare back of her neck.

"The deal was that you weren't to contact Denise directly."

She shrugged him away. "I didn't contact Denise." Anne hadn't said a word to the woman.

"You're following her, that's worse. I don't think I like you spying on my friends, *Cherie.*"

"I don't like being accused—sorry not accused—found guilty of a crime I didn't commit. So deal with it." Anne must have misunderstood. He couldn't have done such a quick about face.

"No one thinks you're guilty, Anne. However, sneaking around, spying on people, acting like a sexy little *Inspector Clouseau*, isn't going to help your case."

Innocent again... *hmmm*... and he thought she was sexy. Anne shouldn't let that affect her but it did. About the spying, she supposed he was right. It didn't help her case but only because she kept on getting caught. That had to stop. Otherwise no one would know. "How did you know it was me?" Anne took off her baseball cap and the wig underneath, tossing them between the seats, shaking her hair down.

"The car got my attention first. I wondered how it passed emissions. Then you fed the meter and bent over." Philippe picked up the wig, looking at it closely. "I'd recognize that *derriere* anywhere."

He recognized my ass? Not my face or my eyes but my ass? Anne was torn between pleasure and dismay.

They pulled into Philippe's driveway, a charming and simple four-bedroom ranch style bungalow located close to downtown. She'd been in it a couple times. Back when she actually thought he trusted her.

"Aren't you coming in?" Philippe offered, as he got out, an imprint of her peanut butter sandwich on the seat of his dress pants.

Was she coming in? For a nooner? It was tempting, the opportunity to touch him always was, but she didn't think so. Yesterday, maybe. Today, no. What had changed? He now knew her to be innocent. If Philippe still had overtly thought she was guilty, Anne probably would have gone inside with him, her feelings safely sheltered by the twin shields of anger and vengeance.

Now, the anger was gone, the thirst for revenge partially sated, which left the raw hurt exposed. It lay out there in the hot sun for all, including him, to see. Anne had to reach for a new coping mechanism before she could reach for him.

"I think I'll pass." Anne stayed in the car. "I don't want to keep this car longer than I have to."

"Good thinking. Replacing it with an equivalent car might be a challenge." Philippe leaned into the open window, suddenly all seriousness.

"Anne, why didn't you tell me about winding up the business?" He had the nerve to sound wounded.

So that was it. The change. Philippe figured out she didn't have anything to gain by the leak of information. He found the proof he needed.

Anne studied his handsome face with sadness weighing heavy on her heart. Nothing changed for her. He didn't truly trust her. She thought about her answer, deciding upon the blunt truth. "I didn't want you to feel guilty."

With that comment, and a backfire to punctuate it, Anne drove away.

~ * ~

She didn't want me to feel guilty. Could he feel any worse? Philippe didn't think so. He watched until that wreck Anne drove disappeared from sight. It didn't look too safe but at least she was cautious enough to avoid the freeway. Philippe doubted it could handle high speeds without peeling apart.

Peeling apart. The thought of something happening to her, his darling Anne, was unbearable. He hurt her enough these past weeks. From the brutal way he fired her to his atrocious behavior upon her return. Philippe remembered how she pushed herself into his office, demanding that he assist her in her investigation, and then, then saying she would do anything. Anything to prove her innocence to him. Anything.

And Philippe took advantage of her generous offer, using Anne shamelessly, uncaring of her feelings, of the pain and betrayal she must have been feeling, concerned only about his own selfish needs and his misplaced anger. She accepted his callousness without complaint, head held high, shoulders defiantly thrown back. Classic, brave Anne.

Merde, she gave him everything, without question, and he, he couldn't even give her his trust.

Sixteen

"An alignment of head with heart, huh?" Stanley hovered over Anne's face with a make-up brush. "An interesting choice of words."

"If you can believe them." Anne wanted to fidget but knew not to move. "They might be only words."

"From Philippe? He doesn't seem the type to chatter."

"Or lie. Why don't you believe him, Annie?" Nancy asked from her vantage point seated at the kitchen table, "Haven't you told me time and time again that Lamont doesn't lie?"

"That's true." Philippe doesn't lie. Tension eased out of her body. So what is going on? Could he actually...

"Sounds like he cares for you, Annie-pie." Stanley dabbed some face paint under her right eye. "What about you? Do you still like him?"

"Yes." Oh, yes, did she ever. In every way imaginable.

"Do you love him?" Nancy tossed out.

Anne hesitated. Love him? Could she love him? After everything? Unfortunately...

"She does," Stanley answered for her. "She wouldn't be in this analysis paralysis hell pit if she didn't. Our darling Annie-kin was never one to dither. Must be love."

"Don't dither yourself out of a lover," her pregnant friend advised. "Lamont likes to make a decision and move forward."

"That'll happen eventually anyway." Philippe moving forward without her. "So why should I even try?"

"Why not? What's the worst that could happen?" Stanley flicked some powder over her cheeks, setting the paint.

"He could break my heart." *There,* Anne said it.

"And what would be the state of your heart if he moved on tomorrow?"

Tomorrow. Not even one more day, one more kiss, or one more touch. "Broken."

"Then you're not risking anything, are you? The downside is the same, and think of the upside," Nancy pointed out.

"And while you're at it, the backside." At the women's gasps, Stanley mocked being offended. "What? Can you honestly say that you haven't noticed that tight little butt of his, like ripe peaches, so round and...?" *Dead silence.* "Okay, okay, enough about that. Open your eyes, Annie-Bananie, Babammie, I'm done."

Anne stared into the mirror, an exotic face complete with leopard spots on her cheek and darkly shadowed eyes reflecting back. "Very nice."

"Nice!" Stanley squealed. "It's more than nice. This is my best work."

"Even better than *Tinkerbell.*" Nancy clapped her hands. "Lamont is going to die."

Stanley took a sip of his white wine before continuing, "For your hair, very simple. We'll twist it up like this." He took a fistful of hair and put it up. "Pins, Nance No Chance." A few were handed over and he secured the do. It looked wild yet confined. "Perfect."

"You're going to wear that dress, aren't you?" Nancy rubbed an excited hand over her belly.

"I don't know. It's a little revealing." Anne bit her bottom lip. She never had worn anything so scanty before. It was almost scandalous. "I'm afraid my underwear will show."

"Then don't wear any, girlfriend." Stanley grinned saucily. "I'm sure Philippe, that handsome devil, won't mind. It'll save him a step."

"Stanley!" But Stanley was right. Anne knew where wearing that dress would lead. Was she ready? Could she forgive Philippe his lapse of trust? Could she not? One more kiss... one more...

Her doorbell rang and Anne shot up straight, clutching her robe around her. "He's early."

"He couldn't wait," Nancy teased.

"Maybe he's expecting pre-show entertainment. You might not want to get dressed." Stanley laughed. "Don't worry, Anne-the plan, I'll take care of your man for you." And he sashayed
out of the kitchen.

~ * ~

Stanley opening the door took Philippe aback. During his short time away from Anne, he came to a decision. *No more guessing.* No more battling the unknown. He'd tell her exactly how he felt and beg for her forgiveness. Right away. But with Stanley there and Nancy calling a friendly hello from the kitchen, that wasn't possible.

"Annie-kitten, your great white hunter is here," Stanley called through the condo.

That's what he looked like, Philippe supposed, with his khaki pants and crisp white shirt. The theme was *Lions for Literacy*, a charity scavenger hunt at the zoo with participants wearing either safari gear or animal outfits, Philippe opting for the more conservative look. He even found one of those *Tilley* hats. Glad he left that in the car. His outfit made Stanley giggle as it was.

Nancy rushed around the kitchen, packing up brushes and make-up. "We're leaving, Philippe, we won't be here much longer." Philippe always liked Nancy.

"We are?" Stanley on the other hand...

"We are." The redhead leveled the man a warning look as she passed what looked like a mid sized toolbox. *Who needed that much make-up?*

"We are." Stanley was pushed toward the door. "Bye Annie-pie," he called out again. "You kids have fun tonight. Don't do anything I wouldn't do."

"Which isn't much." Nancy rolled her eyes.

Stanley opened the door with a flourish, not a bit offended. "Too true."

Philippe breathed a sigh of relief as the door closed behind them and the condo was quiet. But then he felt his stomach clench. What if his distrust had destroyed any feelings Anne held for him? What if she was proving herself out of pride? He wandered through the small place, vaguely noting that the walls were yet another color, and stopped at Anne's bedroom door. *No guts, no glory,* as Anne always said. Philippe took a deep breath and knocked. "Can I come in, *Cherie?*"

"In a minute."

He waited, listening to the noises coming from within. Anne sounded like she was debating something to herself. He could hear her muttering.

The door swung open with Anne hiding behind it. "Philippe, I need your honest opinion. Do you think this is too, well, too..." She walked into view.

And Philippe's mouth dropped.

The woman was wearing a little slip of leopard print silk, more an undergarment than a dress. It was short, not even skimming the knee. Sandal straps, in the form of ribbons, reached up her legs, disappearing beneath the skirt. The top covered everything but didn't cover everything. It was obvious to Philippe that Anne wasn't wearing a bra. If he looked hard enough, and believe him, he was looking, he could see the outline of her nipples poking against the silk. Silk on silky skin, a lethal combination.

Then she turned to grab her purse and he saw the back. There wasn't much of it, the back dropping down to the dimples above her rear. *Mon Dieu, is she wearing underwear?* He didn't think so.

Philippe spun around to face the hallway, the impulse to throw her over his shoulder and slam the bedroom door behind them too strong. They should talk. Get things out in the open. But how could they talk when Philippe couldn't even put two words together.

"It's too much, isn't it?" Anne fretted. "I knew it was. I told Stanley... Oh, I'll change."

Now, she is going to get naked.

"*Mon amour,*" he groaned, breaking. One step and she was in his arms, his lips capturing hers, his hands on that slip of silk. She stiffened at first contact, but with gentle persistence, Anne yielded, softening. Philippe felt the fragile fabric give a little even under his tender onslaught. "I'll rip your dress." *What there was of it.*

"And it wrinkles badly." She stepped back, slipping the dress over her shoulders and placing it carefully on her dresser top.

Yes, she wore underwear but only the thinnest of thongs, her legs bare, her feet in those sandals. They'd have to stay on, it would take too long to remove them.

They should talk. *Mais peut-etre, peut-etre,* he could show her what he lost the words to say.

~ * ~

What was that? Anne shook out her silk dress, too bemused for once in her life to worry about wrinkles. That, what they shared, what Philippe showed her, was unlike anything they ever did before. Sure, they'd had sex before, wild, passionate monkey sex but this… this wasn't sex. Finally, Anne understood what making love was. She slipped the dress over her head, the fabric caressing her body. That was making love.

Philippe tucked his no longer so creaseless shirt into his fawn-colored khakis. "We're supposed to talk, *mon amour.* That's why I showed up early. Now we're late." He checked his watch. "And no clearer."

Mon amour. Isn't that "my love"? Or is it another endearment like Cherie?

"So let's talk." Anne straightened her dress, trying to make the silk cover more skin than it was supposed to. "Do you trust me?"

"Yes, even when logic said not to."

Good answer. Very good answer. "Do you care for me?"

"More than I have for anyone."

Another good answer. So good, it curled her toes.

Should she ask if he loved her? Anne twisted her mouth in thought. Nope, too risky. A good negotiator quit while she was ahead.

"Then that's all I need to know." For now.

"*Vraiment?*" Philippe obviously expected a big blow out. He wasn't going to get one.

"*Vraiment.*" Anne smiled up at him, wrapping her arms around his neck and kissed him soundly. She could feel him responding and tilted her head in question.

"Later," Philippe replied ruefully, "we should go to this thing."

~ * ~

Anne rethought the wisdom of the skimpy dress when she entered the pavilion. Gregory stared at her in a way that made Anne uncomfortable and Philippe's grip tighten.

"Anne, you look marvelous." Denise, in a flowing zebra print, was a picture of light and dark. "I'd like you to meet my fiancé, Derek."

Derek, the mystery man Denise met that day at the Cyber Café. "Pleased to meet you, Derek."

"Believe me the pleasure is all mine." His words were smooth but not too appreciative. Unlike a pair of blue eyes.

"Flying solo, Gregory?" Philippe grumbled.

"Not for long." The blond grinned and winked at Anne. "Plan to go after some big game tonight."

This drew an even darker look from her date. "The punishment for poaching is severe, my friend."

His threat made the lawyer laugh. "Don't worry. If the prey is properly tagged, I'll leave her alone."

"Alrighty then, I think I need a drink. Anne?" Denise hooked her arm, moving them towards the bar. "Men. They can be such idiots," she added out of earshot.

One specific idiot was forefront in Anne's mind. "Philippe doesn't trust me," she blurted out. She didn't know why. She simply had to say it to someone, to remind herself.

"Exactly. Idiots." Denise ordered a vodka martini for herself and a screwdriver for Anne. "Philippe doesn't even trust his own self right now. He likes you Anne."

"How can he when he…" *thinks I'm a thief and a liar and an all around louse?*

"People do many strange things when they're out of their comfort zone."

Anne didn't know about that.

"Look, I understand that you've had a career change." Anne guessed she could call closing down a business and getting fired a career change. "Don't you find yourself doing strange things? Things that don't make sense?"

Like wearing strange disguises and stalking people? "I've painted my condo three times in the past two weeks."

Denise threw back her head and laughed so loudly heads turned. "Anne, you're priceless. I adore you."

Was that a compliment? "Thank you, I think."

Denise didn't pause. "And Philippe likes you. Like he's never liked anyone before. That's why he's acting like an idiot. Derek was the same way when we met."

"Speaking of Derek…shouldn't we get back to your fiancé? He'll think you deserted him." Although the three men were deep in a conversation.

"Nah, he knows them almost as well as I do." Denise intercepted Anne's arched eyebrow look and hastened to correct, "Oh, maybe not as well."

"That has to be awkward." Anne was jealous even now of Denise's relationship with Philippe.

"At first, sure. Especially since I was seeing Philippe." *Then Derek was the one. The one Denise dropped Philippe for. A friend, too. Hurtful.* "But he was fine with me dating Derek. He didn't care."

Denise could tell herself that. Anne knew better. Even if Philippe's heart hadn't been touched, his pride would be bruised.

"Sorry to break up the tea party." Gregory draped his arms lightly around their bare shoulders. "Bogey at nine o'clock, Anne. Your date needs his wing woman."

Anne's eyes darted in Philippe's direction. Suzanne, clad in a skin tight tiger print, was standing too close to Philippe, her hands running up and down his sleeve. All her irritation at Denise's high handedness with Philippe's feelings transferred to Suzanne. *That clinging vine,* she had her shot at Philippe while Anne was out of the picture. Now things had changed. Anne was back.

"If you'll excuse me," Anne told Denise and Gregory sweetly, setting down her cocktail. Her icy smile warning them not to follow.

Philippe's face lit up with relief as she approached. "Anne, I was wondering where you went. You've met Suzanne, haven't you?"

"I have," Anne's voice was husky as she brushed Philippe's lips, her eyes sliding to a spluttering Suzanne. "Suzanne, thank you for keeping Philippe company. I know my interests are safe where you're involved."

"Suze." Perfect teeth bared in a fake smile. "I'm surprised to see you here, Anne. Could damage a company if its leader associated himself with the wrong kind of people."

Was Suzanne accusing her of unethical behavior? Here? In the middle of a party?

"Philippe, didn't you mention exactly that?" Philippe didn't answer, his brown eyes watching them warily. "Poor man, I don't know what caliber of a woman he settled for before he met me." Anne paused for impact and then asked, "Whom are you with tonight, Suzanne?"

Philippe sputtered. Anne ignored him, intent on Suzanne.

She looked less than fabulous tonight, faded and tired. "It's who you leave with that matters, little…" Suzanne looked down at Anne's less than bountiful chest, …"Anne."

The argument had fallen right into the gutter. "Interesting. Who would be so desperate as to steal a date at a charity event?" Anne wondered out loud, "Sounds tacky to me, not classy at all."

"What do you know about class?" Suzanne would have said more if not for the host taking the microphone.

"Enough to know that now is the time for silence," Anne hushed the woman.

~ * ~

Two hours later, Anne and Philippe embraced under the lamps in front of the tiger cage, "I think we've lost the rest of the group." Anne arched her back, gazing up at Philippe, his arms around her tight.

"Fortunately." He nuzzled her exposed neck. "Derek and Gregory were getting frustrated with our lack of contribution."

"And I," she reached down to grab his hard thigh, "was just getting frustrated."

"Suzanne?"

That woman had to be in their group. Anne wasn't proud of her behavior tonight, Suzanne's presence egging her on. "Actually I was thinking about you."

"Were you? Then come, *Cherie.*" Philippe grabbed her hand, dragging her off the lit path into the shadows. "Show me the big dipper again. In case I lose my way."

"It's cloudy." They found a square of grass. He rolled her in his arms upon it.

"I have confidence that you can find it." His hands crept up her dress. "If you look hard enough."

Anne felt him pressing against her. "You look hard enough," the words slipped out before she could stop them. She got her ear nipped for her sauciness. "Philippe, what if someone sees?" Anne protested as her thong was pulled down.

Though the thought of getting caught added more excitement to the encounter.

"Lucky them," and his lips covered hers.

~ * ~

"And that, *M'sieur* Lamont, I believe is where the North Star should be," Anne guessed. She couldn't see the star but that's where it had been a couple days ago. Sated and happy, Anne was half decently covered. Philippe's shirt was off but he had pulled up his pants. They lay there in silence, watching the sky.

"I've a conference call at the office tomorrow." Philippe hugged her closer. "Will you back me up, *Cherie?*"

Back him up. Be part of his team again. *Tomorrow? That could work.*

Ginny was coming over to use her computer, her own in for repair. Anne didn't need to stick around the condo. Her sister would likely appreciate the privacy.

Before Anne could say yes, she heard some rustling in the bushes behind them. "What was that?" She sat up. *Isn't this how horror flicks go? A mad man waiting in the dark?*

Philippe pulled her back down again. "Could be a wild critter. The zoo is full of them. Crazy concept."

"Don't laugh at me," and then Anne laughed at herself. *Axe murderers and serial killers, products of an overactive imagination.* "And we should head back. People will be wondering where we went."

"I doubt they will." Philippe shamelessly looked up her dress as she stood.

"Stop that." She batted his shoulders.

"If I have to." He rose to his feet. "You're hungry, aren't you? That's the rush."

"Nah, my appetites have been satisfied," Anne purred suggestively, her hand rubbing over his bare chest.

"At least one has been satisfied. I ensured that." Philippe tugged on his shirt and Anne buttoned it up for him. "But your man needs to eat."

Her man. That sounded nice.

Philippe took both of her hands and swung her around, her legs actually clearing the ground with the momentum. She laughed. He brought her close. They kissed.

Then they started the trek back to the pavilion, Anne pulling twigs from her hair as they walked. "I should stop here." She tested the rest room door; it was open. "I can't go in like this, full of leaves and grass."

Philippe eyed her and grinned. "It'd leave no doubt as to what we were doing."

"Can't have that. I'd say I tangled with a bush." It would take a while for her to repair the damage and they were mere steps from the pavilion entrance. "Philippe, go ahead. Eat. I'll meet you inside."

Philippe took a deep breath of the night air. They could smell the food through the open doors. "Are you sure, *Cherie?*"

"I'm sure." She gave him a quick kiss and a push in that direction. "I'll be a few minutes. I think I'm in quite the state."

"A state that I plan to get you in again before the night ends," Philippe warned with a knowing grin as he sauntered off.

What a man, Anne thought as she entered the empty restroom. Already twice today and he was promising more. Anne laughed once more as she looked at her reflection. Thank goodness, she decided to clean up. She looked like a wild woman, her hair gnarled and full of leaves and other debris. The dress, well, it was dreadfully wrinkled. The only solution was to wet it down and try to smooth it out. She had to do that first if she wanted it to dry. Anne ran paper towels under the faucet and passed it over the silk fabric. That would work, she noted with satisfaction.

Anne was bent over trying unsuccessfully to rake a brush through her tangled hair when the door opened. She straightened up, groaning as she saw who it was. Of all the people, it had to be Suzanne. And alone.

"Hello, bitch," the blonde woman snarled as her conversation starter. "Did you have fun tonight? With my man?"

"He's not…" Anne didn't get to finish.

"Shut up, just shut up. I've heard enough from you tonight. This time, I'll do the talking." She sounded so irrational, Anne played it prudent and kept quiet. "I hope you enjoyed yourself. This'll be the last time you see Philippe for a long, long time."

"I'm seeing him tomorrow." *Oh, what have I done?* Anne cursed her vanity. Suzanne wasn't in a mood to be messed with.

"Do you think that's wise, plain little Anne?" Suzanne walked toward her. Anne backed up until she couldn't back up anymore, blocked by the tiled bathroom wall. "Do you think that's healthy?" Before Anne could react, her arms were in the woman's stronger grasp, painted red fingernails digging into her skin, drawing blood. Anne tried to twist away but there was at least a foot difference in their heights and a corresponding difference in strength. Suzanne's eyes were glazed and glassy.

"Suzanne…" Anne felt the cold fingers of fear creep up her spine.

"Michael's mine." Anne could smell the liquor on her breath. "I want you to leave him alone."

Michael? Wasn't this about Philippe? Was the woman completely crazy?

"Suzanne—"

But Anne was stopped from continuing. The blonde raised one hand and slapped her solidly across the face. "My name is Suze, get it right for a change, and Philippe's mine. I'm everything he could possibly want. I've guaranteed that, and no one, especially not someone as plain and common as you, is going to take him away from me."

Anne's ears rang from the blow. She had to talk to Suzanne. Calm her down. That was her only shot.

"I—" but again Anne was slapped, this time a full backhand across her other cheek, Suzanne's large diamond ring leaving a stinging trail of scratches.

"No, you listen to me. I want you to stay away." Anne was shaken forcibly, her teeth clattering together, her head snapping back and forth. One more lip splitting slap and Anne fell into darkness.

Seventeen

"There shouldn't be any line-up in here," a familiar voice pierced the quiet night air, causing Anne to sit up straight.

Crap, Suze, Suzanne, whatever that crazy calls herself at the moment, is coming back. And with reinforcements this time. Anne looked around in a panic. She wanted desperately to move from her spot, legs sprawled out, basically bare bum sitting on the cold restroom floor, but couldn't. Her head was spinning and her limbs were shaky. If she got up, nine chances out of ten, she'd faint again. Could she crawl out the door in time? Judging by the closeness of the voices, nope. She wouldn't make it. Anne might as well stay put. She was trapped.

Suzanne filled the doorway, appearing even taller than she normally was, from Anne's vantage point on the floor. Lord, she was an amazon, and she had a cool, calm expression on her face like beating people up was a daily occurrence. Probably was. Crazy woman likely pulled the wings off flies and drowned kittens for kicks.

Anne's fears eased as she realized who was with Suzanne.

"Anne, is that you?" Denise's anxious face puckered around Suzanne's shoulder.

Denise, Denise would help her. Wouldn't she? But then… what was she doing with Suzanne? Denise and Suzanne? Together? Was charming, kind Denise friends with that psychopath?

"It *is* you. Your face." Denise rushed to her side. "My God, Anne. What happened to you?"

Anne peered up at Suzanne's expressionless visage. The unruffled blonde raised a finely plucked eyebrow as if to say, *I dare you to tell her.*

Tell Denise what? What could Anne tell her? That the haughty, sophisticated Suzanne had beaten the stuffing out of her in between cocktails? Denise wouldn't believe it. Anne could hardly believe it herself.

She batted down her anger and tried to smile, her face feeling swollen and sore, her bottom lip puffy. "It's so embarrassing, Denise. I fell down." That was true. Of course she fell down after being punched out. But that didn't need to be mentioned, did it?

"No shit, Sherlock. I didn't think you voluntarily sprawled out on a dirty public toilet floor." Denise crouched down and touched Anne's forehead. Though the cut wasn't that deep, it bled steadily, running in a trickle down her face.

"I must have hit it on the sink as I passed out," Anne offered as an explanation. Could have happened. She couldn't quite recall. For all Anne knew, Suzanne cracked her on the head while she was out cold.

"You poor thing." Suzanne wetted a paper towel under the faucet and handed it to Denise, convincingly playing the oh-so-concerned woman. She was a good actress. Either that or she had some sort of split personality. Like a good Suzanne and a bad Suze.

"Ouch. Why'd you pass out, Anne?" Denise pressed the compress against the cut, trying to slow the bleeding. It felt good, cool against her hot skin.

"Yes, Anne, why'd you pass out?" Suzanne echoed, her voice holding a hint of warning. "There must be a rational explanation. People don't faint for no good reason."

Anne's chin tilted. What was Suzanne going to do if she tattled? Beat her again? "You know how it is, Suzanne." Anne wasn't going to lie. She was done with lying. Let Suzanne come up with the explanation.

"Must have been the heat." Suzanne smiled, her red lips an angry slash against her tanned face. "I felt a bit light headed myself."

"It is quite warm for fall," Denise murmured, "and the scavenger hunt required a lot of running around." Suzanne passed her another wet cloth that Anne used to wipe the grime off her face. It came back bloody. Anne couldn't see herself but she must be a mess. "Better?" Anne asked Denise, ignoring Suzanne.

"Oh, dear Anne, your face... it looks so awful," Suzanne volunteered, too blasted gleefully.

And whose fault is that? Huh? Crazy woman.

"But you're looking better," Denise offered, "Puffy, but not quite as bloody. Next, let's get you up. You can't be comfortable on that dirty floor. Can you stand?"

Anne held out her hands palm down. They trembled. Better not chance another fall. "Nope. Not yet. I think I'll sit here for a bit."

Denise straightened up again and exchanged a look with Suzanne. "We should get Philippe. He'll know what to do. He's good at that type of thing. Suze, could you?"

Anne didn't want to face Philippe. It meant more questions and more lies, but she supposed Denise was right. She couldn't go back into the party. She looked a mess, her dress filthy and torn, her face cut and bruised. Anne checked her forehead with a semi-clean fingertip. No blood. At least her skull stopped bleeding. That was a good thing.

"You go find Philippe. I'll stay with Anne." Suzanne's smile was pure evil, her eyes hard as shiny marble.

Leave her alone with Suzanne? *No freakin' way.* Anne grew alarmed.

What was that psycho up to now? Was she going to finish her off? Right here, on the floor of the ladies' room? Would zoo-visiting moms and toddlers find her dead body in the morning?

Anne couldn't let that happen. It would traumatize the kiddies. "I'd rather Denise stay. I need to talk to her about something."

"Oh, poor Anne, always such a trooper. I don't think you should be talking to anyone about anything right now." Suzanne wasn't about to let her escape. "Denise, you'd be able to find Philippe faster. Go." Anne watched helplessly as her only ally was pushed out of the restroom.

Suzanne turned to Anne with a satisfied smirk, her job accomplished. "Yes, poor little Anne, your face does look bad. You weren't beautiful to start with but Philippe isn't going to think you so cute now."

"Still cuter than he'd think you," Anne snapped, "So now what, Suze or Suzanne, whoever you are, did you come back to admire your handiwork or are you going to finish off the job you started?" If she were destined to die tonight on a bathroom floor, she'd go out fighting. Get a few good insults in before she was smacked down again.

Suzanne didn't look like she was going to smack down anyone. She preened in front of the mirror, powdering down her straight narrow nose.

"Neither, dear hysterical Anne. I came back to ensure you kept your big mouth shut."

"Hmmm... forgot to do that before knocking me out the first time, did you Suzanne? Not great planning on your part."

"It's Suze, and I excel at planning. Though I didn't plan on you being such a lightweight. Thought a woman Philippe screwed would have more fight in her." Suzanne reapplied her shocking red lipstick.

"I wasn't prepared for hand-to-hand combat tonight. Philippe is going to have quite the shocker when I tell him what you're capable of, Suzanne."

"You're many things, Anne, most of them less than complimentary. However, I trust you're not stupid too." Suzanne was unruffled by Anne's threat. "I don't think you'll want to share what happened tonight. Philippe has zero tolerance for weakness; indeed he deplores it in anyone. So even if he believes you, which is unlikely," she flayed out her long fingers, the perfect blood red nails reflecting the fluorescent lights, "he'll be very unimpressed with your inability to handle the situation. Either way, you'll lose."

The woman may be a few bricks short of a load, but she was right. Philippe needn't be involved. Anne would handle Suzanne herself. Once her head stopped spinning.

"Lose? To whom? This isn't a competition, Suzanne."

"Oh, I disagree." Suzanne pulled out a hair. Was it a gray one? Anne hoped so. She hoped Suzanne's entire dyed head was full of naturally coarse gray hair. "I think it is a competition, a very key competition, with Philippe as the grand prize. I don't intend to lose, Anne. He's mine."

"You can't have him. He's with me." Anne had to get that through Suzanne's muddled brain.

"Poor judgment on his part. He'll see the error of his ways and come back to me." Suzanne sounded confident about that. Anne wondered why. Philippe had been so blatant in rejecting her.

"I wouldn't be too sure. Remember what happened with Michael," Anne taunted, dragging up a name that drew Suzanne's ire previously. Anne didn't know the story but she did know that it bothered Suzanne. The comment scored a direct hit.

Suzanne spun on her six-inch heels and approached her, her face twisted in anger. Anne struggled to get out of her way, wiggling her butt backwards crab-like until she reached the wall again. When would she learn to back herself out the door?

"Philippe will be no Michael." Suzanne crouched down. Anne was certain that she was going to be slapped, but for the voices coming from outside and growing louder.

Would Suzanne have enough time to hurt her? She did. She didn't risk raising her hand. Instead Suzanne squeezed Anne's bare shoulder hard. It looked to an outsider like she was being consoled as Suzanne's nails cut into her skin. "Anne, Anne, calm down," the blonde babbled.

"Anne, are you okay?" Philippe's deep voice filled the small space and Anne almost sobbed with relief. *He was here. Finally.*

Suzanne threw Anne a warning look before she turned, a smile transforming her face back to beauty. "Philippe, thank goodness, you're here. Anne was acting irrational, crazy like. I was so scared. I didn't know what to do."

"Was not," Anne muttered between gritted teeth. *Crazy?* Suzanne, that nutcase, dared to call her crazy? She was the only one of the two with any rational thought, and how exactly did Suzanne manage to sound like the victim with Anne sitting on the floor?

Philippe's voice was embarrassingly slow and calm. "*Cherie*, what happened? How did this...?" He reached out to touch her face, tracing from her cut forehead down to her swollen lips.

"I fell," Anne offered the lame excuse again. She couldn't tell Philippe the truth but she wouldn't lie to him either.

"She fainted," Suzanne filled in, "hit her head on the sink, poor little Anne." Could Suzanne make her sound any more pathetic?

"Fainted." Philippe's long fingers flitted lightly over her skin again, resting on the scratch on her cheek. Trust his keen eyes to find the one cut on her face not in line with the rest of the story. Was he looking at Suzanne's hands, at the big, sparkling ring on her right hand? Or was that hopeful thinking?

"You look bad, *Cherie*. How are you feeling?"

"A bit foolish." Anne struggled gamely to her feet. Her legs wobbled, weak, she had a tough time getting them to do what she wanted, and held onto Philippe's arm for support.

"There's nothing foolish about feeling poorly." Philippe swung her into his arms. Nestled against his solid, muscled shoulder, Anne breathed in his comforting musky male smell. As Anne let her defenses down, weariness seeped through her body. Philippe was here. No one could harm her now. Not even Suzanne.

"I stayed with her." Suzanne sounded like a puppy looking for approval. She got it.

"Thank you, Suzanne, that means a lot to me," Philippe murmured. *Is that Suzanne's ploy? To look like the good girl?* Anne didn't know. She couldn't think about it right now. She had a pounding headache that was getting worse by the minute. "Anne means a lot to me." Then to Anne, *Cherie*, I'm taking you home." Denise held the door as he turned sideways to exit.

The cool night breeze splashed against her skin. To Anne's embarrassment, both Gregory and Denise's fiancé, Derek, were waiting outside. She tried to cover up a bit, a futile gesture, as they got an eyeful of bare leg. With the dress being so short, it couldn't be helped.

"Is she—?" Gregory's voice cracked on the question. He sounded sincerely worried.

"She's fine. Banged up a bit but fine. I'm taking her home. Could you call my chauffeur to bring the car around, Gregory? My hands are full."

Blue eyes traveled up her thighs. "Lucky you," Gregory muttered as he flipped on his phone and paced away.

Suzanne disappeared back into the washroom, returning in only a minute, a tan clasp purse in her hands.

"Anne, your purse. You forgot it."

That's right, she left it on the sink, before all this started.

But? Suzanne to remember it? The blonde held out the bag. Why was she being so helpful?

Their eyes met and then, with a smile, Suzanne released the purse. The move was coolly calculated. Anne hadn't a shot at catching it. The bag couldn't have been closed either as its contents spilled all over the sidewalk.

Something rolled out of the purse toward Gregory, a shape Anne didn't recognize. While on the phone, Gregory reached down and picked the object up. After a quick glance, he pocketed it. *Why? What could that have been?*

Anne had to wait for his call to finish to find out. Then Gregory held out his hand to her, his palm down, hiding what it held. "I believe this is yours, Anne." He slid a plastic container into her hand, his blue eyes soft.

A pill canister? In her purse? No. That couldn't be. It had to be some mistake. "Gregory, this isn't mine."

"Anne, I think it is," Gregory insisted.

She knew it wasn't. Anne examined it closer. What did the label say? *Prozac?* Wasn't that an anti-depressant? She glanced up into Philippe's questioning eyes and stated firmly, "Gregory, it isn't mine. I don't take drugs. I don't even use *Tylenol.*"

"It has your name on it, Anne," Gregory's tone was gentle, non-judgmental.

Crap, so it did. Anne looked at Suzanne and her eyes narrowed, no doubt in Anne's mind who planted it. *Blast it, that woman is evil.* She must have planned the entire horrible night from start to finish.

"Gregory, you have to believe me, this isn't mine," Anne repeated. Suzanne whispered something in Denise's ear and the friendly blonde's face changed from concern to sympathy. Anne shifted unhappily in Philippe's arms.

First a fainting spell in the bathroom. Now a pill container full of uppers. They were all going to think her crazy.

"It's okay, Anne. Gregory, could you look into it?" Philippe took the container from Anne and passed it to Gregory, not bothering to hide it from view.

"But," Gregory protested.

"It's not hers," Philippe's voice was firm, "It must have been mislabeled. Find out whose pills they really are, Gregory, and let us know immediately. The pharmacy should be able to tell you, as Anne's legal representative."

"Philippe, please don't embarrass the poor girl," Suzanne purred. "She's obviously under some stress. Anne likely forgot about the prescription, what with her illness and all."

"No, Suzanne." Anne's chin jutted out. "I did not forget. It's not mine and I want to know whose it is. I'd also like to know how the pills got in my purse."

Suzanne was the one squirming now. "I don't think you do, Anne. I don't think you want to air your dirty laundry."

"I haven't any dirty laundry and I'm sure I do." What did Anne have to lose? They all thought she was crazy anyway. Couldn't get much worse.

"If you feel that strongly, I'll help Gregory." Suzanne planned to cover her tracks.

"All it'll take are a couple phone calls." Gregory shrugged. "I can manage that on my own, Suzanne."

That would make her sweat. Anne smiled up at the lawyer. "I'm confident that Gregory will be able to handle it. Can I call you tomorrow?"

Gregory beamed, happy to be at service. "I'll look forward to it."

"Spreading it a bit thick, aren't you?" Philippe grumbled softly in her ear. *What could he complain about?* Philippe delegated the sensitive job to Gregory when he should have handled it himself. Anne gave the lawyer another wide smile as he opened the car door for them.

When Anne and Philippe were finally alone in the car, the driver occupied with the business of driving, Philippe examined Anne's face again, his fingers gentle. "So, *Cherie*, talk to me. Tell me what happened."

Anne pondered the situation. Tempting but Suzanne was right. She should deal with it.

"I don't want to talk about it, Philippe. It isn't important."

She didn't want to talk about it? He was supposed to take her word that those pills weren't hers, even though the label damned her, yet she didn't trust him enough to confide in him? He didn't believe the story about her fainting due to the heat either. Anne may be slight but she was no delicate flower to wilt away in the above average temperatures. Plus the night was not nearly as hot as their lawn sex. If she felt fragile, Philippe would have known then.

The cuts and bruises on her cheek hadn't come from falling. There were bruises and scratch marks on her arms, clear imprints of fingers on her beige skin. Like someone held her against her will. Held her. His Anne. Against her will. And then beat her. In the ladies' room…that meant with another female. But who? Denise?

Couldn't be. Denise was with Derek, waiting for them, when Philippe entered the pavilion. So who else? Suzanne? He couldn't picture Suzanne attacking anyone. She might break a sweat, or God forbid, a nail. She wouldn't have stuck around either, acting like Nurse Betty. Not if she were guilty. *Non*, it couldn't have been Suzanne.

And what was up with the pills? Were they Anne's? Why else would they be in her purse? But she said they weren't and Philippe believed her. If she were in trouble, she'd come to him… wouldn't she? Wouldn't she?

"Anne, if you need someone to talk to…" Philippe smoothed her hair. Anne rewarded him with a lopsided smile. She, thankfully, had no idea how puffy her face was, and her spirits hadn't sagged one bit.

Non, she didn't need anti-depressants. Or did she?

"Thanks Philippe. Your offer means a lot to me. And that you trusted me about those crazy pills, even though the evidence…" She took his hand, her fingertips circling his palm.

"What would a person gain from doing that?" He searched her big brown eyes. They softened and she smiled, her face glowing. *Merde*, she was beautiful, even with her cuts and scrapes and the puffiness, her beauty shone from those eyes.

"Whatever it is, it must be worth the trouble," and she snuggled into his chest, her head burrowing into the nook of his neck. She knew. Or at least she suspected. Was it the same person that attacked her?

"We'll wait to hear what Gregory finds out." He would get answers then. Philippe held her as securely as he dared. He didn't want to hurt her.

"Don't worry, Philippe. I can handle it." Anne yawned delicately, her entire body vibrating against his.

Yes, she could handle it but she didn't need to. Didn't she understand that? Obviously not. She didn't trust him. *Time. It will take time to rebuild,* Philippe reminded himself.

Philippe had plenty of quiet time to keep on reminding himself. Anne fell asleep and didn't wake up when they pulled up in front of her residential complex. She didn't wake up when Philippe carried her to the condo, amazed about how tiny she was, fitted in his arms. She didn't wake up as he juggled her while searching through her purse for the key.

Anne whimpered a bit as he laid her on the bed, the sound tugging at his heart. Did she hurt or was it a bad memory? What could he do? He looked down at her. There was one thing. Her dress was filthy. He should remove it. Then he stopped short, memories flooding his mind. Weeks ago as he did tonight, he undressed Anne. While she was drunk.

He also went through her purse to find her key. No pill containers in that bag. No Prozac.

Then he searched through her bathroom cabinets looking for mouthwash. She was right. She didn't even have a bottle of pain reliever. Her medicine cabinet was bare of any medication. Tension left his body. He had the physical proof to back up his faith in Anne. The pills couldn't be hers.

"*Hmmm*...come to bed, Philippe." Anne reached out for him, her voice drowsy.

She wanted him by her side. That said something, didn't it? Couldn't he bring her comfort? Keep her safe? Philippe smiled at her. "You need to get naked, *Cherie.*"

Anne groaned, her hand at her forehead. "Not tonight, dear, I have a headache."

He frowned. That wasn't a joke, she did have a headache, "and you don't have *Tylenol.*"

"I don't need *Tylenol,* that's a placebo, I need sleep," and she yawned again.

"Come, let's get rid of this dress." He slipped the silk off her, trying not to dwell on her small perky breasts and dark berry nipples. "It smells like the potty." Philippe held the dress up with regret. "I think it's ruined." It was covered with stains from blood, grass and some untraceable dirt.

"First time I wore it too." Anne's bottom lip curled. "I love that dress."

"*Ahhhh...moi aussi.*" Philippe went to work on her sandals. It took some concentration. The straps were very complicated, criss-crossing up her leg. "Don't fret, *Cherie*. I'll buy you another dress."

One index finger raised up. "You owe me a pair of underwear too."

"Underwear?" Philippe didn't remember why the underwear but he would buy her anything she wanted.

"The red ones, you ripped them, while you were punishing me, remember?" Anne smiled as though it was a happy memory.

Strange peculiar woman he had. Here he was twisting himself with guilt over his less than stellar behavior and she had enjoyed herself.

"*D'accord, d'accord*, I'll buy you a pair of underwear."

"And shoes."

He finished the one leg and started on the other sandal. This time it went faster, Philippe having learned the trick behind unlacing them.

"You owe me a pair of black pumps, Philippe."

Oh, yes, the ones they left in the garden, right after looking at the stars and right before she started vomiting. "And a pair of black pumps." Philippe kissed the sole of her left foot, making Anne kick. "Maybe I should buy extras for future clothing mishaps."

"Maybe you should." This good idea earned him a kiss on his chin as he bent over to tuck her into the bed.

"Aren't you coming too?" Her smile held pure encouragement.

Philippe didn't even hesitate. He broke all speed records for getting undressed, peeling off his clothes, leaving only his underwear on. He wouldn't leave her alone tonight.

He lightly glazed the four scratches on her shoulder, the results of a person's not so gentle fingertips. Tonight someone had targeted his Anne, his woman. Despite her wishes to take care of it herself, Philippe would get to the bottom of it. But that thought drifted away as she spooned her body into his.

Eighteen

"You want some corn flakes?" Philippe rattled the box at Anne as she wandered into the kitchen.

"I have corn flakes?" Anne eyed the package with suspicion. She had cereal? Where'd he get that? Not a breakfast eater, she couldn't remember buying cereal. Ever.

"I found it stuck deep in the back of the cupboard, neatly packed away in a plastic container." Philippe opened the flap and tossed a handful into his mouth. He promptly spit them back out into the sink. "I don't think this is fresh, *Cherie.*"

"I'm sure it isn't." Anne took the offensive box from him, checking the "best before" date. "Yep, expired three years ago." Must have been when Ginny came to stay while looking for an apartment of her own. Time to clear out the cabinets. Anne threw the cereal in the trash.

"Is the coffee…?" He eyed the already gurgling liquid.

"Now, coffee I drink. I make it every morning."

Philippe opened the fridge door, looking for something to eat. "You have eggs." He took the carton out, weighing one in his hand. "They're okay. And cheese." He placed a block of cheddar on the counter. "Oh, and a green pepper." The man sounded delighted with his findings.

"I do cook." Anne acted indignant, but was secretly glad she bought the green pepper. She didn't know what she was going to do with it at the time, green peppers having been on sale.

Philippe's expression said he didn't buy her protest.

"Okay, maybe not every single day," Anne admitted, "but I do cook. I even have an onion somewhere and there should be a tomato rolling around in the crisper."

He found it. "You're right. If you grate the cheese, sparrow, I'll make you a killer omelet."

"A killer omelet?" Anne unwrapped the cheese. Was killer a good descriptor for food? She had a taco once that was almost a killer, she was sick for days.

Philippe pulled out the cutting board and quickly diced the veggies. He seemed to know his way around the kitchen. "*D'accord, d'accord,* bad choice of words. It won't kill you, far from it. I'm a terrific cook."

"And a modest one too." Anne wasn't paying attention to what she herself was supposed to be doing. She narrowly escaped grating her fingertips.

Her billionaire venture capitalist could cook? So Philippe was skilled in the boardroom, bedroom, and kitchen. Anne, in contrast, entered her kitchen only to clean. No, that wasn't exactly true. She knew how to open a can in thirty seconds flat. Somehow, she didn't think this skill would impress Philippe.

"Where'd you learn how to cook?" *Did he want all the cheese grated?* Anne didn't know. She'd keep grating until he said stop.

"*Ma Maman*, of course," like it was obvious. "She's a good cook. In Europe, every meal is a celebration. Fresh ingredients, freshly prepared, no cans." He clucked disapprovingly before popping some grated cheese in his mouth.

No cans. Anne guessed she hadn't fooled him at all.

"How did you manage not to learn to cook?" It was her turn to be grilled. "Didn't your mother teach you?"

"Oh, she taught, my poor mom, she taught and taught and taught, only nothing stuck." Anne grinned, remembering her mother's frustration. "But I have other talents. I'm great at dialing delivery."

As if on cue, the doorbell rang. "Saved by the bell. It's probably Ginny."

"*Oui, oui*, go dodge your duties, *mon amour*," Philippe berated.

Anne gave him a hug and a kiss on the cheek as she passed. "It's for the best, Philippe, believe me."

Ginny's eyes widened as Anne swung the door open, reminding her that her face looked bad, bruised and puffy.

"What happened to you?" Her little sister pushed her way into the condo, carrying a clear plastic box of loose papers. No file folders for Ginny. She thrived on chaos.

"I fell." That answer was getting tired.

"Would you like an omelet too, Ginny?" Philippe called from the kitchen.

"No thank you. I already ate," and then Ginny's voice dropped so only Anne could hear, "Whoa, whoa, what's he doing here, Annie?"

They watched as Philippe whisked the eggs in a bowl, a never-before-worn frilly apron over his grass stained, blood speckled white shirt from the previous night, the shirt untucked over equally rumpled khakis. *Domestic Diva meets Outback Jack.*

"After what happened last night." Anne gingerly touched the cut on her forehead. She hadn't put a bandage on it, allowing it to breathe and hopefully heal faster.

"Your mysterious fall, like I believe that." Ginny was clearly disgusted at the lie. "You claim I'm intelligent, yet you try to fool me with that bullshit story. Why would you bother… Oh, no, was it Philippe that…"

"No, no, it wasn't him, Ginny. He didn't hurt me. Philippe would never hurt a woman, he loves them too much." Anne stopped that line of thinking immediately. All she needed now was a visit from her overprotective father.

"Then what happened?" Ginny wouldn't let it go.

"It's all so embarrassing, I'd rather not talk about it." She hadn't told anyone, not even Philippe that it was Suzanne. What was the point? It hadn't had the result Suzanne was counting on and Anne doubted she would try it again.

Ginny studied her, her face scrunched up in thought. Then her expression cleared.

"Got in a fight, didn't you?" Ginny hooted, "My big sis got into a brawl. Oh, man, that's priceless. Did you get a few good licks in?"

"Hush." Now that Ginny guessed correctly, Anne wouldn't lie to her but she didn't want Philippe to overhear. He remained hunched over the stove, and Anne relaxed. "Philippe doesn't know and unfortunately no. I didn't. I'm more a lover than a fighter." Anne was never one to get into physical confrontations.

"I can see that." Ginny nodded to Philippe, rustling through the drawers, finally finding one of those flipper things. "So he stayed over to keep you company, Annie? Strictly platonic?"

"Yep." Anne sighed. Last night, at least. Philippe was treating her like she was made of the most delicate china. He definitely wasn't making any moves on her.

"God," Ginny huffed in disappointment. "He's not another Stanley, is he? Philippe comes across as so masculine."

"No, not another Stanley. Philippe is all hetero." *Oh, boy, is he ever.* "He was concerned about me being hurt."

"How disappointing," Ginny summed Anne's feelings up completely. "Are you that bad?"

"No, no, I'm fine. He's being careful."

"Sweet. I guess I like him, Annie. He's a bit frightening at first, all forceful and angry, but once you get to know him…"

"I know." Philippe was really a nice guy under the bad-ass disguise and Anne was glad her sister liked him.

"If you'd rather I came back," Ginny offered, setting the box down on the floor.

"Nah." Anne shook her head. "Philippe and I are going to his office. The condo is yours for the day, but first, I have to clean up."

"Hey, don't clean up on my account." Ginny opened up the laptop, booting it up. "I had to deal with your room growing up."

"My room?" Anne knew the script. This was a long running

argument.

"Was Anne's room a mess? I find that hard to believe." Philippe wandered out of the kitchen, morning growth shadowing his chin, carrying a steaming omelet on a plate.

Anne took it happily, her stomach growling at the gorgeous aroma. *It smelled good. It looked good.* She put a forkful in her mouth. *And it tasted good.*

"Why?" Anne asked Philippe between bites of egg.

"You're a little anal retentive, *Cherie.*" His boyish smile took the edge of his words. "How's the omelet?"

"Better than an *Egg McMuffin,*" Anne teased, knowing this would prick his pride.

It did. "*Mon Dieu,* is that your only basis of comparison? I don't know when those *McDonald's* eggs last saw a shell."

Ginny watched the two of them, eyes sparkling with humor.

"Ginny, are you certain you don't want an omelet?" Philippe turned that devastating smile on Anne's sister. "You look like a woman who'd appreciate such a work of art."

"No, thanks Philippe, though it does look tempting. I already ate this morning. Unlike Anne, I can cook."

Oh, low blow! "And don't forget, she's the cute sister too." Anne put her hands on both sides of Ginny's cheeks and pressed, making a fish face.

"But golly, *Tin Man,* I have no brain." Released, Ginny's head wobbled like a bobble head doll.

"*Tin Man? Merde.* That means I'm stuck with the sister with no heart." Philippe cursed with a grin. "That doesn't bode well for us, *Cherie.*"

"You mean it doesn't bode well for you." Anne squeezed his hand. "I'm heartless, remember? I'll be okay." She wandered into the kitchen, placing her dirty plate in the sink, the remnants of Philippe's own breakfast already in the basin. "You really can cook, *M'sieur* Lamont."

"Told ya." Philippe followed Anne, leaving a laughing Ginny in the living room. "I can cook. Hate cleaning up afterwards, but I can cook."

"That's okay, I like cleaning," and she did. Putting everything in its proper place was so peaceful.

"I cook. You clean. We make a good team, you and I." She got the impression he meant more than cooking.

Anne rinsed off the plates and stacked them in the dishwasher. "We do. And thank you, Philippe. For everything."

He wrapped his arms around her shoulders. "Thank you, Anne for not giving up."

Not giving up. Like her heart had a choice? Anne was getting weepy and Philippe disliked weakness. "I guess I'd better get ready now, take a quick shower."

"And I'd better watch in case you slip and fall again."

The irony peppering the words told her that Philippe didn't believe her either. That wasn't too surprising. Falling might explain the cut on her chin but not the scratches and bruises across her cheeks.

"I don't think it'll happen again." She shut the bedroom door behind them, blocking out the sound of Ginny, typing away.

Philippe plopped down on the already made-up bed. Anne remembered how they had shared it last night, his arms holding her tightly as she slept, lending her his strength. "It certainly won't. I plan to keep an eye on you."

"Really." Anne turned on the water in the en-suite shower stall. "Do you have your eye on me now?" She let her robe slip to the ground. She wanted to show him that she was none the worse for wear.

"I do but, *Cherie,* your sister's here." Philippe moved towards her with glitter in his eyes.

He'd make love to her on the lawn at the zoo but not with her sister in the next room? *Peculiar, prudish man.*

"Then all you'd better do is watch." Anne wet her hand in the shower and then ran it over her breasts, leaving droplets everywhere she touched.

"You are indeed heartless, *Cherie.*" Philippe reached out to trace the outline of the bruise on her hip. She had landed on it when she fell. "Are you sure you're okay?"

"It looks nasty." The bruise was an angry purple color. "But I feel fine."

"It was Suzanne, wasn't it?" He looked her straight in the eye.

"No." Anne had no choice but to lie outright.

"Yes, it was. Your lips pucker up when you lie, *Cherie.*"

Blast it. The man paid attention.

"*Mais* Suzanne of all people? I saw her hands, Anne. She didn't even chip her nail polish."

That crazy woman had been right. Philippe thought her weak. "She caught me by surprise."

"The first time," he muttered as he belly flopped on the bed.

Yeah, surprise was a good excuse for the first punch but not the second or third. She had no explanation for that. Anne spent the rest of the shower rehearsing witty replies in her head.

When they emerged from the bedroom, Anne felt frustrated yet clean, clothed in a simple t-shirt and jeans, her wet hair pulled up in a ponytail. Ginny, on the other hand, had a worried look on her pretty face.

"Is something wrong?" Anne asked. What had happened, in the space of a shower, to concern her sister.

"I don't know, Anne, you tell me. I turned on your computer and you must have it automatically set up for instant messenger because I started getting notifications right away. I know that I shouldn't have read them, I'm sorry, but…"

Oh, blast. Anne forgot about that.

"Mais?" Philippe's voice was gruff.

Her sister looked at his stormy face and gulped. Anne understood. Philippe was intimidating in his full bastard mode. "But some of them, actually a lot of them, weren't very nice. They were horrible, awful, nasty."

Could Ginny possibly use any more adjectives?

Anne avoided Philippe's searching eyes. A couple weeks ago, about the time she left Lamont Ventures, she started getting nasty e-mails. They weren't that big of a deal. There weren't many of them, maybe a few an hour, and she ignored them, sending them straight to trash.

"Who's sending them, Ginny?" Philippe demanded, "Did you get the address?"

Anne didn't need to hear the addresses. She knew them by heart.

"As far as I can tell, two e-mailers…ok896 and lu1197, no other information." Both Ginny and Philippe looked at Anne for an explanation. She guessed she should give them something, not that she knew much. "I don't know who they are. They never sign their e-mails, and I'm not concerned. These things happen from time to time. Part of making business decisions; no one likes every one I make." Anne tried to ease Ginny's fears. Philippe, she would deal with later. Later became right now.

"Let me see them." Philippe wasn't buying Anne's explanation. Ginny scrambled out of the chair and Philippe took over. He opened the taskbar and scrolled down her messages.

Anne resisted looking over his shoulder. She didn't have to watch. She received enough of them to have a good sense of what they said. They were all basically the same.

He swiveled in the chair. "Anne, these aren't harmless. These are threats. Who is it? Suzanne?"

"I don't think so," and that was the truth.

Sure, she suspected, as Philippe clearly did, that both e-mail addresses belonged to the same person. They were too similar not to be. The sentence structures were the same. So was the tone.

But was that same person Suzanne? No. The e-mails were devoid of all emotion, none of the cattiness Suzanne excelled in. But most of all, the nasty talk talked about her professional credibility rather than her love life. Suzanne's issues with her weren't business. Suzanne wanted Philippe or more likely the mystery Michael person, not Anne's clients.

However it wasn't some random e-mailer either. They started after Denise was betrayed, after Anne was fired by Philippe. It could be a loyal employee objecting to Anne's alleged activities. It could be Denise. Though Anne doubted that. It didn't sound like the woman. Anne had a feeling that she knew who it was though. Some of the words, some of the phrasing sounded familiar. Maybe if she dwelled on it, she'd figure it out.

"Annie."

Anne's eyes darted to Ginny's concerned face. This not knowing didn't help any. Her parents would be getting a full report. "Philippe, don't worry about it."

Wasted words. He was already dialing his phone. "Ginny, are you going to be here all day?" Anne's sister nodded. "A techie from one of my companies will be coming over to have a look at Anne's computer. Make sure he shows his business card before you let him in. You can use the computer like normal, only don't erase anything," and he strode off, prowling around the condo, barking instructions into the phone.

"He's a take charge type of guy, isn't he?" Ginny watched him go, new respect on her face.

Take charge and take over. No asking permission and Anne resented his railroading. "Yep."

"Good, I'm glad. I don't think you're taking things seriously enough, Anne. The messages are harsh."

"They aren't nice, that's for sure."

"Again, you're understating the problem." Her little sister gave Anne a good scolding. "Do the e-mails have anything to do with your face?"

Anne touched the cut on her forehead. "No, this was a silly misunderstanding." *Over a man, of all things, but what a man.* Her eyes followed Philippe pacing across the condo. "It won't happen again."

"So it's someone else. Wow." Ginny's eyebrows raised. "I didn't know number crunching was so dangerous."

Number crunching? Ginny never did understand what Anne's business was about. That reminded Anne. "Anything else on the money transfer at *Wedding Pings?*" The temp work slowed but Ginny stayed in contact with some *Wedding Pings* employees, trying to dig up the information for Anne.

"Nothing. No one knows who got the million. Wait a minute, do you think that had to do with…?"

Could be.

Anne didn't have to answer as Philippe interrupted them. "Ginny, the tech should be here around ten o'clock."

"Ten o'clock? On a Saturday?" Did no one work business hours any more?

Philippe ignored Anne's question. "Also talked to Gregory and he hasn't tracked down the container yet," he continued.

"Was Gregory even out of bed yet?" Anne couldn't keep the sarcasm out of her voice. It was barely eight o'clock. On a weekend. After a late night party. Gregory wouldn't have been too happy with that **early** morning call.

Philippe had the good grace to look abashed. "No, he wasn't."

He raked his fingers over his five o'clock stubble, and then sat back down at the computer, scrolling again. As he did so, he moved his head back and forth until his neck cracked.

The man was upset. Anne leaned against his back, rubbing his shoulders. Yep, his muscles were stretched tight. "Philippe, I appreciate the concern. I do, but I can handle this."

Philippe gave her a doubting look. "I know that you think you can handle it yourself, Anne."

"Because I can. I can take care of myself, I'm..."

"Your own woman, yes, I know." Philippe placed a hand on hers. "But you are my woman too and you don't have to. We're a team now. I cook. You clean. Remember? I help you. You help me."

"By doing what?" Anne's laugh was shaky. She had complicated his life since entering it, "Facilitating corporate espionage? Forcing you to fire your V-P? Decreasing employee faith in your judgment?"

"Fire the V-P? My God, Anne," Ginny broke in, "Were you the one that got Kevin Maple fired?"

That sounded so harsh. Anne's chin rose. "I might have been involved."

"But it would have happened anyway," Philippe defended her.

"Were you the only woman involved?" Ginny's hands twisted together.

"Well..." *What was Ginny getting upset about now?*

"Were you?" her sister insisted.

"Yes, I was the only woman involved." *How is this relevant to anything?*

Ginny was about to tell her. "God, Anne, Kevin Maple hates you with a deep seated passion. I didn't know it was you. He never mentions your name, calls you that haughty bitch. I never realized it was my own sister he was cursing out all this time."

"He's angry..." *Kevin is still harboring a hate for me? It's been over a month.*

"He is and he's not calming down." Ginny didn't reduce Anne's concern. "It's like you're an obsession with him. Talks about you all the time. Says you're going to get what was coming to you. His assistant, a sweet woman, thinks he's a couple of cards short of a full deck."

First Suzanne, now Maple... what is with all the crazies lately?

"Cherie, are these from...?"

"Maybe." Anne tilted her head, her ponytail swinging to the side. Maple, the mystery e-mailer? He hated her. He was connected to Lamont Ventures.

"That bastard!" Philippe paced away from her. He took out his phone again.

Anne ran after him, snatching the phone and turning it off. "But it might not be him, Philippe. We don't know."

"Give me the phone." He reached for it but she put it behind her back.

Anne placed a palm on the center of his chest, holding him back. "Calm down, Philippe. Let's get the facts first."

"If I find out—" The unspoken threat in his words frightened Anne.

"Then you will talk to him in the sensible, rational manner I expect from you. He hasn't done anything to me, maybe talk a little smack, some much understandable venting after his dismissal, but …" She spun around, her arms outstretched, the phone in one. "That hasn't harmed me any."

"Yet." Philippe didn't lunge for the phone signaling that his temper was back under control.

"Don't be so dramatic. He won't harm me. He's a middle aged executive, not some gangster. This is so silly, I can't believe we're discussing this."

"I can't believe you never told me." Philippe frowned.

Tell him? When? Up to two days ago, he thought her guilty of espionage. Anne decided to be the bigger woman and let that go. "I'm sorry, Philippe. I thought I could handle it, and you've been so busy. We're both busy. Look at us now. We're already late for your conference call and we have to stop at your place." Anne tried to distract him, picking up her purse.

"We need to talk about this," Philippe warned her as she tugged him towards the door.

"Yes, yes, we'll have plenty of time for that," but she planned to avoid any further discussion. She'd handle it and that was all he needed to know. "We can do that once you're smelling a bit better."

"What are you saying?"

Anne opened the door. "You smell, Philippe. As in, you stink. Ginny, make yourself at home. Will you be here when we get back?" *Please say no, sweet sister.*

Ginny wasn't that sweet. "Do you want me to be?" She showed Anne her dimples.

"No." Anne was blunt.

Her sister laughed. "Then I won't be. Bye, Philippe, hope you smell better later."

Philippe sniffed one underarm, shuddering. "Do I smell that bad, *Cherie?*"

Nineteen

Tuesday morning, a partial answer about the e-mails came. Philippe walked into the condo, plopped a fat file in Anne's pajama-clad lap, and said gruffly, "They were funneled through the Cyber Café," and walked away without another word.

He didn't have to say more. The file said it all. The most telling bit being in the conflict of interest section. The Cyber Café was owned by Derek, Denise's fiancé. Add to that, Philippe recently cutting off the Cyber Café funding, and Denise had more than enough motive. There was no concrete proof though. Using a cyber café, a place where anonymous computer usage was the product being sold, meant no link to an individual.

Anne needed to talk about it. Not with Philippe, he was too emotionally involved. Not with Nancy, she was busy moving. That led to an appointment with The Angel. Anne walked into the luxurious hotel lobby and stifled the impulse to walk right out again. There, sitting with the self contained Ms. McKenzie, was another suspect, Kevin Maple, looking slick and polished in his charcoal gray suit.

Maple's smile faded as Anne approached, her heels clicking confidently on the marble floor. "Miss James, what a delight to see you," his tone said that it was anything but, "you do get around."

Nice. Let the slander start. "Ms. McKenzie, Mister Maple," Anne's acknowledgement and greeting deceivingly civil.

Their relationship past needless formalities, the financier didn't rise to greet Anne, but remained seated, ankles crossed, a dainty teacup cradled in her manicured hands. "Anne, child, have a seat. Mister Maple and I are finished." She didn't look at the man for confirmation. From the Angel's uncharacteristic and telling silence, any conversation the two shared must have been decidedly one sided.

"Just about done, yes," the executive softened Ms. McKenzie's harsh words before launching into his next attack, "Anne, Missus Dumont, the President of *Wedding Pings*, sends you her best."

Smiling sweetly at the man, Anne sat back straight upon the chair, good posture being one of the Angel's things. Maple was making trouble, implying the worst. "You must be mistaken, Mister Maple. I've never met your Missus Dumont." True, Mrs. Dumont hadn't time for a student reporter.

"Really." A silver eyebrow rose. "She was certain she knew you. Quite well, in fact. Said you've been very helpful to her organization, and that much of her site's recent success could be attributed directly to your efforts."

"Interesting. But then I have a common name. It's an easy enough mistake to make." She kept her face smooth as glass. "And I'd like to thank you for the daily e-mails, Mister Maple," Anne pushed, trying to put him on the defensive. "It's nice that we stay in touch after our so very brief working relationship."

There was a flicker on that lined face. Was it guilt or confusion?

"Well, you know what they say about keeping friends close." Kevin Maple's right foot tapped nervously. An annoying habit.

Keep your friends close but your enemies closer. The message was received. "So true, Mister Maple." A lack of a denial was as good as an admission of guilt to Anne. The executive stood. "Oh, are you leaving?" she managed to input disappointment into the question.

And now he was beating a hasty exit. More evidence.

"I fear that I must. Opportunities never rest. Ms McKenzie." The Angel inclined her head, not deeming it necessary to speak. "Miss James."

Ms. McKenzie didn't even wait until he was out of earshot. "Distasteful. I trust that didn't affect your appetite, child?" She set the teacup on the side table and rose to her feet, smoothing down her baby blue suit.

"I'm made of sterner stuff." Anne walked with her to the restaurant entrance.

The maitre d' took one look at Ms. McKenzie and hustled to seat them.

"I heard." The maitre d' was not needed. Ms. McKenzie seemed to know the path to the table. She was so buttoned down, detailed driven, that Anne wouldn't put requesting a specific seat past her.

She had heard. What? Must have been... Anne touched her face. Stanley assured her that her bruises weren't noticeable under the foundation. "How?"

Ms. McKenzie kept the lunch menu shut, folding her hands on top of it. "Philippe mentioned it briefly. That that Suzanne creature was the cause, shocked me."

Philippe mentioned it? What was he doing? Anne wanted this to be kept private.

"Don't look so upset." Ms. McKenzie tapped Anne's arm, her small effort at comfort. "Philippe felt it prudent to tell me. It was my right to know. I introduced them."

Ms. McKenzie introduced Suzanne to Philippe? Was Suzanne one of the Angel's rare female friends? But Ms. McKenzie talked about her with such derision, calling her *that creature*. "No, I didn't know."

"It was not intentional, mind you." The woman poured, the tea having arrived without being requested, offering some to Anne. She declined. "A chance meeting. Suzanne recently had arrived in town and I felt a rare spurt of generosity, always a mistake, that. If I knew…bah, all that is hindsight and I never live in the past."

The waiter arrived and they put in their orders. Living in the past or not, Anne wanted to know more about her nemesis' sure-to-be sordid history. "How did you know Suzanne?"

"Oh, from her New York days." Ms. McKenzie lit up a cigarette. This must be one of the last smoking restaurants in the city. "Of course she wasn't quite as curvy as she is now and not nearly so blonde."

At the financier's candor, Anne almost spit out her mouthful of water. "What do you mean?"

"The blonde hair, the boobs, even the tush, it's all brand spanking new." A circle of smoke swirled around the Angel's head. "She was one of those skinny model types before, you know the type." Older eyes swept down Anne's less than ample figure. "Like you, except taller."

Anne considered herself as far from a model type as possible and she couldn't even imagine Suzanne looking like one. She'd be an entirely other person.

"Why the drastic change?" Though a part of Anne could understand it. She often looked at other's womanly curves and wondered what it would be like to be so blessed. However, the difference was that Anne never wondered long or hard enough to warrant an extreme makeover.

Ms. McKenzie shrugged, smiling a thank you, as the Waldorf salad was set before her. "Who knows what went through that brain of hers. All I know is it happened after that disaster with her fiancé."

A fiancé. Anne took a not so wild guess. "Michael?" It had to be him. It explained Suzanne's emotional reaction to the name.

"Yes." There was a pause as an apple piece was delicately bitten into. "The woman he left her for was one of those *Barbie Doll* types." Anne suspected that the Angel was once a *Barbie Doll* type, though one with a cuttingly sharp brain. "After five years of engagement. Men, they can be such bastards." Ms. McKenzie scoffed, having two ex-husbands, she knew that better than most. "I suppose Suzanne decided why fight it? Might as well become the enemy."

"That makes sense, in a warped sort of way." Anne had settled for a plain garden salad. She hankered for a club sandwich but didn't think Ms. McKenzie would appreciate the visual. Her self-appointed mentor was trying to stick to a healthier new diet.

"Sounds like it did warp her. She always was a bit over the top, the real reason I think Michael might have left her, but fighting? And to think I had associated with her." Suzanne would no longer be associated with the social conscious Ms. McKenzie. "So share the details. Did she really slug you out?" The Angel's eyes gleamed in interest.

Anne laughed, the finance power woman had a bloodthirsty bent to her. "Unfortunately yes. Much to my embarrassment, I didn't even get a shot in myself."

An hour later, they still were chatting over coffee.

"So you think Maple was serious about working for you?" Anne asked. That was an important piece. If he was, then he couldn't have had the *Wedding Pings* gig already lined up, could he?

"Sounded serious to me. There was that fear in his eyes that older executives get, like if they don't get another position soon, they might not ever."

Anne had seen that expression too many times. Sometimes it led to wild and fanciful business ideas.

Ms. McKenzie studied her with interest. Anne got the impression that the woman was bored and enjoyed the distraction. "Why?"

"Working on the task you assigned me, figuring out who sold Denise out," Anne shared, "Maple is suspect number one."

"He does have motive. He hates you."

Lord, another person thinks that. How had she made such an enemy out of the man? "He told you that too?" How had that confidence come about? It wasn't normal interview talk.

"Didn't have to tell me. I have eyes. I can see it. Hate, pure hate, plain as day. If he knew, he would have helped that Suzanne creature out."

Anne shuddered, the thought of the two psychopaths teaming up too much to handle. "Don't say that."

"It's the truth." Ms. McKenzie didn't appear concerned. "So if Maple's suspect number one, who's number two?"

Anne hesitated. This was awkward and she didn't know if she should mention it to the Angel. Philippe's group seemed pretty tight. Though Ms. McKenzie could add her input.

Anne risked it. "Something isn't quite right with Denise and her fiancé."

"Derek?"

Did Ms. McKenzie know everyone? "Yes."

"I don't wonder. He approached me about financing." The Angel took a sip of espresso. "Quite desperate for it. Upon his pleading, took a look at his business plan. What a mess!" and then her lips puckered. "It wasn't one of yours, was it?"

Ms. McKenzie would re-evaluate her job offer if it were. Anne shook her head. "Nope, didn't touch that one."

"Didn't think so. A waste of paper. Don't know what Philippe was thinking." She paused and then rolled her eyes. "Actually I do. Philippe must have been thinking with his heart on that one. He doesn't have a chance at getting his money back." Ms. McKenzie's mouth turned downwards. "Did a few of those myself, back when I was green."

Must have been a while back. Ms. McKenzie was known for her cold, logical business decisions.

"So you turned him down," Anne stated the obvious, snapping a piece of biscotti off to dunk in her coffee.

"Of course. He's not my friend, child. Though I do like Denise. She wasn't good with my Philippe, too weak, but she is charming on her own."

"She seems like a nice person," Anne murmured. Could a nice person let another person take the blame for what she'd done?

"A nice person that you have as a suspect number two? You are a practical one, Anne. That's what I like about you. No delusions about human nature."

Was that a compliment? Her mentor thought so.

"Let me guess," Ms. McKenzie warmed to the discussion, "Denise's motive for cashing in was to supply financing for her fiancé's money-sucking white elephant?"

"Yep. Would you do it?" Anne asked the businesswoman. This would be the logic test.

"Sell out my own secrets for a quick dollar infusion? No question. I'd do it in a second. You hadn't signed a financing contract, had you?"

"Nope. Was about to."

"But you hadn't signed yet, so no harm, no foul. Her decision to make. Her idea to sell. What does Philippe think?"

"He doesn't want to talk about it."

"*Hmmm...*" Ms. McKenzie sipped the hot liquid. "What does that tell you?"

"That he doesn't rule it out." Philippe thought it was possible. Now, Ms. McKenzie agreed. But Anne liked Denise. *Oh, why couldn't it be Maple?*

"Exactly, he doesn't rule it out." The older woman beamed with approval. "So prove it, and then come work with me."

"Trying to steal her away from me, *mon Ange?*" Philippe kissed his friend on her cheek and pulled up a chair from the empty table next. "*Mon amour.*" He clasped Anne's hand. "Whatever she offers, I'll happily double."

"Difficult to do as I don't technically work for you, Philippe." He fired her or had he forgotten? "How did you find us?" Anne hadn't been answering her phone this morning.

"Called Nancy. Your voicemail gives her home number." Since Nancy was at home and moving soon, that number was best. "She mentioned you were having lunch with *L'Ange.*" His smile was fond. "And it is Tuesday."

What did Tuesday have to do with anything?

"I'm a creature of habit," Ms. McKenzie explained. She came here every week? No wonder she had a table reserved for her use.

"*A* creature *si belle*," Philippe cooed, lifting Ms. McKenzie's fingertips to his lips.

"You are too much, Philippe." Anne noticed the delighted woman didn't pull her hand away.

"I find he's not enough," Anne shared with her mentor, a dare in her brown eyes.

"*Vraiment?*" He turned his attention to Anne's fingertips. "I must correct that bad impression immediately."

"Well, do that somewhere else, will you?" Ms. McKenzie's smile softened the words as she pushed her chair back. "I must get to my next meeting."

"And Anne and I must go shopping." Philippe managed to tuck both of their arms into his as they walked out.

"*Vraiment?*" Anne mimicked, her bad French accent making the Angel laugh. "I think you are mistaken. I was to meet with Nancy this afternoon."

"Nancy sends her regrets. She discovered a sudden conflict in her schedule. Have I mentioned that I like Nancy?"

"Only a half dozen times," Anne grumbled but she was thrilled he liked her friends.

"Finally, you have a little play friend to argue with you, Philippe," the Angel teased, "I am so happy for you and for me. I find it tiring," the woman confided in Anne.

"You love it, *mon ange*, but we will let you rest." Philippe kissed Ms. McKenzie on the cheek as they parted.

"Be off, you rascal. Have fun, Anne. Oh, and I do think your number two should be number one."

So Ms. McKenzie was betting on Denise being guilty.

"Number two?" One of Philippe's dark eyebrow twitched.

Anne steeled her mouth into a straight line. "Yes, she thinks Gregory has a lot of potential."

"Not nice, *mon Cherie*." He slapped her bottom as they walked through the lobby, not heeding the concierge's disapproving frown.

"I'm also a bastard, Philippe, remember?" Anne tossed back Denise's words. "And as a bastard, I prefer some forewarning. Would it have been too much to hear that Angel knew about the Suzanne situation before I lunched with her?" Philippe slept over again last night. He had plenty of opportunities to share the information.

"*Je m'excuse*, an oversight." He didn't sound that contrite.

"Any other oversights that I should know about?"

Philippe paused outside the entrance of the hotel, tossing a plastic number chip to the valet. "I went to see Suzanne this morning."

"Why?" Anne peered up at him. Not that she had to ask. She knew it had to be about her.

Philippe shifted, not meeting her eyes. "The original prescription label was underneath. I made her aware that I knew the pills were hers."

"And?"

"She won't be bothering you again."

Bossy, controlling man, this was her business, not his. She should have been at least consulted before he took action. And why'd he see the woman on his own? Did he not think she could handle facing Suzanne again?

"I wanted the satisfaction of confronting her myself." Anne stuck her chin out stubbornly. "I deserved that much."

"I didn't see it that way, *Cherie*. I forgot about you being a warrior woman." Philippe's admiration shone in his eyes.

A warrior woman. She was a warrior woman, darn it. "Forget again and you'll have me to battle with."

"I'll remember." Philippe watched her cautiously, clearly expecting a blow out.

What was the point? What was done was done.

And they were going shopping, Philippe and her in the middle of a workday. Anne was determined to enjoy the stolen moments. They spent enough time on Suzanne and Maple and Denise.

So she tactfully changed the subject. "I'm curious. Why the sudden urge to shop, Philippe? Why now? Shouldn't you be at work? Why couldn't it wait?"

She was rewarded with an amused smile. She didn't know why but her questions always made Philippe smile. "I don't have to be anywhere, *Cherie*. I'm the boss." He opened the passenger door for her and slipped the valet a bill. The valet thanked him, calling Philippe by name.

"Been here before?" Anne asked, keeping the mood light.

"I've had a Tuesday meeting or two with *L'Ange*." Philippe gripped the steering wheel, "Where to? Rodeo Drive?"

Rodeo Drive? Anne had shopped there once or twice. Not what she would call an enjoyable experience. Too uptight to be comfortable. Anne only had to glance at him to get that message across.

"Right. What was I thinking?" Philippe grinned. "No Rodeo Drive for my peanut butter girl. What about Century City? I took my eldest sister there once when she came to visit. She liked it. It's got a few burger places."

Better but still ritzy. "*Johnny Rockets*, not an *In N Out*, a bit upscale for my humble tastes."

"Humor me, *Cherie*, I'm treating."

He was treating. Anne didn't know if she liked him buying her things.

Didn't leave her much control.

Philippe read her mind again. He did that a lot lately. "*C'est matin*, I was…"

"I understand." He didn't have to say more. She wouldn't make him apologize.

He nodded his appreciation. "Besides, *Cherie*, I owe you a dress, have to repay my debt."

That was right. He did. "And a pair of shoes," Anne reminded him, "and a pair of underwear." Especially the underwear.

"*D'accord, d'accord*." He was a gracious winner, feigning disgruntlement. "This will be an expensive outing."

"And I assume Century City has a *Victoria's Secret?*" Anne put her hand on his thigh, feeling the muscles underneath the fabric flex.

Twenty

Shopping let them forget their troubles for the evening. But only for the evening. The next morning, the troubles came back, with interest.

"That bastard!" Anne paced back and forth in the Lamont Ventures boardroom. This wasn't Lamont Ventures business, well, not really, but the location would have to do. She no longer had a boardroom of her own to pace in.

"It wasn't me, *Cherie*." Philippe watched her from his vantage point at the table.

"I know that." *Really couldn't Philippe take anything seriously?*

"And I don't like being put in the same bastard category as this hacker person. What do you think, Nancy?" He was too blasted flippant.

"Not now, Philippe." Anne cut him off. Her sense of humor temporarily had fled.

"I'm so sorry." Nancy shrunk even smaller in the chair, her face rosy. "I should have cut external access, leaving the database alone for history."

Yeah, she should have. And Anne should have make certain that was done. Her friend was dealing with classic baby brain. What was Anne's excuse?

"What's done is done, Nance. No use going back in time. We have to concentrate on the future. Philippe, how long was he in for?"

He studied the file, having been prepped by the company president, wanting to handle this himself, giving Anne the much-appreciated privacy to vent. "Two hours, he did his research and picked the perfect time to escape detection. Three o'clock in the morning, right before shift change."

"Two hours. Two friggin' hours." The speed of Anne's stride increased, as she thought of the confidential information residing on their server. "He could get everything in that amount of time. What did the bas— sleezeball access?"

"Everything," Philippe didn't mince words and for that, Anne was grateful. She needed facts now. "It was a total security failure on our part."

"Everything. Every blasted thing—" Anne flopped in the empty chair across from Philippe, folded her arms on the table and rested her forehead upon them. Neither Philippe nor Nancy spoke, letting her sort out her thoughts. It couldn't be as bad as she thought. Anne heard of hackers entering sites and not wreaking havoc. Some of her composure restored, Anne raised her head. "Did he deface the site?"

"No." Philippe sighed. "*Cherie*, this was no white hat pointing out security gaps. He purposely was looking for information."

"And he wouldn't be looking for information if he didn't plan to use it," Anne concluded. Use *her* information. Information her clients entrusted with her. Information she once again had failed to protect. It was a good thing she was getting out of the business. She wasn't as good as she once thought herself to be.

"And use for a return. The hacker was a pro."

What was Philippe saying? That an amateur couldn't access her site? Anne didn't quite know, not anymore.

Her doubt must have shown. Philippe forced out between clenched teeth, "My system isn't that easy to get into, *Cherie*." This was a failure Philippe would take very personally, his origins being in software development. "The man was skilled and will expect to be well compensated for his efforts."

Well compensated? There was one person out there who is a million dollars richer.

"But, by whom and for what piece of information?" Could it be someone after one of her clients? Or was he after her?

"We don't know that yet. My people are watching the net for any information drops." Philippe was on it, trying his best to recover. Anne gave him credit for that.

"Do we have an I-P address?" That cyberspace fingerprint would be key to catching the hacker.

Philippe ran a hand through his short brown curly hair. "The Cyber Cafe was the funnel, the origin elsewhere, untraceable."

"That...that sleezeball." This got Anne pacing again. Back and forth, back and forth, her thoughts moving as quickly. "The same place as the e-mails; they must be connected. This is personal then. He's after me."

"Annie..." She had forgotten about Nancy. Her friend's eyes were round.

This shouldn't happen, getting Nancy alarmed. That was all Anne needed, to put additional stress on a pregnant woman and have that to worry about too. "Don't worry, Nance," Anne rushed to assure her former partner, doing her best to trivialize the matter. "It's silly corporate games. You know I enjoy those."

"I don't know." Nancy bit her bottom lip. "You sound pretty upset."

"Of course, I'm upset. Right now I'm losing." She dredged up a smile. "But not for long. I'm too good for that."

Anne exchanged a loaded look with Philippe and he stepped in to back her up. "And I'm even better. It's playing with money, Nancy, and I can outlast anyone in that arena."

Cocky bastard. He downplayed the situation and pumped up his ego at the same time.

"Well," Nancy caved, but not completely, "as long as there's no physical threat to anyone."

At this, Anne could grin with a clear conscience. She almost was certain the hacker was about financial retribution, not physical. "No physical threats, Nance. I wouldn't risk it. I didn't win the last fight, remember?"

"I remember. That was foolish on your part to even put yourself in that situation." Since Philippe, Ginny, and the Angel knew, Anne figured telling Nancy wouldn't do any additional harm. Her friend had been overprotective of her since.

"And I wouldn't allow Anne to put herself in harm's way again, Nancy. Believe me," Philippe at his most domineering.

He wouldn't allow her, would he? As if he had any control over her. She'd get into trouble if she wanted to.

But Philippe's comments satisfied Nancy. "So this is a game?"

"A game," Anne reassured her. A terrible, awful game with money, reputations, and businesses at risk.

"Okay, then. You and Philippe may be good at these games, Annie." Nancy stood, her hand moving over her stomach instinctively. "But I'm not. I'll leave you to your plotting. If you need me, give me a call." She squeezed Anne's shoulder as she passed.

Philippe and Anne waited until the door was fully closed before continuing.

"Thank you for that." Anne nodded towards the door. "I didn't want to worry Nancy. She has enough on the go."

"You're a good friend, *Cherie.*" Philippe sighed.

"But a terrible businesswoman." Anne hated that this happened.

"You made a mistake. We all did. Nancy, you, me. We're all responsible, and you and I will fix it." You and I... they were a team. That thought eased Anne's mind a little. Only a little because the worst was yet to come.

"It must be Kevin Maple." Her worried glance darted up to Philippe's. "I'm sure of it. He hates me. He'd strike out at my clients just to get to me."

And Philippe knew this was the core of Anne's worries. If it was only about herself, she could handle it but the thought of her precious clients being harmed scared her.

Philippe moved around the table to the chair next to Anne and took her hand. It trembled in his, like a tiny frightened bird. "We don't know that for certain, *Cherie.*" Though Philippe planned to have a talk with Kevin immediately. "And we don't have proof. But we will, I promise you. My people are working on it."

She wouldn't meet his eyes. "I appreciate it, Philippe."

"You're a priority for me, Anne." He raised her hand and kissed the inside of her wrist. Her pulse was strong. Anne was strong. A woman he could count on in adversity. A true warrior. But a warrior without a battle plan.

"What can I do?" Her helplessness struck a chord with him. He felt helpless too.

Anne wanted to take action, do something. Philippe understood but he didn't want her involved further. "Look at the rest of your information. Ensure that it is secure," he advised, giving her lower level tasks. "That will prevent a repeat attack. I don't know if Nancy is giving the business wind-up the attention it needs."

"She has other priorities." The corner of Anne's mouth quirked up. "I'll look into it but what I really meant was, what can I do about Kevin?"

He knew what she meant. There was no distracting his single-minded woman.

"Nothing. You can do nothing." Philippe was firm, remembering Anne's previous horrible attempts at investigation. Gregory found her out, he himself found her out...if anyone else, no, that couldn't happen. "We," and by *we*, he meant *she*, "will wait and see. We wait for the experts."

"Or wait for him to make a move." Anne frowned. Philippe knew waiting wasn't Anne's strong point. "Whichever comes first."

Anne could be right. The next move could be Kevin's. One thing Philippe drummed into Kevin's thick skull over this past year was once a plan was set, to implement and implement quickly. Anne gave a heart-wrenching sigh and Philippe pushed all thought of Kevin from his mind. He would deal with his former executive later. Right now, Anne was his focus. *Mais*, what to do for her, his poor little sparrow? To relieve Anne's stress? To relieve his own stress?

There was only one action he knew that did that quickly, and it sure wasn't a strategy planning session. Would she be up for it? He could ask. "*Cherie?*" his question came out as a groan.

"Philippe," her reply said it all. She needed him. As much as he needed her.

Philippe swiveled Anne's chair around so they faced each other. "We wait. What to do, *mon amour*, while we wait?" He pushed her silky brown hair back away from her face, not hiding what he wanted but not rushing her. He let her take the next step. And she did.

"I can think of a few things."

With his assistance, Anne eased her body into his lap, straddling him, her skirt pushed up, exposing those fabulous hose-clad legs. He smelled her, a mixture of her fruity shampoo and her own special scent. Their lips came together, hungry, frustrated, vicious, their tongues dueling inside her mouth, fighting for control.

He was hard for her, he always hardened for her instantly, so he grabbed a handful of her lushly rounded buttocks, pressing her against him. *Mon Dieu*, this was exactly what they needed, to spend their fury.

"Only a few things?" he ground out against her mouth.

Anne started moving back and forth. "Maybe more than a few."

~ * ~

Wait and see? *Screw the wait and see.* She was taking action. If sitting here, waiting, counted as taking action. Anne's car was parked outside the Cyber Cafe, her phone on the dashboard in front of her. She hadn't bothered with a disguise this time. Stanley was busy, plus she didn't plan on leaving the car.

No, her plan was to log the goings and comings at the Cyber Cafe, taking digital photos of anyone she knew, waiting for one of those hateful e-mails. When it came, and by the previous frequency that wouldn't be long in coming, Anne would know for certain that it was Maple. She'd have proof, a time stamped photo of him entering and exiting, and the e-mail.

It wouldn't hold up in court but it would make him nervous. That could be all that was needed, to make him nervous. If she had proof, would Kevin be so brave? Anne doubted that. He never once signed an e-mail, relying on anonymity.

So far, no sign of him. She saw Derek and Denise a couple of times. Once she saw Denise, at least she thought it was Denise, go in twice without exiting. Anne couldn't be quite sure, the L.A. area had an abundance of tall blondes, plus she had to admit that she wasn't that great at this detective work. She was too easily distracted.

But that got Anne to thinking. Maybe Denise exited without Anne seeing her. It was possible. Fire code required at least one other entrance. *And would Kevin use such a back door? No, there was no reason to.* He didn't know he was being watched. Plus he didn't seem like a back-alley type of guy, schlepping around in the grime and stink.

Though he didn't seem like a harassment type of guy either. There was no accounting for appearances. What did they say about mass murderers looking like the sweetest, quietest, nicest guys? Not that he was a mass murderer, at least Anne hoped not, but then he didn't look like the nicest guy either.

Lord, this is boring. Luckily this time, she had her own car. The seats were more comfortable, and actually clean. The radio worked. "Karma Chameleon" came on. Anne tapped her hands on the steering wheel to the beat. What a good song. She hadn't heard it since, she couldn't remember, quite a while. *The All Eighties Power Hour.* She reached down to turn the volume up a bit and almost missed a distinctive gray-topped head enter the Cyber Cafe.

Anne fumbled for the camera. Damn, too late to take his photo. She did it anyway, only getting the closing door but at least it was time stamped. She'd take another, this one of his face, when he came out. She could also, to add evidence, get Denise or Derek to confirm that Maple was there. Sign, what did the T-V shows call it? An affidavit?

Anne logged the details in her little notepad, pleased with herself for being so organized. Small details were often the difference between selling a business plan and not. Maybe this time, the details would put additional fear in Kevin Maple.

The irritating "You've got mail" digital voice filled the car. Anne picked up her phone to check the source. Nope, not her stalker. *Spam.* She certainly got a lot of those garbage e-mails. She should figure out how to update her filter. Not that Anne normally used her phone for e-mail, the small screen making her eyes dingy, the brightness turned up too high. Today was an exception. She didn't plan to haunt the Cyber Café any longer than necessary, only until the e-mail came in.

Her phone rang but Anne ignored the even more annoying ring tone. What was that song? *Push it, push it real good.* Anne definitely didn't load that. Must have been one of her teenagers. Even if she knew how, it wouldn't have been her first choice. The music stopped. No matter. She wasn't answering her phone. Anne had to stay focused. The stalker wouldn't be calling her.

Her phone rang again. Okay, she'd check the number. *Blast, it was Philippe.* She wouldn't answer it. She didn't want to lie about what she was up to. But he might have news. Maybe she didn't have to sit in this overly warm car. Maybe he got the person. Though how could he? Maple was inside. Maybe he got sufficient evidence and he wouldn't need her detective.

Curiosity piqued, Anne picked up. "Hello Philippe."

"*Salute, Cherie.*" The door opened and Philippe slid inside, his phone pressed to his ear. Anne threw him a disgusted look and ended the call.

Busted yet again. "How did you know I was here?" How did he always know where she was? "Are you following me?"

"No need, *mon amour*, I could see your car from my office."

Philippe indicated the building hosting Lamont Ventures. Following a hunch, he had scanned, via his handy dandy telescope, the street running in front of the Cyber Cafe. When he spotted the black Volvo parked right outside, he knew immediately to whom it belonged. Maybe he should be following her or having her followed, to ensure she stayed out of trouble. Anne was a half decent bluffer but a disaster at detective work.

"Oh." His darling woman looked adorably sheepish.

Hungry Like The Wolf filled the car. "A Duran Duran lover, Anne?"

"It's the radio," Anne turned the volume down.

His girl had it cranked, probably belting out the tunes the only way she knew how, horribly off key. Philippe couldn't believe he loved someone so clearly tone deaf.

An overwhelmingly annoying ring replaced the eighties music. Anne glanced at her phone and ignored it.

"If you give me your phone tonight, I'll download something a little more..." It rang again and Philippe winced... "pleasing." This made Anne laugh, her head thrown back, her hair falling like satin around her. Now that was a pleasing sound. He should record that for his own phone. He'd answer every call with a smile.

"I usually have it on 'vibrate.'"

No kidding. "I can tell. So what are you doing here, *Cherie*? So bored with your business closed down that you hang out in parked cars?"

"No, I have plenty to do." Anne shook her hair, the sun reflecting off the gold strands. "I'm checking out a theory."

"Hunting my friends again, *Cherie*?" Philippe hunkered down in the car. "Should I be hidden?"

Anne ignored him and he straightened back up again, running a hand over the dash. It came back clean. "Couldn't get the station wagon? Did it finally go to the big junkyard in the sky?" He was glad she wasn't in the rust bucket. It wasn't safe to drive.

"Stanley wishes," Anne grumbled.

"It was Stanley's car?" Not that he cared but this surprised him. Stanley appeared even more anal about order and cleanliness than Anne.

"*Geez*, no." This drew another laugh from his uptight girl. "It belongs to a friend of Stanley's but sometimes he insists on doing the driving."

"If Stanley stops calling me sweetie, I'll have it stolen for him." Philippe picked up the digital camera and scrolled through the photos. There were quite a few of pavement and sky. *Did she not know how to delete them?*

"Steal it? Philippe, your connections scare me sometimes." Anne snatched the camera from him.

"And your thought process doesn't scare me?" Philippe had to give the woman points for creative thinking, though he would deduct them for lack of knowledge. "Let me guess. You're tracking everyone going in and out of the building, waiting for your mystery e-mailer. How do you plan to figure out which person it is?"

"You've got mail," came from her phone and Anne looked at the display. Her smile was satisfied as she undid her seatbelt. *Where did she think she was going?* Anne was almost out the door before Philippe could grab her. She struggled but Philippe held her tight.

"Philippe, I have to—he's going to get away," Anne spluttered.

"Clever plan, my tech-stunted *Magnum P.I.*" Philippe tried not to laugh, she was such a fireball. "But it won't work."

"Let me go. It'll work," Anne protested, watching the door with growing concern, wiggling in his arms. It shouldn't be arousing his passion but how could that writhing body not?

"It won't work." Philippe waited for her to ask why but her mouth clenched tight. "Why Philippe, do you ask? Well, *mon amour adorable*, it's because all the e-mails thus far have been time stamped for random delivery."

Anne's jaw loosened and she stopped trying to pull away from him.

"*Parfaitement.*" Philippe knew she understood. "The person's no amateur. And the program to accomplish the delay is custom written, no back tracking, no tracing."

"You've gone down this route before," came out as an accusation. Philippe accepted it for the frustration it likely was.

"Some time ago, though not..." He picked up the camera again, snapping a photo of her sweet face. "...with such verve. I'm glad you're on my team, *Cherie*."

"Am I on your team, Philippe?"

"*Bien sur*, of course you are, *Cherie*." He took another photo, this one zooming into her gaping neckline, focusing on a swab of exposed lace. "An integral part."

"Then why didn't I know about the time stamping?" She pulled her blouse together. "How do you expect to catch Maple if we don't share information?"

Speaking of sharing information. "Check your e-mail, *Cherie*. What does it say?"

Anne squinted at the tiny screen. Did she need glasses? "Prepare to pay."

Prepare to pay. An ominous message. *That had better only be about money.* "Does it say how?"

"No. Do you think Maple..."

Philippe interrupted her, lowering the camera lens, clicking a photo of the curve of her knees. "I don't think Maple's your man, *Cherie*."

Anne flipped her skirt to cover as much leg as possible. "How can you say that? He's a customer. I saw him go into the café."

Philippe put the camera down so he could look directly in her eyes. "After coming from my office. I met with him this morning."

She wound up and slugged him as hard as she could in the shoulder. Which wasn't hard at all though Anne shook her hand from the impact.

Was that all she had? No wonder Suzanne beat the pooh out of her. Philippe's six-year-old niece could hit harder. "Cherie, I think you should take a self defense class," he said, knowing full well that this tangent would lead away from his conversation with Maple.

"I might do that," she growled in irritation, "and then you'll be sorry. First thing I'll do is beat your ass."

The thought of little Anne giving him the beats made Philippe laugh so hard that his eyes watered. At first, she was silent, disgruntled with him, but eventually a smile upturned those beautiful lips.

"I'm not very strong," Anne admitted.

"And you're terrible at stakeouts and cooking and …" he kissed the top of her head …"you can't sing to save your soul."

"Hey," she protested.

"But I love you anyway." Philippe continued to kiss her, moving to the tip of her nose as she tilted it up at him.

"You do?"

"Of course, I've told you that plenty of times, *mon amour*, my love." His fingers explored the softness of her hair. Did she not know that? That he loved her? "I don't call everyone that."

"You've never called anyone your love?" She looked at him in wonderment.

Damn woman would call his bluff. She was too smart by half and that endeared her all the more to him. "Not since high school." He used those words to land girls before he realized how very powerful they were. Such was the callousness of youth.

"You love me," Anne repeated it like she couldn't believe it was true.

He would have to keep saying it then, until she did believe him. "I do," and he paused, "so?" Philippe looked at her expectantly.

"So?" Big brown eyes blinked up at him.

So? Anne loved him back, didn't she? A tiny kernel of doubt shifted inside of Philippe. His little brown sparrow simply wasn't using him, was she? "Do you…?" But he couldn't come out and ask. What if she said no? He didn't want to know.

Anne laughed at his distress. She was evil, his woman. "You know that I love you, conceited man."

Philippe nodded like yes, he had known it all along, his confidence restored and then some. "I'm a bastard. We know these things."

"But bastards still like to hear the words, don't they?"

"*Peut-etre.*"

Anne wrapped his arms around her. Philippe's body responded. *Couldn't happen, could it? Not again.* She placed his hand on her breast and his fingers moved of their own volition, kneading, caressing.

What was his little brown sparrow doing? It was broad daylight, they were parked at the side of a busy street. Any number of curious pedestrians could spot them. No, better to wait. *Mon Dieu*, she felt good. If only they were in that underground parking over there? Philippe stared at the sign with yearning, aware of the softness under her blouse fabric. Her hand rested on top of his right thigh.

The Volvo was no *Maybach*, not that much leg room. To do anything would be a challenge. Wouldn't be very sensible, would it? He had to be sensible. Anne's hand moved upwards.

Time to move the car.

Twenty One

The e-mail came in the morning, after Philippe left Anne's condo for the office. Anne hadn't told a soul, not Philippe, not Nancy, certainly not gossip queen Stanley. No one. She didn't want to talk about the problem until she had a couple of possible solutions. Or one solid, workable solution.

Philippe phoned her, several times, the duration between calls shortening. Anne wasn't picking up. What did she have to say? She had nothing so far, no action to suggest.

"Hello, hello—Earth to Annie-kin." Stanley snapped his fingers in front of her face, finally breaking her concentration.

"Oh, Stanley." She blinked her eyes a couple times, coming back into the present.

"What's up, girlie?" He rested his wrists on his slim hips. "You're in dreamland."

"She's been like that all day." Nancy popped her head up from behind a stack of boxes. They almost had finished packing-up her living room. Next was the dreaded kitchen.

"Sorry, I've been distracted." Anne moved a few more books off the shelf.

"I'd say." Stanley flounced to the sofa. "So share." He slapped his knees in anticipation. "You looked so frowny-faced. Not good." A finger waved, "That'll give you wrinkles and you don't want those. So what could make our Annie-bananie grumpy? Is it that gorgeous hunk of a man? Is he giving you trouble?"

Philippe? Anne's face softened at the thought of him.

No, it wasn't him. "No reason for frowns there. He used the 'L' word last night."

"The 'L' word!" This brought a round of squeals and both friends grabbed Anne's hands, singing, "He loves you, he loves you." She spun around until they toppled to the sofa, collapsing on each other, laughing.

"Oh." Nancy made a pained sound, grabbing her stomach.

"Nance," Stanley and Anne froze, horrified. *Is Nance…the baby…?*

"Psyche." That dratted redhead laughed, pinching them both. "Got'cha."

"That's not funny, Nance," Anne protested. "We were worried."

"Not funny to you." Nancy grinned. "You didn't see your faces.

And I have to have my fun since I'll be big as a house while wearing my bridesmaid's gown."

"Dum dum te dum," Stanley hummed the wedding march, walking more like Hitler than a bride.

"Not yet," Anne groaned. "Too early, guys."

"But getting closer, don't you think Fancy Nancy?" The makeup artist lifted Anne's hair, twisting it. "Yes, definitely up."

"Getting closer," her other friend agreed. "Not that much more time to plan. And up is so classy, shows off her neck. Anne has a nice neck. She could wear my pearl studs."

"I was thinking diamonds," Stanley disagreed, "to match the dress."

Dress? What dress? And about the hairstyle? Diamonds? Anne looked at them in confusion.

"Yes, that's right." Nancy tapped her forehead. "I forgot that the dress has rhinestones, not that many, just around the waist."

Around the waist? Rhinestones? Again, *what dress?*

"With the simple draped bodice, more isn't needed. It'll make her boobs look bigger too."

Boobs bigger? Anne looked down at her flat chest. *Maybe that isn't a bad idea.* They couldn't appear much smaller. Wait a minute though. She didn't need a dress, did she? Anne had to break into this crazy conversation before it went any further.

"What are you two talking about?"

"Your wedding dress." Stanley waved her off. "Nothing for you to be concerned about."

"My wedding dress?" Anne was worried about getting blackmailed and they were busy designing her wedding dress. "No, no, no. It's too early."

"It's only in the planning stages," Nancy tried to assure her.

Stanley grabbed Nancy's hands. "But didn't I tell you? I got the silk in Hong Kong…"

"You did?" The redhead smiled. "You said you were keeping an eye out for it."

"And the rhinestones when I was in Austria last. They have the best selection, darling, you should have seen it! Bling, bling. Like Liberace's bedroom."

"It's going to be so beautiful. Have you cut the fabric?"

"Indeedie, I did do." Stanley twirled. "I used that dress you gave me, Nancy, for sizing."

"Which dress?" Anne shouldn't be encouraging this but couldn't help herself.

Nancy looked everywhere but at Anne. "The taupe, the one that fits you like a glove…"

"Nance…" Anne wondered where that had gone.

"Don't be mad, Annie. It was only for a few weeks, until the sizing was done."

"Final sizing will be when you try it on, Annie-kin, but we know how you don't like standing still."

"Final sizing?" Anne's brain was about to explode. "I don't think I want to talk about this anymore."

"We know." Stanley gave a pitying glance. "Oh, how we know. You have no interest in weddings, that was clear from Nance's. That's why we decided to be good friends and plan everything for you."

What? "When did you decide this?" And why hadn't she been involved in the decision? Shouldn't she be involved in planning her own wedding? Wait a minute. Shouldn't she have a fiancé first, before planning a wedding?

"When? Oh, a while back, Annie-dynamie. As soon as I saw you and that hunky money-man together. We knew. It was like magic!" Stanley swirled his arms around, doing some hocus-pocus.

"Remember at the bridal show, when he saw the make-up job you did on Annie, Stanley?" Nancy's face glowed. Anne's friend was a hopeless romantic.

"Girlfriend, he didn't have a chance. That man was so far gone." Stanley giggled and they high-fived each other like they were directly responsible.

"Shouldn't you guys wait until I have a ring before planning?" Anne decided to rain on their parade and point out the obvious.

"Oh, no." The two looked at each other in horror. "That'll be too late, Annie-pie. You'll end up with some city hall wedding or, or, or…"

"Vegas," the two squealed together.

"Hubba hubba burning love." Stanley was off doing his best *Elvis* impression, surfing on the couch.

There was no use talking to those two. Anne snorted with disgust, piling more books in the box. This box was going to be as heavy as sin. Thank goodness Nancy had movers. Hope none of them had back problems.

The doorbell rang, breaking up the party as Stanley was doing his best *Scarlett O'Hara*. Nancy hustled to the entrance, dusting her hands off on her tee shirt.

"Where the hell is she?" Anne heard the bellow as clear as day across the breadth of the house. He would track her down. *Arrogant*…so she didn't answer her phone, that didn't give him the right to interrupt her day.

Determined to ignore the source, Anne continued packing.

Philippe filled the doorway and glared at her. She didn't have to look up to know that. Stanley and Nancy watched them in fascination like it was a real life soap opera unrolling in front of them. She half expected them to break out popcorn and beer.

"When were you going to tell me?"

Blast it, he is furious. Why? What exactly is his problem? Anne's anger rose. He wasn't the one getting blackmailed.

"Philippe, this isn't the time." Anne nodded toward her friends and they busied themselves shuffling objects around. Like that fooled anyone.

"*Merde, Cherie,* you don't understand, do you? We don't have time. We need a plan. A response is expected."

He was right, but Anne didn't have one yet, not a single plan. And part of her hoped that if she ignored the problem, it would go away.

"*Maintenant, Cherie.*" His jaw clenched.

Maybe the problem would away if she was very, very lucky. Philippe certainly wouldn't. He had to be dealt with and dealt with quickly. From the rate of his rapidly darkening look, she would say that he was about to completely lose it. That couldn't happen here, in front of an audience.

"Nance." Anne turned to her friend, her face a carefully contrived picture of calm.

"Don't worry." Nancy smiled in understanding. She was such a good person, her Nancy. "Go take care of what you need to take care of. There'll be more packing you can do later."

Philippe didn't wait for anything else to be said. He grunted something Anne couldn't make out and grabbed her, slinging Anne over his shoulder like she was a big sack of those potatoes she saw in stores. Very undignified, what with her butt in the air and everything. Anne was not impressed.

Nancy and Stanley watched him stomp off, their friend kicking and struggling, concern and amazement written across their faces.

"That was interesting." Stanley's eyes didn't need liner to look bigger. They dominated his skull.

"Yes," Nancy fretted. "We don't have much time left."

"I think you're right, Nance Valance." Stanley nodded his platinum blond head, "Anne's dashing Frenchman is not what I would call a patient man. He won't give us much notice at all."

Nancy picked up her phone. "I'll warn Ginny. She's got the most difficult job. The hall looks like it will be last minute."

~ * ~

Philippe was on the phone, barking instructions with machine gun rapid fire into the mouthpiece. Anne sat in the passenger seat and quietly fumed, arms crossed, a sullen look on her face. How dare he treat her like that in front of her friends? What was he, some throw back to the Middle Ages? She opened up her mouth to tell him that. Somehow he managed to squeeze off the first question.

"When were you going to tell me, *Cherie?* I should have been called immediately. Instead I hear the news from an employee." His expression was nothing but raw hurt, pure and simple.

Anne felt guilty, she should have told him. He kept talking about how they were a team. She was about to apologize when the rest of the words sunk in. *Hear from his employee?* What did he mean, hear from his employee?

"Are you reading my e-mails now? Monitoring my every movement? Invading my privacy?" Her voice raised but she didn't care. She was having a very bad day.

Philippe didn't deny it. "From those addresses, *oui*, I am. I'm reading them, I'm tracking them, I'm running algorithms on them. Obviously I have reason to."

They glared at each other, both very upset.

And why is he upset? A small voice inside her asked. Because he cared. So sweet. Bossy but understandable. Besides, of course, he would monitor those e-mails. He felt responsible. They came from the Cyber Café through his network. She should have known he'd do that.

"I was going to tell you first. I haven't told anyone else." Anne looked out the window at the passing houses. Children skipped rope. An older gentleman was out with a hose, watering his vibrantly green front lawn. The peaceful scenes taunted her inner turmoil. "I had to think on it a bit."

Philippe heard the fear in Anne's voice. He continued staring at the road directly ahead, not wanting to see the worry on her face. It would remind him of his failure. He should have settled this by now.

Anne was his woman and he was supposed to take care of her. But take care of her how? They didn't know who the blackmailer was, where he was, what he truly wanted. Nothing—they knew nothing. Frustrating. All Philippe could think of to do was call in a crackerjack team. That was something, not much, but something. Together they might be able to formulate a plan. *Mais peut-etre* Anne already had one.

"What do you want to do?" The sensible, rational part of Philippe wanted to hear Anne had a solid plan, one that only needed implementing. But the very primitive part of him wanted to hear her ask for help, to give him the chance to be her white knight.

Without turning his head, he felt those big brown eyes looking towards him for a solution. A cool soft hand covered his on the steering wheel. "I don't know what to do, Philippe."

White knight, it was.

Two hours later, they were no closer to a solution and Philippe was even more frustrated. He ran a hand through his hair. "*D'accord*, let's go over the facts again. Anne could you read the e-mail?"

"If I lose, you lose. Transfer one million dollars to the site listed below on Tuesday at exactly 3:00 p.m. or all confidential information will be posted on the same site." Anne's voice was steady; her soul was not. This couldn't be happening.

"The website is owned by a dummy corporation," Gregory added, "that's owned by another corporation owned by an overseas corporation situated in Kazakhstan. No remote tracking is possible from that point. I have a call in with the local government."

"We won't get a response in time," Philippe dismissed that avenue.

It was Pete Thorne, Philippe's top information technology point person's turn to recap. "The site was easy to hack into, no real controls to speak of. A basic site, the inputted information sits in a database. Any average programmer would be able to access it. The site has no links or auto transfer to any other external site. I expect the information will be picked up and moved manually."

"So we don't know where it's going," Philippe concluded, "what are our choices, Detective?"

Detective Marlow clicked his pen a couple of times. "Don't pay."

"And punish innocent companies, innocent people for my mistake? It would ruin them." That was no solution for Anne. "No. Unthinkable."

"Then pay it," Marlow gave the other.

Everyone turned toward Anne. "It'd wipe me out but I'd do it if I thought it would stop the blackmail. However, there's no assurance that the information won't be posted." She thought of Kevin. He hated her enough to be vindictive even with the million dollars in the bank.

"It's Kevin, I know it is." Anne was sure.

Philippe opened his mouth, Anne was convinced, to contradict her, instead to her surprise, he agreed, "You might be right."

Whoa, where had that come from? *"Why?"*

"I drove by his house," Gregory piped up, "the lights were on, the curtains open. Boxes were everywhere, the walls were bare."

"He's moving," was Anne's conclusion. "Why would he move when he has a good job here?"

"Exactly." Philippe nodded. "And he didn't mention a move during our meeting. Looks like he might be cashing in and leaving town." He addressed Marlow. "Can we hold him until the deadline passes?"

"On what grounds? You have nothing on him." Marlow was right. They didn't.

"Couldn't we track the receipt?" Gregory asked.

"In a click of the mouse, the money will disappear. It could be picked up whenever and where ever." Lamont's Head of Information Technology shot down that idea. "We have no control over the transfer."

"I wish there was a way we could," Anne muttered.

"Is that a possibility?" Philippe asked Marlow, "Could we counter-offer with our terms?"

"Blackmailers aren't usually open to counter offers. It isn't a business negotiation. They hold all the power and there's a lot of emotion involved," the detective explained.

Anne walked through the steps from start to finish in her mind. Something didn't feel right, but then, she wasn't the most tech savvy person in the world. She already slowed the process down by asking basic questions.

They tried to humor her, these highly intelligent men plotting to help her, but one simple question from her might push them over the edge. Yeah, she should leave it to them. Philippe and his I-T wiz, Pete, would know more about that than she would. *Although...* That nagging feeling wouldn't go away. The locked down, detail person in her wasn't happy with the gap in logic. *And what do I have to lose?* They were at a standstill. Maybe this would get them thinking in a different direction.

"One thing I don't understand." Anne stopped as Gregory shook his blond head.

"Anne, this not the time..." the lawyer cautioned her.

Philippe gave Gregory a look that said he overstepped his bounds. "Let Anne speak. Anything will help at this point."

Was that faith in her? She guessed so, in a very understated way. "What I don't understand and maybe someone could explain to me. How does he expect us to transfer a million bucks blindly to a public access site? How do we know it'll go to the right person? Couldn't anyone pick the transfer up?"

Silence fell in the room and Philippe stared at her, his mouth slightly open. Was he amazed at her insight or amazed at her incompetence? Anne didn't know. Philippe slapped the table, making Anne jump. *Here it comes*, she readied herself.

What she heard was, "Anne, you're brilliant!"

Pardon? Is that sarcasm? It sure sounds sincere.

"Anne has it exactly right. The wire transfer information isn't going to simply sit there. It can't." Philippe laughed, sounding pleased with the situation. "He needs to pick it up and move it immediately. That's why he needed exact timing."

"But he could pick it up from anywhere, undetected," Pete pointed out again.

"He could," Anne agreed, "if we didn't know who he was. Only we do. We might not have proof to arrest him but if we followed him and caught him in the act..."

"Provided you have the right person. And if it isn't who you think it is?"

"We give the person only a short window for pick up and end up transferring nothing." Philippe smiled. "Only a flashing error message, like the transfer failed. He'll think it's a computer glitch and ask for a re-send. Pete, can you design that?"

Philippe's tech person grinned. "Of course. Not only that but I'll put a bug on the transfer site. As soon as the website is accessed, I'll get the I-P addie. It won't be long enough to get to a location but if you're already there..."

"We'll be following him," Anne piped up, happy to take action.

"Not we, Anne." Philippe shook his head sternly. "You've done enough."

"But—" Anne stopped when she saw Philippe's eyes, black as coal. It was a losing battle and distracting him from the real issues.

"What do you think, Marlow?" Philippe asked the detective.

The man smiled for the first time that meeting. "I think you're onto something and the department will help all we can. We don't have the computer support but we can give you any officers you need."

Twenty Two

"So if Philippe is following Maple, what are we doing here?" Nancy, her car seat pushed way back, rested her bare feet on the Volvo dash, wiggling her purple painted toes while she could still see them.

Anne would have the car detailed after the constant grazing her pregnant friend was experiencing. There were candy wrappers and empty *Ziploc* baggies everywhere. "You didn't need to come."

"Oh, yes, we did, Annie-kin, especially if we valued our lives," Stanley piped up from the backseat, his hands manipulating Anne's long hair into a collection of tiny braids.

"Philippe wouldn't really kill you."

"How do you know? You didn't see him." Nancy mumbled through a carrot-stick-filled mouth. "Philippe was worried about you. Told us not to leave you alone." She placed an index finger on her chin. "Why is that Annie? Is it because he thought you wouldn't stay at home like he requested? *Hmmm*, could there have been some weight behind that theory?" Nancy turned her head to the left and right.

Blasted man knew her too well. Anne wasn't about to sit at home, waiting for a phone call. Uh huh, not her. "Okay, okay, he might have been right about that but I had a hunch."

"A hunch? Sweetie, next time, could your hunch lead you to a spa instead of..." Stanley wrinkled up his nose,"... this pathetically decorated Cyber Cafe? Can the space theme be any more obvious? It's begging for a make-over, to bring it back from the heinously color blind future."

That sent Nancy off on another tangent. "That reminds me, can your interior decorator friend come over to look at the house before I have the open house? I want it to..."

Anne's attention drifted away from her friends' banter. Keeping an eye on the front door, she studied the e-mail threat again. Somehow she couldn't picture Kevin, a hardnosed executive, writing it. "If I lose, you lose." The game talk was a common business analogy, sure, but the use of you and I? It sounded too personal, too emotional.

When Anne broached the topic with Philippe this morning, he didn't want to hear about it. After last night, he was completely focused on Maple, certain that Maple was the culprit. That was Anne's fault. She had used her skills to sell him on Maple as the guilty party. And yes, much of the evidence pointed in that direction but this note, well, this note didn't sound right.

"Oh, there's Denise," Stanley squealed, "I have to talk to that girl." Before he could open the door, Anne pounded her fist on the controls, activating the power locks.

"Hey." Stanley's bottom lip curled. "Why'd you do that for? Didn't you see that darling purse she was carrying?"

"Stanley, we're on a stakeout." There was silence in the car as Anne's unspoken message was absorbed.

"Shut up! You think Denise...?" Stanley's expression was incredulous.

Anne felt bad. Denise was Stanley's friend. "She's the only other person with something to gain."

"If they're blackmailing you for a million cool ones, everyone has something to gain," Nancy pointed out. "Even I would be tempted."

"Girl, I'd sell you out for a lot less." Stanley's gamine grin flashed. *Is he wearing lip gloss?* Anne wouldn't put it past him.

"I'd sell you out for one shiny quarter," Nancy snapped back, her eyes dancing.

Anne rolled her eyes. This was like going on assignment with two-year olds. She loved her friends but she was too strung out to enjoy their antics. She had a bad, bad feeling they had the wrong person, and that had led her to waiting here. Would that person be brazen enough to use the same entry point? It was a long shot, but all Anne had to go on.

The person should be logging in soon. Anne checked her watch, thirty minutes to transfer time. Getting close.

"Did you see what beautiful was wearing?" Stanley's mouth moved non-stop. "That pink suit, I swear is *Armani*, the detailing is exquisite, the lines." He kissed his fingers.

"She sure knows how to dress." Nancy sighed.

"Unlike that other tall blonde. Did you catch her getup?" His nose wrinkled.

"Other tall blonde?" Anne's head snapped up, her thoughts flying to another tall blonde she knew. *Could that be Suzanne? Could Suzanne be mixed up in all this?*

"Blonde for today." Stanley snorted. "The ragamuffin was completely synthetic and clearly deranged. I mean why get all that work done if you are going to dress it up in bag-lady threads? A hoodie and ripped jeans? What is she, a member of a teenage skater gang?"

A hoodie? Ripped jeans? No, definitely not Suzanne.

"Maybe she's a famous actress." Nancy wiggled in her seat.

"Infamous, more likely, Nance Valance. I've had more than my fill of ugly for the day. Do we have to do this stakeout thingie much longer?"

"Yeah," Nancy's normally bubbly voice held a bit of a whine, "I need to go to the bathroom."

"Cutie, no wonder." Stanley petted the top of her hair. "You've devoured most of La La Land."

"I'm eating for two." Nancy swatted his hand away.

"More like twenty, mommy dearest."

Anne's phone rang, a classical rendition of "Twinkle, Twinkle, Little Star" filling the car. She answered it with a sharp, "Anne James."

After the call ended, Stanley hung over the seat back. "Please tell me super duper studmuffin got his man and we can go?"

"No, he didn't. It wasn't Kevin Maple after all." Anne took a deep breath. Philippe was understandably ticked off. "They've narrowed it to this area, the person is signing in from the Cyber Café."

"So it's…" Stanley's voice drifted off.

"I guess it is." Anne was disappointed too. She liked Denise. The woman seemed so nice, so genuine. For all her suspicions, Anne never really thought her responsible. "I'm sorry, Stanley."

Nancy wasn't. She unbuckled. "What are we waiting for? Let's go get her and then take a potty break."

Anne didn't think it would be quite that simple. "No can do, Nance. I told Philippe that I wouldn't approach Denise." Her word was binding. Philippe knew that; that's why he forced the promise from her. "I'm to wait, make sure she doesn't leave before he gets here. Don't know when that'll be, what with traffic and everything. He's clear across town

"It'll take him forever to get here." Nancy huffed, blowing her bangs up. "My bladder's going to explode by then. 'Sides, why would he think Denise'll wait around that long? She'll get her money and go."

Anne's thoughts exactly. "Nance, I can't even talk to her. I promised."

"You can't talk to her, Annie-kin," Stanley's voice was unusually solemn, "but we can. Let's you and I, Chancy Nancy, pay Denise a surprise visit."

Her friends would do that? Touching, but Anne couldn't let them. "This isn't fun and games, Stanley. Blackmail is illegal, a sign of a desperate woman. It's dangerous."

"Dangerous, bah," Stanley dismissed the concern. "She might be hard up for the cash, but violent? This is Denise we're talking about, right Nance Valance?"

"Well." Nancy rubbed a worried hand protectively over her tiny bump of a belly.

"Fine," Stanley huffed. "Be that way. I'll talk to her my own sweet self. I could offer to do her hair or something. Spiff her up for her mug shot."

He could distract her, keep her in the building 'til Philippe arrived. Stanley was impossible to get rid of when he didn't want to go. Denise would never know. Yeah, that could work. Anne's eyes lit up. "She's probably accessing the net from the back office. If you can keep her there, Stanley, I'll hustle the other people out and then lock the front door."

"And I'll lock the back door. The washroom's gotta be there anyway," Nancy added, not willing to be completely left out.

"Greedy Miss Beautiful won't be going anywhere." Stanley's grin was the saddest Anne had ever seen it. "Not with this team."

Anne checked her watch, fifteen minutes to go. "This team has to get moving."

Stanley popped his head in first, signaling to them that the coast was clear. While he chatted up the attendant, Nancy headed toward the washrooms. As predicted, situated in the back.

Now what? Anne looked around. Stanley disappeared into the office area. The attendant plus five others were left. Best to clear out one person at a time to avoid suspicion.

She started furthest away from the on-line solitaire-playing attendant. Her reasoning was that it was closest to the door, the area with the most potential for action. A pimply-faced teenage boy furiously typed away on a computer, intent on playing a shoot 'em up type of video game. Anne sat in the empty seat beside him. "Excuse me, can I talk to you outside for a moment?"

"Busy." He didn't take his eyes off the screen.

Anne leaned closer, placing a hand on his shoulder. "Please."

This got his attention. He looked at her like in a drunken stupor, his bleary eyes clearing. The boy swallowed a couple of times and agreed.

"Take your stuff," Anne kept her voice low.

This granted her a perturbed look but he did as requested, following her. Once outside, Anne quickly explained the situation. Maybe she exaggerated the danger a bit but it got results. The boy high-tailed it out of there, not looking back.

Anne's next target was across the room. The businessman, easier to convince, didn't take as much time. Anne checked her watch, time she no longer had. The three other patrons would have to stay. Anne couldn't risk being outside. The door needed to be locked.

Anne sat in the chair vacated by the teenager, his computer active, and for want of anything better to do, picked up the piece of paper beside the mouse pad. A flyer, *Cyber Café* franchises for sale, so this was... no, later.

Anne would think about that later. Right now she focused on the remaining people. The attendant with a piercing through his bottom lip and a tattoo on one forearm looked like he could take care of himself. There was an elderly man, a coffee at his side, slowly hunting and pecking on the keyboard. Anne doubted she could warn him without him making a fuss.

Next was a teenage girl, fingers flying, instant-messaging friends like crazy, while chatting on her phone. It would take too long to even get her attention.

The fourth must be the hoodie Stanley referred to. She was tucked in the corner, her face shielded from view, a portable privacy screen on her monitor. She sat there, her fingers resting on home row, her back straight.

Waiting. What was she waiting for? A growing unease built in Anne. There was one person she knew of in the Cyber Café waiting. Anne checked the time. One minute to. Could be. Keeping an eye on the back room door, Anne casually approached the mysterious hoodie.

Mere steps away, the woman's computer started going crazy. Alarm sounds blared making everyone jump, even the self-absorbed teenage girl. Perfectly manicured fingertips frantically grabbed the manual volume controls. No matter what the hoodie tried, the alarm continued.

To seal her fate, the privacy screen fell off, exposing a bright red blinking failure notice, a notice that Pete Thorne had designed. Anne didn't need further confirmation. It hadn't been Denise after all. Then who? As the mystery woman struggled with the computer, partially rising out of her seat, her hood fell back.

"Suzanne." Anne's gasp turned the blonde's head. Their eyes met. Anne braced herself. She was prepared. She could handle the crazy woman this time.

Suzanne pounced, surprisingly quick for such a tall woman, something silver flashing in her hand. *Blast it all to hell, a gun.* Anne might have been able to handle Suzanne but she couldn't handle Suzanne armed. Philippe had been right. She shouldn't have approached her blackmailer.

"You had to have it all, didn't you, bitch?" Anne felt the cool metal press into her side.

"I don't know what you're talking about." With their height differential, Suzanne's free arm easily wrapped around Anne's shoulders, squeezing her neck. The gun wasn't needed; all it would take was one sharp snap.

"You have Philippe, though who knows for how long." Suzanne moved Anne back toward the door. "You had to deny me my money too?"

"What money?" Out of the corner of her eye, Anne saw Stanley and Denise watching white faced. *Don't come closer*, she silently pleaded.

The grip around her neck tightened. "Don't pull that crap with me. Despite my blonde hair, I'm not dumb. I own a successful consulting company."

"Owned." Anne didn't know where she got her nerve from. "You won't own it long from jail."

"I'm not going to jail." The laugh was thin and brittle. "Philippe wouldn't risk the negative publicity."

Suzanne dragged her backwards. Anne had to think fast, they were almost out the door. "He won't have a choice if you kill me."

"If you co-operate, I won't have to, will I?"

"Suzanne, don't." Denise, the Denise that Anne thought guilty, stepped forward, her hands outstretched, her palms up. "It's not worth it."

"It's Suze, and how would you know what a million dollars is worth?" Suzanne stopped moving to confront Denise. "A million dollars is nothing to you. You tossed away a million dollar idea like it was garbage. Why would you care? When you can steal a wealthy man, not caring about the precious years another woman invested?"

Crap, this was all about a man? *"Not everyone's Michael."*

"Shut the fuck up." Anne was lifted up by the neck, the lack of circulation making her woozy and limp.

"But I didn't toss my idea away, did I, Suze?" Denise again drew the woman's attention away. "It was taken by you. That business plan I gave you never got to Philippe, did it?"

"I don't know what you're talking about?" Suzanne mimicked Anne's voice.

Was that what she sounded like? Like Minnie Mouse?
It was a surprise anyone took her seriously.

"I think you do," an achingly familiar voice joined the conversation.

Philippe! Oh no. Anne's knees almost buckled. He was not supposed to be here. How did he get in? Must have been through the back way. Nancy was to have locked the door. Now he'd put himself in danger, risking his own life to save hers.

Philippe's heart stopped when he saw the pistol pressed against Anne's slight frame. His fearless woman was in big trouble this time. He forced himself to think, pushing the blinding rage away. He had to. It was up to him to get Anne out safely. Her white knight.

"Golly, gee, the gang's all here," Suzanne's normally cool voice sounded slightly hysterical. Not like the Suzanne he knew. She didn't look like his Suzanne either, her hair ratty, her clothes faded and torn.

His eyes must have reflected his thoughts because Suzanne continued, "I was myself with Michael. He didn't like it. I made myself gorgeous for you, Philippe and you didn't like it. Men—you're never satisfied, are you?"

"It isn't the outer beauty that I'm interested in, Suzanne." Philippe took a step toward the two of them, avoiding looking at Anne. He was well aware that Detective Marlow had guns aimed and at the ready. Once Suzanne pulled her own gun, there was no other choice. This would not end well for his ex. All that mattered was that it ended well for Anne.

"My name is Suze." The woman tightened her grip on Anne's

delicate neck and his sympathy for Suzanne fled. "Not Suzanne. Suzanne was that woman back in New York. I've told you people that time and time again."

"I didn't..." Philippe kept her talking. If she transferred her rage to him, Anne would be safe.

"Listen. No one ever listens to me." Suzanne allowed Anne to breathe again. Philippe heard her ragged gasps. "Never. All you want is a pretty face."

"Not true, Suze." All Philippe wanted at this moment was Anne, safe and sound in his arms.

"How could it be? Look at me." Anne's voice was raw, husky. "I'm about as far away from a star as possible."

A star? Like a North Star? Philippe looked into those beautiful brown eyes. Damn woman was going to do something foolish. Philippe squeezed and released, squeezed and released the set of keys in his hands, thinking, thinking. He had to distract Suzanne. That way if anything happened, it would happen to him, not his brave woman. The keys were gripped so tightly they cut into his fingers. *A star.* Philippe looked up to the ceiling for inspiration. The glass covering the fluorescent lights, his keys...

Philippe caught Anne's eyes and nodded. Quickly and without further warning he threw the keys into the light fixture. The sound of broken glass and loud popping noise got Suzanne's attention, long enough. Long enough for Anne to move, twisting away from Suzanne's grip and slamming the blonde right under her nose with her palm. The hit must have been hard because Suzanne dropped the gun to grab her face, howling in pain.

Anne kept moving, sinking to the ground, sliding the gun across to Philippe. The handle was moist and warm to his touch, the safety still on. Philippe aimed the gun at the cursing Suzanne. Though it was clear that she wasn't going anywhere, he wasn't taking any chances.

By the time Suzanne straightened up, police had her arms pulled back and her wrists cuffed. Her nose dripped blood and was noticeably crooked. Anne did that. His Anne.

"You'll pay for this," Suzanne screamed as she was herded out.

Phillipe watched her go with sadness and relief. Whatever happened to Suzanne, he didn't know. She seemed to have everything a woman could want. But Anne was all *he* wanted.

"Self defense, Cherie?" Philippe eyed his brown haired girl with respect.

Anne nodded, grinning, her face unnaturally pale. "I do listen to you from time to time, you know." Her voice was hoarse, her neck already turning a nasty purple color.

"Not that often unfortunately." Having given the gun to Marlow,

Philippe's arms were now free to wrap around her.

Anne trembled uncontrollably. "Anne, you okay?" *Mais oui*, they had an audience, Philippe had forgotten.

She nodded, slowly, like the action pained her. "Thanks to you, Denise. I don't know what would have happened if Suzanne had gotten me out the door."

What would have happened to his Anne, his love. He almost... A shudder ran through Philippe's body. "*Mon amour...*" he groaned.

"Philippe." Anne's eyes sent the same message, the others forgotten. They had wasted so much time fighting their feelings.

"Hey, what did I miss?" Nancy wandered in from the back room.

Philippe's eyes met Stanley's over Anne's bent head. "Come with us, Nance Valance. Beautiful and I will fill you in." For once, Philippe was in perfect agreement with Anne's carefree friend.

They stood there, clasping each other, Anne borrowing Philippe's strength to supplement her tapped reserves. He was here, Philippe, safe, and he wasn't going to leave.

Anne attempted a joke. "You don't have any more crazy ex-girlfriends that I should know about, do you?"

"I don't know, *Cherie*. I've dated a lot of women," Philippe gently teased Anne.

This earned him a slap on the chest. "Bastard," said with affection.

He held her apart from him, looking down at her with brown eyes glowing gold. "I can promise you that I won't have any new ex-girlfriends."

No new ex-girlfriends... that would mean. "What are you saying, Philippe?"

"That I'm not going to risk losing you again, *mon amour*." His palm cradled her cheek. "Today," his voice cracked.

"I'm ending the day in your arms," Anne reassured him. She had never seen him so affected, that the thought of losing her was the cause, well, that meant... "Are we in contract negotiations? Should I have a lawyer present? Maybe Gregory..."

"Screw Gregory. You're not bringing him into this," but Philippe smiled that ice-melting smile of his, the one that flipped her stomach and made her toes curl.

"You might claim undue stress." Anne brushed her lips against his.

"I might if this wasn't clearly pre-meditated. I have the consideration in my pocket." Philippe slipped a hand into his coat, bringing out a blue leather box.

"Whoa, whoa, whoa." He was serious. This was actually happening. Plain Anne James was about to be proposed to by the dynamic Philippe Lamont. Perceived weakness or not, her eyes teared up. "You're missing a few steps. We have a lot to settle before that."

Philippe's disbelief reminded Anne of a certain night when she bravely showed him exactly what she wanted in lovemaking. *"Comment?* Like what, *Cherie?* I love you. You love me. What else is there?"

"How about my start date? My title?"

"Your title will be Missus. Your start date, tomorrow."

Anne thought of Stanley, Nancy, a wedding dress with rhinestones, a bouquet with roses. Her friends were going to kill her. "I'll need at least a week to tie up loose ends."

"Three days."

"One week and that's final." Anne pressed an index finger against his lips. "I'm not haggling with you, Philippe."

He nibbled at her skin. "Mais non, mon amour, I can think of better things to do."

"Vraiment?"

"Vraiment." And what Philippe presented needed no counter-offer.

Also available in paperback

God's Gift by Mario S. Fedele

ISBN: 1897261888

A touching memoir of overcoming insurmountable odds and how faith, love and family can be the glue that binds.

Full Circle by Joyce L. Rapier

ISBN: 189726187X

Tired of running from the past, Todd Jenkins faces the most difficult time in his life, confronting and resolving his own fears of his deceased father.

Celestial Dragon by Ciara Gold

ISBN: 1897261942

When a Deliphit with forbidden powers seeks acceptance, she finds true worth in the arms of a mighty warrior, a man with the heart of a dragon and the soul of a king.

My Lady's Will by Marjorie Jones

ISBN: 1897261780

A battle of wills, a battle of the heart, and unconditional surrender . . . if it's not too late.

On Eagle's Wings by Rebecca Goings

ISBN: 1897261446

Will Eagle's Wing be able to fix the time-line he's derailed without losing his heart in the deal?

Mistletoe Magic by Rebecca Goings, Phyllis Campbell & Liz Hunter

ISBN: 1897261454

When life gets too complicated, you can always count on the enchantment of Christmas to lighten the heavy burden. MISTLETOE MAGIC is three incredible stories of lost faith, snowy mountains and the quiet magic of the Christmas season.

Noblesse Oblige by Lynne Connolly

ISBN: 1897261772

When she enters a new world, Marianne finds love, luxury beyond her imagining – and murder.

Fraternity by Lori Derby Bingley

ISBN: 1897261497

One man. Six women. And a fraternity of brothers who will do anything to keep their secrets.

The Confession by Lori Derby Bingley

ISBN: 1897261829

A father's startling confession makes one woman face a past she longs to forget, by trusting the one man who forces her to face it.

About Kimber

Aspiring writers are told "write what you know". Kimber Chin took that advice to heart. She knew two things… business (based on decades in new business development) and romance (based on falling and staying in love with the man of her dreams).

Kimber Chin helped lead product launches at numerous Fortune 500 companies. She enjoys drafting capital winning business plans and assisting start ups. She is an entrepreneur, a blogger, and a wife.

Visit our website for our growing catalogue of quality books.
www.champagnebooks.com